Buttmen 3

erotic stories and true confessions
by gay men who love booty

edited by alan bell

WEST BEACH BOOKS

Buttmen 3 is a West Beach Book

West Beach Books
PO Box 1726
Port Hueneme CA 93044
www.westbeachbooks.com
www.buttmenfunzone.com

Designed by Alan Bell
Copy Editor: Robert Gaylord

All stories featuring public figures are fantasies and purely the product of the authors' imaginations.

First Paperback Edition: June 2003
First Paperback Edition ISBN 1-931875-07-3
ISBN may vary on electronic editions.
LCCN: 2003101917

Cover and back cover photos courtesy Jet Set Productions (www.JetSet2000.com)

Buttmen 3

erotic stories and true confessions
by gay men who love booty

Table of Contents

A Note About Safer Sex

Buttmen 3: Erotic Stories and True Confessions by Gay Men Who Love Booty bears witness to various aspects of men's sexuality as it relates to the male ass. This anthology strives to provide insight into our fantasies and realities by allowing the authors to communicate freely about what they think about and what they do to explore their love of men, ass and sex.

West Beach Books acknowledges that some of the sexual acts within these pages fall outside the current definitions of safer sex. Our intent is not to condone, condemn or judge individuals or individual choice, but rather to present a forum for free expression of sexuality and sexual matters.

We do, however, encourage all Buttmen to educate themselves in all matters of sexual health, to know current medical positions on safer sex, and to take personal responsibility for one's actions with full knowledge and awareness of the potential consequences of those actions.

Heaven in a Jockstrap

MATTHEW STEWARD

It's not difficult to resist the temptations of the casting couch. As a talent agent, all manner of opportunities present themselves. But it seems too easy to exploit the power imbalance between myself and the struggling young actors and models I deal with every day. While the notorious stories of "the couch" are truer than not, most agents and casting directors remain above the fray. Beyond having a conscience, most of us grow somewhat inured to the constant flow of pretty faces and bodies we encounter as a part of our jobs. And because it is part of our jobs, the assessment of such lovelies becomes almost clinical and detached. It's better—and more professional—that way.

Besides, most of these guys are in their twenties and I've always been ambivalent about younger men. They are pretty and all, with lovely young booties, but I've usually preferred men closer to my own age. Still, since hitting my late 30s a few years ago, they've been swarming around me like bees to honey. A friend told me that I'd hit the "Daddy Zone." While the relationships have been usually short—in both time and of substance—these young men were hot as hell, eager to please Daddy. Not my cup of tea, but every once in a while, a stunning young man catches my eye.

His name was Marcus and he was a friend of a friend of a friend—one of the many requests I receive to assess the chances of some young hopeful. The women are easy, since I remained very detached. Most of the guys are easy too, since I'm either not attracted to them or if I am, the thrill is gone quickly—once they speak. They are often either too full of themselves to be truly appealing, or dumb and untalented. But Marcus was one of those stunning exceptions that not only caught, but also *kept* my eye.

Because it was a favor, I hadn't seen his picture beforehand, as is standard procedure. I'd been told he was very good-looking, but I was unprepared for the knockout that walked into my office. Before I even got to his body, I took in his incredibly handsome face, highlighted by a gleaming smile. He was very dark, beautifully dark, and given his last name, D'Angelo, I gathered he was Italian, maybe even Sicilian. His classic features were perfectly arranged, with penetrating brown eyes and a delicious mouth featuring a seductively pouty lower lip. And then there was that body. It was a testament to his facial beauty that it took me a good minute before I got there. Even under his khakis and button-down shirt, he looked every bit the jock: broad shoulders tapering to a narrow waist that sprouted tree-trunk thighs.

He reached my desk, extended his hand and I felt his solid, masculine grip. My knees buckled. I invited him to sit down. To top it off, he had an orgasmic speaking voice: deep, with a bit of a grumble but also with shades of sweetness and intelligence. This guy was rockin' my world and we'd barely said hello!

Marcus told me about himself and his career aspirations. As he spoke, my internal panting took a respite as I got to know him. While my attraction increased exponentially, it's difficult to thoroughly objectify someone once you get to know the real person. That's especially the case when they seem vulnerable, pouring out their dreams to you. As with so many of my younger clients, my paternal feelings came to the fore. I wanted to be responsible for his care and feeding (pun intended). So, while I'd always kept my nose clean before, the mother of all temptation was sitting in front of me, enthusiastic and smiling luminously.

Marcus told me about playing football at a small college. Being a big sports fan, we spoke at length about athletics and I fell deeper and faster by the minute. While he demonstrated an appealing confidence, there was none of the false bravado and machismo often found in studly men. There was something else. He was an eager puppy—warm, excited to please.

I told him that I needed to see him do a monologue, so we made an appointment for him to return the next week. Then we stood up and shook hands and he turned and walked away from my desk. Thankfully, he couldn't see me falling back into my chair. His ass was spectacular!

Though his build hinted at something good back there, I'd missed stealing even a sideways glance when he walked into my office. Now it was confirmed: his ass was beyond good. Even through his pants, where the impact of a fine ass can be muted, his butt was reaching out to me: big, firm, wide bubbles with a shelf-like quality. Cocktails could easily be served on them. Judging by the back belt-loops scrunched together, he had difficulty finding pants that fit well, and after he was gone, the image of his ass danced in my head until my buzzing phone jarred me back to reality.

As is customary, I took Polaroids of Marcus. All day long I kept sneaking peeks. But rather than quenching my desire, they only fueled it further. Would it wear off in a day or two? I wondered. One of the advantages of being around so many hot guys is that, inevitably, another one comes along to distract me from the last. But days later, Marcus remained all I could think about. And I needed to see that butt again. That brief glimpse was etched into my memory and

I craved more. But that craving made me afraid of what I'd do. For the first time, I considered dipping my toe into that previously-forbidden pool.

The day arrived for Marcus to do his monologue. When he showed up, I was in the middle of doing a deal over the phone, so my assistant put him in the conference room where he was to perform. Knowing Marcus was waiting for me, it took every ounce of strength I had not to cave into the demands of the negotiator. When I finished, I slammed down the receiver, rushed to the conference room and took a moment to collect myself—a notion that was all for naught after I opened the door and saw Marcus standing there clad only in a pair of thin gray shorts. Fortunately, my being a little late was a good cover for my startled reaction.

"Sorry to keep you waiting," I said breathlessly, lunging into the room.

"No problem," Marcus beamed. "I needed to get ready. I hope you don't mind the casual attire, but it helps me get in the right frame of mind since the scene takes place on a beach."

Mind? You gotta be kidding.

I pulled a chair from the conference table and sat facing the small clearing in the room that would serve as his stage. He took a moment before beginning the monologue and I was finally able to fully drink in the beauty before me. The promise of what lay beneath his clothes was more than realized. His muscles were beautifully formed from head to toe: huge biceps; full, round pecs with pointy nipples (did they look a little chewed-on?); and incredibly solid thighs—all cloaked in remarkably smooth, deep olive skin. I was growing hard in my pants and crossed my legs to mute it, but, of course, I wanted to see that ass. As if on demand, Marcus turned around and bent over to pick up a bottled water he intended to use as a prop.

The straps from his jock just barely peeked out from under his shorts and I could feel pre-cum oozing from my dick. I desperately squeezed my legs further together. Maybe I was the naive one, because Marcus seemed to stay in that position—not ten feet directly in front of me—a little too long. Even covered by those shorts, his ass exceeded my week of fantasies. So big, so round, so full, so perfectly shaped, so damn fucking inviting that I had to resist every urge to kneel behind him and bury my face in those incredible mounds of flesh. I wondered if his ass was smooth like the rest of him. And what of that hole?

The monologue began and I remained hard and dripping throughout, trying my best to gain a semblance of composure in order to concentrate. But it was an uphill battle. He impressed me with his piece about a young man on the cusp of serious life decisions—very touching. There's something about a "beautiful slab of beef"—as one of my colleagues would come to refer to him—being so comfortable with emotion and vulnerability. Though he was green, he clearly had a certain *je n'est sais pas*. My lapse into an honest, critical appraisal made me realize that it wasn't just the lustful haze speaking. I knew I could have him on a soap in less than six months.

I did wonder, though, why he wore those shorts. Yes, the scene took place on a beach, but there was no reference to attire. Hmmm. Toward the end of his reading, he knelt down, playing it directly to me. That's usually a no-no, since it can make the recipient uncomfortable, but I was taken in by his trance. When he finished, we were locked in a stare. It took everything I had to break it, ever so gently.

"That was very good," I said, almost in a whisper.

"So glad you liked it," he said eagerly.

"You showed nice range. You've got real potential."

"That's so cool. I want you to be proud of me."

The statement hung in the air. It was a bit odd but very endearing. And then it hit me. We had just entered the Daddy Zone.

"Um, you can get dressed now, if you'd like," I said, trying to regain my professional aura.

"Oh, okay." Reluctantly he gathered his things and sat next to me, still clad only in his shorts. He smiled. I melted. This kid was something and I was deep in uncharted waters. After a long moment, I spoke.

"Listen, Marcus, I'd really like to work with you, but I'm concerned about . . ."

"How I'm looking at you?" he asked calmly, those brown pools fixed on me.

". . . and how I'm looking at you, " I confessed.

He sat back in his chair, completely unafraid to show off that body. I was drowning in a sea of my utmost fantasies, not sure if I wanted a lifeline.

"I don't want to be unprofessional," I said soberly, fighting for my sanity.

"Yeah, okay, I understand," he said, with a hint of disappointment. After a thoughtful pause, he resumed: "I mean, I really appreciate your being so cool. I've heard stories about the casting couch and all, but . . ."

"But?" I repeated, really thinking: *Butt!*

"I don't wanna overstep boundaries or anything," he continued, "but I'm . . . I like guys . . . I mean . . . I had this thing with one of my professors . . . and I know this is gonna sound really weird, but you sort of remind me of him and . . . I mean, I don't wanna screw anything up, but . . ."

I pressed my fingers against his lips. My God, they were beautiful—so full and moist, just amazing. "Listen," I began, "you're . . . incredible-looking . . . and smart and charming and talented . . . but I've always resisted anything . . . I like to think I have some integrity and don't want to be one of those scumbags who . . . "

This time he put his hand on my lips. I was dying.

"It's okay," he said. "You're not. I mean, you're so not like that, which is why I'm into you. I trust you." He took my hand in his. It felt electric.

"I'm starting to feel like I'm the sheep and you're the wolf." I was a fucking puddle.

"I've always been confident and go for what I want," he said.

From most other guys that would've sounded like arrogant puffery, but from Marcus it seemed natural and sweet. Where the hell did this kid come from?

"So, now that I know that you like what you see ..." he said, as he deposited my hand on his leg, the warmth of which spread to me like a wildfire. His thigh was like marble, smooth and solid. I never wanted to let go.

"Maybe we should go back to my office."

I made Marcus put on his shirt and sweatpants—so as not to be completely ogled in the hallway—and hurried him into my office. I peeked around the corner to my assistant and told her to hold my calls. When I returned to my office, Marcus was undressed again, sitting at my desk, looking as delectable as ever.

"I see you made yourself right at home," I said, closing and locking the door.

"Yup," he said, smiling lasciviously.

He threw his big, beefy leg over the side of my chair, revealing that he'd stripped down to his jockstrap. I was speechless. Every part of his body was thick and solid, draped in that gorgeous swarthy skin. I drew closer, wanting to take it all in slowly. He continued to smile, running his hand across his chest, tweaking at one of his erect nipples.

"So, how much do you like what you see?" he purred in that sexy voice.

"I think the bulge and wet spot in my pants should answer that question," I replied, more comfortable playing the seduction game.

I stood in front of him. Our eyes locked. He reached out to fondle my crotch. I grabbed the bulge in his jock, feeling his hard, throbbing dick in the pouch. He pushed himself up and kissed me passionately, thrusting his pouch deeper into my hand. We fell back into my guest chair and began laughing. Then I realized I'd been so distracted by the turn of events that I'd forgotten about his prime asset—among a host of prime assets. I pushed him off of me, eliciting a puzzled look.

"Turn around and let me see that ass, baby."

"I *knew* you were a buttman!"

"A card-carrying member."

He turned slowly, revealing the single most spectacular ass I'd every seen in the flesh. It was everything I'd imagined and more, but now it wasn't just a heated jack-off fantasy.

"Kneel on my chair and show it to me."

Like a schoolboy anxious to please the teacher, Marcus hopped up on my chair, displaying his incredible globes framed in that jock. I had to sit down. He knew about his ass and clearly loved to show it off. Heaven in a jockstrap!

"I've been told I have a nice ass," he said nonchalantly. "Does it meet with your approval?"

"Fuck, yes," was all I could mutter, transfixed by its splendor.

The next thing I knew I was down on my knees getting a better view. His cheeks were indeed smooth like the rest of him, but his crack had a healthy dose of fine black hair. The overall effect was astounding. Beneath the hair, I could see his hole peeking through. He was clearly no virgin. The hole was small but pronounced, a tight ring just begging for my tongue. I wasted no time burying my face deep in that hairy crack, nuzzling inside for dear life. Marcus sat back on my face, which made my dick jump. Then I allowed those stupendous cheeks to envelop my face.

As I lapped my tongue along his crack the first time, Marcus emitted a low, rumbling groan. I cautioned him to remember where we were and to keep the noise down. Then I took his big glutes in my hands and pushed them upward. As my tongue stopped at that juicy hole, I dug in deep, luxuriating in his glorious taste and eliciting another moan. I handed him his shorts and told him to stick them in his mouth. He did so willingly.

I sat down on the floor, leaned my head back on the seat of the chair and told Marcus to lower that ass on my face. He was clearly familiar with the practice and I thoroughly admired the view as he lowered himself onto my face and waiting tongue. I heard him moaning through the shorts as I demonstrated my expert ass-eating technique. All former concerns and inhibitions had flown out the window—or up his butt, as the case may be.

I grabbed those tree trunk thighs, pulled him farther down and burrowed my tongue deeper. He continued to moan and wiggle his ass on my face, which felt like it would disappear inside his hole. He took the shorts out of his mouth, breathing heavily. I was about to tell him to put them back in when he whispered in a child-like voice, "Please fuck me, Daddy!"

Hearing the request from Marcus's lips was a revelation. I wanted to be his Daddy and didn't have to be asked twice to fuck my boy's splendid ass. Like any good gay Boy Scout, I carried condoms in my briefcase. Always be prepared, right?

Marcus turned around in the chair, again in the original position in which he'd shown off his ass. It was a view worth ogling for a moment. I would have looked longer, but he began his pleading again and I'm not one to deny the pleas of a hot and horny man-child with the ass of life begging to be fucked. I dropped my pants and prepared for entry.

Not being a good enough Boy Scout to have come prepared with lube, as well as condoms, I stuck two fingers in his luscious mouth and told him to wet them for me. He sucked my digits hungrily, moaning something about knowing that they were going up his hole in a minute. I removed my fingers from his mouth and gently placed them up his ass. His hole was on fire—tight, but pliable. I could've finger-fucked him for a few hours, but his pleading grew louder.

"Please, Daddy, fuck my hot hole."

"Be a good boy and put those damn shorts back in your mouth while Daddy puts his dick up your ass."

He pushed his ass out farther. I ran the head of my dick up and down the crack, eliciting more muffled moans and pleas. It was truly a sight to behold: all that beautiful ass, there for my taking. Then I teased his hole with my head before pushing it in. I kept just the head in there so I could memorize the sight before me. Reaching up to his broad, strong back and then down his big, muscular arms, I thrust my cock all the way inside Marcus's ass. He emitted a grunt, then a long, low moan. I held him, not moving, with my cock up his ass, feeling its exquisiteness. Marcus was right there with me, sucking my dick with his ass muscles, moaning underneath me. He needed to be fucked.

He started riding my dick and through the shorts in his mouth, urgently pleaded, "Fuck me, Daddy, fuck me!"

I gave my boy what he craved. I rammed back and forth, fucking that glorious ass the way it needed to be fucked. Great ass deserves a great fuck. Marcus threw himself back toward me with increasing vigor. I seized those amazing ass-mounds, more than my hands could hold, and watched my dick open up his gorgeous hole. His muffled moans drove me crazy. It was a cornucopia of sensations.

I reached around and grabbed his bulging jock pouch—my other arm was wrapped around his chest—and piston-fucked that ass. A moment later I felt him shudder violently. He came in my hand, through his jock. I was so startled, stunned and turned on that I gave one final thrust and filled the rubber inside him. I held him by the crotch, running my other hand over his chest. Then I slowly moved my hands to his ass—always back to the ass—where I was buried deep within. He collapsed in the chair, panting, and purred like a kitten.

I pulled out of him slowly and crawled next to him on my chair. Marcus reached up, pulling me closer. He turned his head to face me. I was awestruck by his beauty, as if it were the first time I'd seen him. That pouty lower lip hung seductively and moved toward me. Marcus kissed me sweetly, flicking his tongue inside my mouth. He trailed his tongue up to my ear and whispered, "Thanks, Agent Daddy."

Baby

MEL SMITH

"Fuck! I've been hit!"

I belly-crawled to Hayward. He twisted on the ground, blood soaking his uniform pants.

"My ass, Vreeland! Fuck! I've been hit in the ass!"

I pulled out my buck knife and sliced open the seat of his pants. A thumb-sized hole in Hayward's right butt cheek oozed blood. I rolled him over. A fist-sized hole gaped in his right thigh, blood, bone fragments and fatty tissue spilling out.

Another volley of shots sent dirt and leaves flying around us. I hefted Hayward over my shoulder and grabbed his rifle. My left hand rested on Hayward's bared ass. The tips of my fingers wedged into his crack as I ran for cover, Hayward wailing in pain. Bullets whizzed by me. Hayward's blood soaked my uniform. I felt ready to puke, but, God forgive me, my cock was hard.

I made it to the farmhouse that Hayward and I were approaching when the shooting had started. I ducked through the sagging door frame and found we were in a kitchen. A cellar door was open to my right. I shifted my grip on Hayward, sat on the ladder leading down to the root cellar and made my way to the bottom. I dropped

Hayward on the dirt floor—harder than I meant to—and went back up the ladder to close the cellar door.

Hayward whimpered in the spot where I'd left him. His ass faced me, all curves and clenching muscles. The blood looked painted on. His brown-black skin glowed through the streaks. How many times had I jacked off to the vision of that ass? How many loads of cum had I frantically wiped off my hands and stomach, terrified that someone would find out? How sick was I that I would be squeezing my crotch over a man's ass while he lay in agony, possibly maimed for life?

Pretty fucking sick.

"Fuck, Vreeland. It fucking hurts so bad."

I let go of my crotch, thankful that Hayward's blood hid the wet stain left by my cock. I kneeled next to him. He looked up at me, tears turning his brown eyes to watery gems.

"It hurts."

I took off his helmet and touched the tight curls on his head. My cock got harder.

"I know. I know. They'll be here soon, though. We gotta be quiet."

He nodded. My breath caught in my chest when he held my hand.

"Shh," was all I could manage. We heard footsteps overhead. Hayward squeezed my hand tighter. His eyes were shut and tears streamed down his cheeks. He pressed his lips to my hand, trying to hold back his moans. With my free hand, I followed the contours of his ass, my trembling fingers hovering less than an inch from his flesh. We were about to die or be taken prisoner and one thought pounded in my brain to the rhythm of my throbbing cock: so fuckable, so fuckable, so fuckable.

Engines sounded in the distance. Plane engines. Voices whispered frantically above us. The engines neared. The whispers became shouts. Footsteps ran, then the world exploded . . . .

When I came to, I had trouble breathing. It was darker than before. A solid darkness.

I tried to talk—"Hayward?"—but my voice was muffled. I moved my arms and realized I was under dirt. I pushed my way out and spit clods from my mouth.

"Hayward?"

He moaned back. I felt my way to his voice. My eyes began adjusting to the darkness. I found Hayward, partially buried as I had been. I dug him out, but he was barely conscious. I found my way to the ladder. It was broken but I was able to climb to the top. The cellar door would not budge. We were trapped.

Accustomed to the darkness, I could see most of the cellar. I whispered a prayer of thanks when I realized the cellar had been converted to a bomb shelter/hideout. A good deal of it was covered in dirt, but I found candles, matches, a large supply of water in various bottles, and packets of dried food, mostly fruit and meat. There was even a small first-aid kit with alcohol and rags torn up for bandages.

I went to work on Hayward's ass. The dirt had stopped the bleeding. I used water to clean up the wounds then poured alcohol in them. Hayward regained consciousness, screaming. I dressed his wounds with the rags and calmed him down. I wrapped him in the one blanket I found, but he still shivered, probably from shock. I laid him on his left side and spooned him. He held my arms tight to his chest and whimpered, "Thanks."

My crotch pressed against his ass. The thin blanket and my threadbare uniform were inadequate barriers. My cock felt the tight muscles and that wondrous curve of flesh and it responded. I shifted my body but my cock found its way back to Hayward's crevice. My hard-on pushed against my zipper and nestled between Hayward's cheeks.

"Vreeland?"

"Yes?" My voice cracked and was much too loud.

"Are you scared?"

"Yes, Hayward. I'm scared."

He scooted back, forcing my cock deeper and, I swear to God, I felt his asshole.

"Me, too," he said. His body trembled in waves, vibrating my cock until I was so hard I had to breathe in gulps. Hayward's hands slipped into mine. "Am I going to die?"

"Not if I can help it." Warm teardrops fell onto the backs of my hands. I pulled him even closer to me and his tears ran down my arms. I laid my lips against his ear and sighed "not if I can help it" as I came in my pants.

Hayward fell asleep. Biting my lip until it bled and holding back tears, I soon dropped off, too.

Hayward's body temperature woke me up. I felt his face. It was on fire.

I gave him some water and made him eat some jerky and dried figs. His eyes glowed in that feverish way that comes with only sickness and love. I knew which one I wished it was. I laid a wet rag on his forehead and removed the bandages from his ass. Blood and pus oozed from the bullet hole. The smell and color were foul. I touched his flesh around the wound; it burned. Tears stung my eyes. I still wanted him. I hated myself because I still wanted to fuck him.

"How's it look?"

I wiped away my tears. "Not bad."

"Vreeland?"

"Hmmm?"

"I . . . I gotta take a shit."

I helped Hayward to a corner of the cellar. Pain made it impossible for him to get in a decent position for crapping and I knew I would have to clean him up afterwards. I left him in the corner and turned my back. I fought the urge to watch. My hand hovered near my crotch, twitching with the need to masturbate.

Hayward cried out in pain. "I can't do it, Vreeland. God, it hurts."

His wounds were bleeding again.

"Just relax, Hayward. Don't strain."

"I can't." He curled into a ball. "My stomach . . . Please, Vreeland."

I tried to soothe him but his cramps got worse. I looked around the cellar. I grabbed two bottles of water, the alcohol and some rags. I knelt next to Hayward.

"We gotta clean you out. We can't let that shit build up inside of you."

"I can't." He was crying again. "I'm sorry, Vreeland. I'm sorry."

"Don't be sorry, baby." I froze at the slip of my tongue. Hayward was suffering too much to notice. "But . . . well, I'm gonna have to give you an enema. At least as best as I can."

He didn't seem to hear me. His moans were soft and child-like. I sucked on the end of the bottle. It was a beer bottle serving duty as a water bottle, about to become an enema bag. When I had the end of the bottle lubed up good with my spit, I laid my fingers on Hayward's tailbone. My body trembled. My cock swelled. Cutting through the smell of gas and infection was the unmistakable odor of a man's asshole. I closed my eyes, zeroed in on that smell and inhaled. The memories of every asshole I'd ever experienced were in that smell. They represented opportunity to me. The chance for love and discovery and intimacy. The chance to feel normal existed in those holes. When I tasted a man's asshole or watched one of my body parts slip into it, I knew—for that moment—who I was.

I opened my eyes and ran my fingers down Hayward's crack.

His cheeks were solid but incredibly soft at the same time. They clenched against my fingers. I whispered to him. "Relax, Hayward. It might hurt a little but it's gonna help. I'm sure of it."

He sobbed softly, then nodded. My fingertips found his hole. I couldn't breathe. I'd been in love with Hayward since the day he joined our unit. Nineteen, shy but eager, he had huge, wonder-filled eyes. His skin was dark, dark brown and perfect. I had never seen skin that looked so soft on a man before. I yearned to touch it, to taste it, to press against it. His lips were full and always had an up-turned sweep, as if he were ready to smile at the slightest encouragement. And when he did smile, it was as if his entire body went into the effort. He was an exuberant angel, a puppy who devoured love and begged for more. Everyone in the unit was in love with Hayward, although I was the only one who loved him with my cock in my hand in the dead of the night, cumming in buckets to the vision of his sweet-angel ass, praying and hoping and needing to feel normal.

I lined the bottle up with my fingers and tried to push it in. Hayward screamed and jumped.

"Shhh. Shhh. I'm sorry. But you need to relax."

"I can't. Please, Vreeland, I can't. It hurts too much. Everything hurts too much."

"I . . . I think we need to start smaller; see if we can get you to relax."

The soft sobbing was back. Hayward did not say anything.

Feeling guilty and elated and aroused, I undid my pants. Hayward's face was buried against his arms. His ass rested against my thigh. I put the bottle down, then stroked Hayward's undamaged left ass cheek with my left hand. My right hand slid over my cockhead, gliding on pre-cum. My left hand worked its way into Hayward's crack. My thumb found his hole—puckered so tight, it felt like a pebble—and I massaged.

Hayward's breathing slowed. His sobs quieted. My right hand pulled down the length of my cock. I gathered my balls in my palm and squeezed them together with the fat base of my cock. My hand dragged back up to the head. My balls swung free, engorged and exquisitely painful. I gathered more pre-cum and continued to stroke my cock while I finger-loved Hayward's hole. His sobbing stopped. His breathing sort of sighed. His body relaxed and pushed back against me. His face stayed nestled against his arms.

I sat back on my heels. My cock grew and my knees bounced. My thumb massaged faster, matching the tempo of my cock-beating. I felt my full balls fill even further and my ass came off my heels. I pumped hard and massaged frantically. The pleasant pain in my crotch became an excruciating, frightening tear for one split second, then cum exploded from my cock as my thumb popped into Hayward's asshole. I felt free and I soared as I pumped the fluid from my cock. A delicious, heart-pounding warmth spread from my thumb and seeped through my body. I fell back against my heels, exhausted and elated. My thumb was up to the hilt in Hayward's ass. I looked at it and I cried. It looked so right to me—it had felt so true—so why did it now feel so wrong?

I kept my thumb in Hayward's hole, working it slowly in and out. I smeared my cum all over the bottle neck and placed it next to my thumb. Slowly, I pulled my thumb out, pressing harder and harder with the bottle. At just the right moment, I yanked my thumb out and the bottle went in. I pulled Hayward's ass onto my lap and raised it as much as I could without causing him too much pain. I tipped the bottle and watched as the water flowed into Hayward. He began to moan and squirm. When the bottle was empty, I gently laid him on the ground and stepped away. Hayward twisted, then curled up tighter. A horrible stench filled the cellar, then shit erupted from Hayward's ass.

I waited until he was spent, then I moved him to the center of the cellar. I soaked some rags and washed Hayward's ass and legs. I cleaned his wounds, poured in some more alcohol, then put on fresh bandages. By the time I was finished, Hayward was asleep. I watched his angelic face for a while, then I went to a corner and sat. I hugged my knees to my chest and cried some more.

Hayward began to shiver and mumble my name. I wiped my face dry and went to him. He looked up at me, hugging himself and shaking.

"I'm cold."

I smiled—with great effort—and laid down behind him. I pulled him tight against me and my cock did what it couldn't help but do. Hayward snuggled back and we became one body, parts falling into places where they seemed always to have belonged.

"Vreeland?"

Making sound would have hurt too much so I did not answer.

"I'm going to die."

My lips touched the back of his neck and still I couldn't answer.

"I'm not scared anymore, Vreeland."

My tears trickled down his neck as his tears dropped like kisses onto my hands.

"Vreeland? Would you call me baby again?"

Spring Break Buttfest

JAY STARRE

During spring break in Florida, I got my own big break. I love ass and I'm always on the lookout for new and unexplored derrière territory. After all, that was why I was heading to the beach that warm and sunny afternoon. Even still, I was taken by surprise when I parked my car along the strand and noticed a large banner proclaiming: BUTTFEST 2003: COLLEGE MEN BARE THEIR BOOTIES.

It was happening on a stage in the middle of the beach. A massive crowd of drunken young students were cheering, jeering, whistling and screaming as a swarm of swimsuit-clad college lads paraded by. I stumbled forward on lust-weakened legs to clamber over the short seawall. A few dozen anxious steps later, I joined the raucous gathering and was gazing up at the young men strutting on stage. It was awesome. The skimpy swimsuits did little to cover their otherwise nude bodies, glistening with suntan oil and sweat. I was in a daze of desire, craning my neck from side to side in an attempt to ogle all that Buttfest 2003 had to offer. The contestants were walking back and forth and playing to the crowd, swivelling their hips lewdly and waving their asses sexily above us. There were big asses, small tight asses, muscular butts, brown butts, white butts and black butts, all barely concealed by apparently obligatory bikini swimsuits.

A gaily-dressed announcer appeared on stage, his booming voice rising over the shouting crowd. "Individually now, each delicious, hunky college boy will display his charms for you to admire! The louder you cheer each lucky lad, the more likely he will be to win the prize. Now here they are, the finalists for Buttfest 2003!"

I glanced around me. There appeared to be about an equal number of inebriated men and women in the crowd, and conspicuously, a number of drooling gay men. I decided it was safe to stay put, so I self-consciously licked the dribble off my lips and looked back up to the stage.

The first young man paraded in front of us. He was tall and lean, with a tight high ass that looked like it was formed of solid marble. He was slightly sunburned, which gave him a flushed, sexy appeal that had my cock leaping in my shorts. He turned his back to us and waved that incredible butt in sexy circles, then suddenly whipped down his suit and bent right over, flashing us with his moon-white ass. The crowd went berserk. I shouted right along with the rest of them. That dimpled can waved at us in all its pristine pale glory, outlined by tan line and devoid of any blemish or trace of hair. To my disappointment, he didn't spread his cheeks and offer us a glimpse of his no-doubt tight asshole. But the sight of his ass itself was definitely a treat.

The next finalist was short, stocky and blond. He was also pink with embarrassment and seemed much too shy to have entered such a brazen contest. But with a little encouragement from his buds in the audience, he did an about-face and pulled down his trunks to offer us yet another a glimpse of naked male ass. His was big and fleshy with a coat of pale blond down, the chunky cheeks a true delight. Before he hustled off the stage, I imagined burying my face between those nervously clenched mounds.

The visual feast continued, to my giddy fascination. Each and every ass was truly a wonder of nature. But about half way through the twenty men, one in particular waltzed onto the stage and captured my undivided attention. Rather tall at about six feet, with wavy auburn hair above a handsome Latino face, he was incredibly well-built with broad shoulders and well-rounded hairless pecs. But it was more than his looks that attracted me. He was beaming with self-assured cockiness as he waved to the crowd and bent over to blow a kiss while showing off his ass in the swimsuit. Then he stood up and prepared to turn around for the unveiling of his naked young ass. As he rose up, his eyes met mine. I was in the back of the crowd, but he found me. His soft grey eyes—very unusual with his dusky colouring—locked with mine. He pursed his lips and offered me a phantom kiss, then he winked, very languidly and purposefully.

My cock was jerking against my fly. I thought I would cum right then and there. He was still watching the audience behind him as he bent over at the waist, unlike the others who had looked away as they bared their buns. In fact, he kept his head turned toward me, grinning wickedly as he reached behind himself and pulled down the skimpy nylon of his tight swimsuit. I tore my eyes from his so I could check out his naked butt. I fell instantly in love. The swell of the plump mounds was perfectly proportioned to the rest of his body. His narrow waist accentuated the roundness of those globes, yet his thick, muscular thighs brought their girth into perspective. Those ass-cheeks were fucking flawless! I memorized every inch of his expansive ass, the dimpled sides, the creamy sepia tone of the smooth flesh, the light brown hair that swirled just perceptively around the crack. He was still looking at me as he wiggled his ass seductively and became the first and only contestant to spread his thighs and show the audience his wide-open crack and small, puckered butthole.

The crowd laughed and cheered. I was delirious with lust. He stood up and waved, making certain to nod to me in particular as he strode off the stage. Although another handful of men bared their asses for the crowd, I could only think of him. When the winner was announced, I was shocked he didn't appear. As I watched the winner accept a six pack and a wad of cash, I wondered how any of the others could compare with such a raunchy, sexy butt-boy.

"Hey, man," a sultry voice drawled in my ear. "Like what you saw up there?"

I turned and was amazed to see the object of my ardour standing right beside me. He must have slipped away from the stand when he realized he hadn't won.

"I loved what I saw," I said. The fact he had sought me out emboldened me. "I can't stop thinking about what I would like to do to your butt. With it. Inside of it."

"You're one hot Daddy! Would you like to meet a couple of my friends as well?"

Could things possibly get better? I thought. Before I could speak, my new pal waved his arm and two young accomplices magically appeared from the edge of the crowd.

"Meet Julio and Brad. I'm Carlos, by the way."

"And I'm Jay," I replied breathlessly. I eyed his two gorgeous friends, one blond, the other Latino. I was probably twice their age, although I knew I looked great for 40. Their eyes wandered up and down my body appreciatively, telling me all I needed to know.

We piled into my car and raced to my oceanfront hotel. I was giddy with lascivious imaginings, and cannot recall much of what went on until we found ourselves in my room and I was in the arms of the three young college studs. All of us had been lightly clad in the balmy spring warmth, and it only took moments to get naked. Before I knew it, I had Carlos, the Buttfest contestant, on his belly straddling my lap on the bed with his naked ass wide open before me. It was all I had imagined and more. Carlos might not have been the winner that day, but I certainly was.

"What a sweet, sweet butt," I groaned as I kneaded the lush flesh of his brown cheeks.

"Play with my ass. Stick your fingers up my hot hole. It's all for you," Carlos dared me with a twinkle in his eye.

"You can play with ours too, stud," the white boy grinned as he stood close beside the bed whacking his very hard cock. Julio was on the other side of the bed, naked and pulling on his brown boner. Both turned and waved their naked asses at me. I was busy prying into Carlos's hairless crack but took a moment to check out the two other asses being offered to me. Brad's chunky white can was pale as milk and rather large, as he was short and built like a tank. There was a dusting of nearly-invisible blond hair over those expansive mounds, but when he reached behind himself and spread open his deep crack, I could see that it was pristine smooth and most likely shaved. I groaned out loud at the sight.

But I had to check out Julio's ass as well. He moved in closer so that he was beside Brad. Then he bent over. His butt was compact, sepia-coloured and hairless. Julio opened up his crack with both hands and flaunted his pulsing butthole. I moaned my approval while still exploring Carlos's hot butt-crack with my fingers. Then I found the hole at the crinkled entrance and Carlos shoved his butt up to meet my hand. Just as one fingertip slid beyond the spongy anal lips, Brad shoved his big white ass toward my face, which was in the perfect position for an impromptu act of analingus. I jammed my face between those chunky, milky buns and began feasting on ass.

"Yeah, eat that white boy's fat ass," Carlos muttered lewdly. "Finger my hole!"

I noisily slurped deep into Brad's parted crack, tasting sweat and butt-musk while I worked one finger deeper into Carlos's pliant slot. I was past the second knuckle, twisting it in circles to open him up, prompting grunts of appreciation. A finger in the hole, my tongue exploring another. Could it get any better?

"Got any lube?" Carlos huffed from his position facedown on the bed. "I want you to really fuck my ass with your fingers, but I like it wet and slippery."

"In the stand beside the bed." I managed to pull my face from the delights of Brad's sexy crack long enough to answer. Then I was back to butt-licking. From the corner of my eye I noticed Julio moving away, no doubt to fetch the lube. Then I heard him laugh and proclaim excitedly:

"I know exactly what we can do with this."

When he rejoined us, he was brandishing a big flesh-coloured dildo which I had forgotten was in the drawer. He lubed it up with enthusiasm, making sure the shaft was shiny and glistening. I expected him to hand it to me so I could shove it up Carlos's hot hole, but he squirted a generous supply of lube into Carlos's crack without relinquishing the dildo. Maybe he wants to shove it up Carlos's willing slot, I thought.

Instead, he turned around, bent over and jammed the slippery dildo into the palm of my free hand, aiming the head of the rubber toy toward his parted buns.

"Ram it up my ass. I love a big dildo up my butthole."

I removed my face from Brad's wet asshole long enough to oblige Julio. Taking hold of the base of the hard rubber dick, I pushed upwards into Julio's wide-open ass. His amber cheeks quivered with anticipation as the dildo slid around in search of a target. It took only a moment to find the wrinkled hole, and then I just shoved.

"Oh, fuck!"

Half the dildo disappeared up Julio's quaking butthole, his gaping lips stretched tightly around the white rubber shaft. Then, amazingly, he began to fuck himself. Talk about a real butt-pig!

A pair of white hands pulled my face back into white, fleshy ass crack. Brad wanted more tongue up his ass. I opened wide and clamped my mouth over his pulsating hole. I tickled it with my tongue and when it gaped open in response, dove in deeper to taste his exquisitely heated innards. While I tongue-fucked his eager hole, I was also busy sliding a second finger up Carlos's now well-lubed anus. The snapping rectum was fluttering open and closed as Carlos squirmed in my lap.

"Those fingers are way up my ass." Carlos groaned. "Feels awesome. So does your hard cock rubbing against my belly."

His smooth stomach rubbed back and forth against my stiff boner. He humped my lap eagerly as he took two of my fingers deep up his hot hole. I could feel his hard cock sliding around against my thighs at the same time. It was all a blur of ass and hole as I ate one, dildoed another, and fingered a third. I was drilling Julio's willing brown butthole with rapid, deep thrusts to his grunted squeals, and eating Brad's pink little slot as he writhed against my face and moaned for me to shove my tongue deeper. And Carlos's butt was wide open as he spread his thighs as far apart as possible in order to take the third finger I was forcing inside him. He was almost on his knees by then, begging for me to fuck his ass with as many fingers as possible.

My cock began to betray me at that point. I was having the buttfest of my life and would have loved for it to go on forever. But Carlos's stomach rubbing incessantly against my stiff prick was driving me to the brink. And all those willing holes were such a turn-on, I could not stop the wave of orgasm that caught me up in a sudden surge of rapture. I shoved upwards with my cock against Carlos's stomach and erupted. At the same time, I rammed three fingers against Carlos' prostate.

"I'm cumming!" he shouted. "I'm shooting my wad with three big fingers up my ass!"

Carlos was joining me in orgasmic ecstasy. I held my fingers deep inside his ass as the quivering slot went wild. He was bucking all over my lap. As I coated his stomach with jizz, he sprayed my thighs with his own juice.

"Oh yeah, I gotta blow too." Brad moaned between his legs. His head was down and his ass was in my face as I sucked hole for all I was worth. I felt his anus spasm around my tongue as he shot.

It was Julio's turn. He rammed his ass back over the entire shaft of the ten-inch dildo and I felt his tight butt-cheeks against my palm as he jerked his cock to satisfaction. The stench of cum filled the air.

I collapsed back onto the bed. The three college students joined me in a tangle of arms and thighs.

"What a hot Daddy," Carlos whispered in my ear as we lay together and caught our breath.

"What a bunch of hot asses," I chuckled back.

"There's only one thing." Carlos grinned at me mischievously. "We haven't had your big Daddy-cock up our asses yet. How about it?"

After a short period of recuperation, a few beers and some light conversation, I had all three of them kneeling on the bed with their asses in the air. My cock was stiff and eager.

"Fuck us good!" they all said, almost simultaneously.

Two brown butts and one chunky white ass! All wide open and waving at me. All three had gaping, just-worked-over holes glistening with lube. And I swear those slots were smiling at me!

I fucked them all.

Neighborly Rim

TOM G. TONGUE

Hello. My name is Tom G. I'm not going to give you my last name because I'm not queer . . . I mean gay. At least I don't think I am. But more about that later. I'm twenty-six, married with a four-year old son, Tom, Jr. I'm 5'11", weigh 185 muscular pounds (less than 2% body fat). I'm smooth with little body hair and have brown hair and blue eyes. Paula, my wife, tells me I'm good-looking, and women seem to take to me right away.

All right, we've had enough with the physical descriptions. So, why am I am sharing what happened to me on a message board? I heard somewhere that if you are confused and write down what you're confused about, it helps you to understand yourself better, or some shit like that. All I know is that I've got to get this stuff out of my head or I'm going to go crazy.

It happened late last week—just a couple of days ago. As I sit here and write, I still don't believe what happened to me. My entire world has been rocked.

I was coming home from the gym—I had the afternoon off—dressed in just a jock, my shorts and tennis shoes. I stopped at the apartment mailbox, and among the bills and junk flyers, there was a hand-written envelope addressed to Alan Evans. Not me. Looking closer, I realized the letter was for the new couple down the hall. Paula said she'd seen them moving in two or three weeks earlier. Taking the elevator to our floor, I figured I'd just push the missive under their door. Just as I was kneeling to shove it through, I heard a masculine voice, slightly muffled, but still clear enough for me to understand: "Ah, honey, I just got out of the shower. I know nothing was delivered during those 10 minutes. Okay . . . I'll check. Hold on."

The door flew open, and, I swear, time stood still. Behind that door stood a man . . . no, not a man . . . a *god* with a cordless phone propped against between his head and shoulder! I don't go around staring at other guys, if you know what I mean, but in this case, I couldn't help myself. "Alan Evans" was naked as a jaybird with just a towel the size of a postage stamp held in front of his crotch. He looked to be the perfect model of an Italian male—tall, tan, curly jet black hair, blue eyes, aquiline nose, high cheek bones, pouty lips, muscles of death highlighted by dense curly hair plastered to his chest, abs, arms and legs. I hadn't seen the butt, but I would've bet it was covered with curly black hair, too.

Our eyes met and something happened to me. Some switch clicked inside me, I don't know what. I just know that my dick got hard—rock hard—in less than five seconds! I was still crouched in front of him, and, looking down, I saw that my prod had broken free of my jockstrap and was exposed to the world. And Alan. From the bottom of my suddenly-too-short shorts against my right thigh, you could see four or five inches of my soon-to-be-dripping prick. I quickly glanced up and down the hallway. We were alone. I looked up at his face and it was obvious that he was looking right at my crotch. He smiled—no, make that leered—at me. Then all of a sudden, he threw the tiny towel behind him, put a finger to his puckered lips, and signaled me to be quiet. Then he reached down, grabbed my arm and, in one swift motion, pulled me to my feet and inside their apartment.

"What . . .?" I tried to speak, but he put his free hand, the same one that had been holding his towel, over my mouth.

Closing and locking the door and speaking into the phone, he said, "Honey, can you hear me closing the door? I checked out in the hall and there wasn't any package there." He winked at me . . . he honestly winked at me! "Didn't you tell me that you had a couple of hours before the seminar started?" he asked her. "Goooood!" He looked me directly in the eye, placed his index finger in my shorts and jock, pulling them down slightly, and rubbed the back of his finger along the top of my pubic bush. He spoke into the receiver with a husky voice: "Why don't you get undressed for me, baby?"

I guess you realize by now that he was standing there buck-naked. His dick . . . his dick was beautiful! It's hard for me to say that, but that's what it was. I'd never really looked at another guy's penis before . . . well, okay, I had. But I'd never seen one like Alan's. It was long, fat, veiny and thick as hell—just a little shorter than my nine inches but a lot thicker. His balls were low-hanging and lemon-sized in their hairy sack. Did I mention that it was steel-hard and pointing upward? Did I mention that since he threw his towel away there was little else I could see but that beautiful organ? I am not gay! But, why—for what strange reason—did I want to bend down and lick the drop of pre-cum that appeared at the rosy tip? Why was my dick hard—make that diamond-cuttin' hard?

He pulled down on my shorts and I realized that I hadn't moved since he'd made the request. Using the toes-to-heels technique, I removed my tennis shoes and kicked them across the floor. I grabbed both pairs of shorts at my hips, and he stepped back slightly, giving me room to push them down and step out of them. They joined my shoes.

He stepped back farther, looking me up and down and said,

again into the phone: "Hi, you undressed? Great! Baby, you have the most beautiful body. I just love touching you all over." Cradling the phone again, he reached out and began caressing my shoulders, neck, pecs and tits. I never knew that my nipples were a source of pleasure, but the pinching, stroking and tweaking he was doing was sending electric sparks throughout my body. More pre-cum flowed. Tentatively, I reached out to feel the hair on his chest. Surprisingly, it was soft and it felt good to run my fingers through it. Grinning like a little boy, and pushing my hands away, he spoke again: "Baby, your tits are amazing. I want to suck on them and make you beg for more." With that, he changed sides with the phone as he bent slightly and took my left nipple into his hot mouth. He licked and sucked it loudly, making slurping noises.

"Oh, you like to hear me?" he said with a panting voice. " How does this sound?" He dropped to his knees and buried his face in my crotch, sniffing loudly. My hard-on was rubbing against the side of his face. I felt like I would cum if he touched my dick directly just once. I had my head thrown back and was biting my lower lip to keep from screaming for him to suck my dick. "Oh, honey, you smell so good," he moaned, looking up at me. "You know what I'm gonna do now?"

He paused, running his tongue across his lips seductively. "I'm gonna lick that sweet clit of yours. Listen." Instantly, he tongue was everywhere at once. He licked my crown, slurping up my juices, a slight moan emitting from his throat; he licked my hairless balls, pulling them into his hungry mouth and moaning again; he licked up and down the shaft of my dick, stopping occasionally to stab at that spot just below the head that is so sensitive. I had to bring my hands to my mouth to muffle myself. I had never known such bliss, and I'd never even spoken a word to this guy! Un—fucking—believable. Even I wouldn't have believed it, except it was happening to me! When he swallowed the head and about five inches of my dick,

I nearly did scream. He slowly pulled off me, with a long tongue-wiggling slurp; I pushed forward to get some more of the feeling.

Back to the phone: "Yeah, I want my sweet baby to cum for me." Peering deep into my eyes, he swallowed my prick to the balls! I was amazed! Paula hates giving head and, when I could talk her into it, it was nothing like this! He groaned and fucked his face with my cock. All too soon, I knew I was going to blast off, and I didn't think he'd want to drink it. I placed my hand on the top of his head to push him back, but he swatted me away and moved faster, moaning louder. I came! It was a toe-curling: from the tips of my hair follicles to my toenail cuticles, I felt the waves of passion and shot at least seven spurts. The first two went into his mouth; the rest splattered on his face and chest and the phone as he spoke again while pulling on my wet cock: "Yeah, baby. Give it up! Cum for me!"

As my silent orgasm subsided and he was dragging my dripping prick across his cum-stained face, I could actually hear a woman's voice on the receiver as she screamed in ecstasy. Alan smiled at me as he stood, leaned forward and kissed me. I was kissing a man! I was kissing a man and I loved it! Okay, I liked it. I could also taste my cum, something I'd never done before.

Okay, so I cleaned his face, chest and the phone receiver with my tongue, no big deal, right? It tasted . . . okay. No, it tasted fucking great, and I was about to drop to my knees and start sucking his . . . like, buddy payback, you know? I'm lying again. I wanted his fat dick in my mouth! He placed a hand on my chest to stop my descent, and smiled again. "Did you enjoy that, darlin'?" While she was saying whatever she was saying, I nodded and looked into his eyes again. I reached forward and took his erect penis in my hand—yes, another first. It was smooth, soft and hard all at the same time. It was hot and sticky wet from pre-cum. I didn't understand why he'd stopped me from sucking it, but he seemed to enjoy my touch because his eyes were rolling back and his mouth was hanging open. I wanted to kiss him again, but he was in control and I waited for him to lead.

To the phone (and to me): "Okay, now that I've gotten you warmed up, it's time for phase two." He turned me around and pushed me toward a couch I hadn't even noticed before. We had been in the fucking foyer the whole time! After less than ten steps, I ended up bent spread-eagled across the back of the sofa, my face in the cushions, with my ass exposed and vulnerable. Realizing what his intentions were, I resisted. He pushed me back down as I attempted to straighten myself. "Phase two, baby, phase two." He was somehow holding my hips in place, still holding the phone. "It's pussy-eatin' time!" Totally shocked, I felt his hot breath on my open ass. He lightly kissed my cheeks, and before I knew it, his tongue was out and he was taking long licks up and down my crack, not quite touching the hole. More talk: "Oh, baby, you smell and taste so good! I'm gonna eat that sweet hole. I'm gonna lick it out like crazy!"

Suddenly, I was impaled on his tongue and experiencing feelings I didn't know existed. I wanted to scream, but knew I couldn't make any noise in order to continue our little game. Actually, it added to the excitement. He was turning on this woman with the sounds he made pleasuring my body! Talking to my asshole, the phone and me, he said: "Soooo sweet. The sweetest pussy ever! Let me eat it some more." He drove his entire face into my ass trench, shaking the back of his head from side to side as he tried to get deeper. "Sweet pussy!"

I could actually feel my hole opening to his thrusting tongue. I reached back and pulled my cheeks as far apart as I could so he could get deeper. I wanted to feel his entire head up my hole. His tongue was driving me crazy. In my head, I was yelling at the top of my lungs: "Oh, man! Get that tongue up my ass! Clean it! Lick it!" But in reality I was making tiny whimpering sounds.

"Oh, sweetie, you taste soooo good."

He stood, grabbed my shoulders, lifted me to my feet and turned me around again. He pushed my chest until I toppled backward across the back of the sofa—my shoulders landed on the seat cushions; my ass was on the back, my legs and feet were akimbo in the air. He pulled my right foot toward his face and sucked the big toe into his molten mouth. Running his tongue in a circular motion, he cleaned it thoroughly, sending electric sparks up my spine, and even my asshole. Dropping my foot and smiling he said, "Now it's time for the big finish!"

Curling the phone upward until the earpiece was still by his ear and the mouthpiece in his hair, he put his hand under his mouth and ejected three big wads of spit against his palm. I knew what was coming, and somehow, for some reason, I wanted it to happen. Massaging the self-produced lube onto his throbbing pecker and lifting my ankles until they rested on his shoulders, he lined his weapon up to my quivering asshole and waited. Righting the phone, he spoke again, hypnotizing me with his gaze: "Oh, baby, I'm gonna fuck that pussy now. You ready for it?" I nodded and bit my lip. "You want it?" Again, I nodded. "Here it comes. I'm gonna shoot a gallon of my spooge in you!" Alan drove forward and suddenly, I felt his pubes against my smooth asshole. He was all the way in, and, goddamn it, it felt good, great, fantastic! He brushed across something deep inside me that made me feel like I was shooting off, but I wasn't. It was even better than anything I had felt before. All these new feelings were incredible and I knew at that instant I wanted to do it again!

"Oh, sweetheart, you are sooooo tight. I love feeling us connected this way—it feels sooooooo great!" As he spoke, he undulated his hips gently, stirring that big meat around in my hole, brushing over that "place" again and again. Gradually he changed his motions from circular to in-and-out, pulling his piece almost all the way out and driving it deep inside me. Soon I was pushing upward to meet those thrusts as they increased in speed and intensity. I was looking directly into his intense blue eyes, mouthing the words, *fuck me, fuck me hard!* I didn't want these feelings to ever stop, but I felt my second orgasm dangerously close and I wasn't even touching my dick! I was still making a small grunting noise every time he hit the "spot" and wanted him to know. I mouthed, *cumming!* I don't know whether he understood or not.

Head thrown back, he moaned into the phone: "Oh, darlin', I'm gettin' close. Yeah, you too? Great! Cum, baby! Oh! Here I cum, shooting a big load, a big load in my baby!"

Feeling his fat prick spurt deep inside me, my cum shot out of me like I've never seen it. It flew over my head, landing somewhere behind me, on my forehead, nose and lips and flooded my chest and belly. Amazing! I had come only a few minutes before and I was in awe. Alan leaned forward and as we listened to his friend scream in pleasure, he rolled the phone upward again, and we shared another slurpy kiss with my errant cum as the main ingredient. Slowly he pulled himself up and free from my clutching hole. I felt empty. Then he said, "Oh, baby, you're just dripping with my semen. I need to take care of that mess for you."

Oh, my God! He drove into my ass again with his mouth and loudly slurped and sucked his load from my still-stretched hole. Murmurs came from between my legs: "Oh, baby's hole tastes soooo good! Did you enjoy that, honey?"

Straightening again and smiling at me, he turned his back and with a few words I could not make out, finished his conversation. Upon hearing the beep of the phone disconnecting, I tried to lift myself free of the uncomfortable position I was in. Seeing my dilemma, Alan, jumped to the rescue and pulled me up and into his arms for another tongue-slashing kiss. I felt his dick, still hard, against my stomach and knew what I was going to do. Kneeling, without a word being spoken, I looked closely at his glistening hard-on. As I said before, it was beautiful. I knew where it had just been, but I didn't care. I took the head into my mouth and savored the multiple-flavored treat. It was delicious . . . manly, musky and alive. Yes, I am now a cocksucker.

I worked him over with every trick I'd seen in porno flicks. I was able to get most of him in my mouth and was soon bobbing up and down, getting him deeper down my hungry throat with every stroke. Hearing his gasps and sighs of pleasure above me turned me on. Grabbing his muscular ass and rubbing my hands across it, I began pulling him into my mouth. Soon, he was fucking my face as violently as he had my ass and I heard, "cumming!" just before his love-lava hit the back of my throat—another tasty treat. I rode the wave, swallowing rapidly to keep up with him. I pulled on the shaft and made sure that I got the last emissions. I didn't want to miss a drop. Alan pulled me up, and again we kissed like long-lost lovers.

Backing away from me, he smiled broadly and said, "Hello, I don't believe we've been formally introduced." We both laughed . . . deep belly laughs. It felt great!

"Welcome to the neighborhood, Mr. Evans," I said. "My name is Tom. My wife and son and I live just down the hall."

Smirk-smiling at me again, like he knew a joke, he said, "Hey, partner. Looks like you made a mistake. Who the hell is Mr. Evans? My name is Gino . . . Gino Pastorelli. My girlfriend, Tina, and I just moved in here a couple of weeks ago."

"Oh my God!" I said. "This was all a mistake?" I explained about the letter which I had earlier dropped in the foyer. When I finished, he pulled me to him and replied with a kiss.

"No, Tom, this definitely was not a mistake," he said. "You're the best welcome wagon I've ever seen."

When I left, I took Alan's letter with me, along with Gino's phone number. Tina is away on Monday nights, besides traveling one week a month with her job. Gino said *Monday Night Football* would be starting again next week and asked if I'd like to "join him."

That's my story. I'm posting it on this board because I'm a happily married man who just got off with a guy and loved every minute of it. I'm confused. Am I gay now? Oh, did I mention that I saw Gino's ass while we were dressing? It's just as hairy as I thought it would be. I wonder how it tastes?

Jailhouse Rock(hard)

D'JAHMA SENTWALI

*I*t's very early Saturday morning. I've been arrested.

Last night, after the gym, I took a hot shower and went straight to bed. It was a long day. I was beat. About 12:45 a.m., the phone rings. A recorded voice queries, "You have a collect call from . . ."

It's my cousin Paul.

"I'm so fucked up I hadda get the operator to dial you," Paul slurs. "Robert went home with some female and stranded me at this bar. It's off Bedford Ave. Can you get my keys off the coffee table and pick me up?"

"What?" I can tell from the sound of his voice that he is wasted. "I'll be there, day'am!" Angrily, I jump out of bed, slip into my flip-flops and throw a bathrobe over my boxers. I cuss him all the way downstairs. I hop into his Mazda. *Homeboy owes me big time for this.*

When I get to the bar, he isn't there. I drive around the block. Three times. Dressed in a robe, I can't get out, so I honk. *Where the f is he?*

A cop car pulls up behind me. "Keep your hands where we can see them," a voice instructs over crackling speakers.

I pound the steering wheel. *Paul, I swear: you're dead meat!*

"License and registration," the skinny young cop demands when he reaches my door.

Day'am! I forgot my license.

"Officer, this is my cousin's car. He's drunk and I . . ."

"Step out of the car please," he orders.

"It's a long story, officer. I was in bed. My cousin called. I hurried . . ."

The cop raises his hand, stopping me mid-sentence. He makes me turn around while his older, stockier partner pats me down. They handcuff me and read me my Mirandas. *How was I supposed to know this was a no-cruising zone? As soon as I get outta of this here mess, I'm taking a bottle of whatever Paul was drinking and smashing him upside the head with it.*

The two cops lead me through the station house with me still dressed in my bathrobe. *This is humiliating. Everyone thinks I'm a fucking flasher.* They handcuff me to a bench to await processing. There are a dozen or so other detainees, some asleep, some drunk, some out of their natural minds. One fool is literally barking at the moon. *I don't belong here.*

I glance at the clock. *Day'am, it's been over 45 minutes and they've still got me sitting on this hard ass bench.*

"Excuse me, but when do I get to see the judge?" I ask the nearest cop, a fat sucka with a belly that's processed too many donuts.

"Afraid you're gonna be the guest of the county until sometime Monday. Judges have all gone home for the weekend." He smirks and hands me and my paperwork over to a tall, medium-toned, muscular brutha. He's gotta be six-foot-four, and like, 220 and some change. His big beefy chest can feed a small nation. His angular face dons a smug smile and he signals me to follow him down a long hallway. Halfway down, he glances at my unknotted robe and approaches me. His hands rest coolly against my privates as he reties my terrycloth belt. I jerk.

"Can't have you upsetting the rest of the inmates." He stares at me. I reject the notion of allowing my eyes to meet his.

We proceed. He's in front of me and I can't help noticing how his V-shaped back melts into his uniformed pants. His firm, brown rounds are sticking out like a pair of reinforced steel-belted tires. He stops in front of a heavy, greenish-gray metal door and presses a large, red button. A bell goes off and the doors slide apart. We walk through. The door slams behind us.

On second thought, Paul better not even be in the country when I get outta here.

He leads me to a room where an elderly Latino takes my mug shots and fingerprints.

"Here."

My escort gives me a wet towel to clean my fingers. Afterwards, he places his hand just above my ass and ushers me into another room. There are two guards sitting atop the lone desk: a five-eight or nine, 178 pound, dark-skinned brutha with a baldy and goatee, and a five-eleven or so, 190 pound, tanned-skinned Puerto Rican. The Rican's short-sleeves are rolled up to his biceps. Tattoos of Chinese characters are stenciled all over his biceps. He directs me over to the desk. The brutha who escorted me there gives them a "thumbs-up." They snicker and whisper while exchanging my paperwork.

My escort takes his time removing my handcuffs, his forearm nestled in the groove of my ass. The goateed brutha steps from behind the desk. The Rican glances at me and wets his lips. He nods to the other two.

"We're gonna have to put this one in protective custody." The goateed brutha seizes my chin and turns it from side to side. "I hate to think what would happen to this pretty ass . . . in a cell full of horny guys."

"Yeah." My escort clears his throat and masturbates his nightstick. "Strip, pretty boy."

I do a double take. "Excuse me?"

"You heard what I said."

I hesitate. He insists with silence. I undo my robe and pass it to him. He tosses it. I pause with my thumbs inside my boxers.

"All the way," the goateed brutha chimes in.

I hesitate again, then lower my boxers. I reluctantly pass them to him. He sniffs them, laughs, then tosses them atop my robe on the floor.

"Got damn, look at them muthafuckas." The Rican strokes his chin while eyeing my ass. He smooches his lips and orders me to grab a corner of the desk. Then he takes it upon himself to place my feet on the white line that's painted on the floor while his naked biceps spread my cheeks apart.

"Martinez . . ." My escort nods for him to step aside, then takes his nightstick and slides it between my crack. "Open up."

I glance around. "But . . ."

"Shut the fuck up." He delicately rotates the tip of the stick around my anus.

The Rican grabs my neck. "You heard the man. Open up!" Then he whispers in my ear. "This is what you wanted tonight, eh?"

The other two snicker. The Rican and the goateed brutha kneel beside me. I can feel the heat of their breath against my crack. The goateed brutha takes a whiff of my ass.

"Hey, T'Ray, shower-fresh, just like you like 'em." He darts his hot tongue into my hole. "Hmm, smells like homeboy been bathing with some of that lilac soap."

Did Paul set this up?

His fingers probe my anus. The Rican begins stroking me.

"A clean hole is a good hole." T'Ray—my escort—opens up a desk drawer and dips his fingers into a jar of petroleum jelly. The Rican and the goateed brutha spread my cheeks apart. T'Ray grabs my swaying balls, then rubs the jelly all over my hole. Next comes a finger. My anus reflexively winks.

Paul couldn't *have set this up, but I still don't believe this is happening. This is real life, not some porno flick.*

T'Ray steps back far enough to give me a clear view of the erection straining against his pant leg. *Day'am! Stretching all the way across his massive thighs.* He gets up next to me and slides his index and middle fingers inside me. I tense up.

Okay, Paul, this has gone far enough, you muthafucka. I'm going to kill you.

T'Ray smacks my ass with one hand while spreading me with the other. He slides his index finger in and out of me. My dick flinches. It starts to feel good. So good, I involuntarily gyrate backwards. Now, I'm dripping.

Maybe before I kill Paul, I'll thank him.

The imprints of all three men's erections are threatening to rip through their uniforms. The goateed brutha strokes my dick and plays with my balls. The Rican pinches my erect nipples and catches a long stream of my pre-cum dripping from my piss slit. He jabs his coated finger in my mouth. "Suck it." Then he torturously rubs his slick digit around my cockhead. My knees buckle. I protest with groans, yet my dick pulsates in spite of my objection. T'Ray thrusts three fingers up my ass and begins snaking in and out of me, over and over. I'm on the brink of losing my mind as his extra-large tentacles send chills up my spine. *I can't take this much longer.*

"Stop, stop, he's about to bust," the goateed brutha observes. "Don't let him cum 'fore we get some of that!"

T'Ray reluctantly pulls out and releases my balls. Embarrassed, I can't move. He rubs, then slaps my ass, then strokes his throbbing member through his pants. Pre-cum outlines its oversized head. *Day'am, it's gotta be 13 inches or more.*

My dick is so stiff, it hurts.

"He likes your fingers up there!" the Rican says. "Let's see what else he likes."

Still clothed, they crowd me. The Rican and the goateed brutha begin dry humping me with their erections. T'Ray grabs my dick. He squeezes more pre-cum onto his fingers and sticks them inside me again.

Now, he's unzipping himself.

He pulls out his dick and starts grinding his fat cockhead against my twitching hole, then sticks his entire shaft between my thighs. I can see it jutting out just below my own dripping sex. The goateed brutha squeezes pre-cum from his boiling balls. He coats both T'Ray's and my dick with it, then stuffs us both in his mouth. T'Ray lifts my chin, his light-brown eyes searching mine.

"You should feel honored. He don't do that for everybody."

The Rican and the goateed brutha pick me and plop me down on a wooden bench. T'Ray takes off his boots and pants. Once done, he straddles me and puts his jimmy on my lips. A gob of his salty-sweet juice falls into my hungry mouth. He moves forward so that his ass is hovering above me. His hole is winking and I can smell his sweaty, moistened balls as he rubs them against my nose and lips. He reaches behind and strokes me as he slides his hot butt crack back and forth over my mouth. His hard dick, heavy balls and wet asshole bear his distinct brand of musk and sweat and the smell has me reeling. I can't resist sticking out my tongue and licking his hot canal.

He tastes funky but sweet and clean.

T'Ray moans, turns around and sits on my face. His dick is so hot, it heats up my chest. Sticky drops of pre-cum dot my abdomen.

"Toss my salad, boy," he commands me. I do as he says. His cheeks are smooth, his crack slightly hairy with dark curls that are coated with sweat. His hole is tight. My tongue has to work overtime to penetrate his anal ring. I'm up for the job. He's moaning and groaning loudly. "Now hold your head back," he says after a while. He leans forward, thrusting his hot blazing sex down my throat. His hips thrust back and forth. His balls slap my forehead.

"We'll get him ready for you T," the other two men say almost simultaneously.

His buddies pull my legs apart. They're both buck-ass naked now, rubbing and spanking my ass with their dicks. The goateed brutha is cut and about 9 inches. The Rican is uncut with a large, pink head. T'Ray alternates between slapping my face with his manhood and thrusting it into my mouth. Meanwhile, one of his buddies attempts to enter me. It hurts, but the scent of T'Ray's jimmy, balls and ass is driving me wild.

"Let me do him first," T'Ray orders.

They switch positions. T'Ray gets between my thighs. His buddies stand on either side of me and pinch my rock-hard nipples. Then they cram their dicks down my throat. I suck them for a while, then they both straddle my face, the goateed brutha's front to the Rican's back (both of them facing T'Ray). The goateed brutha slides his steely dick inside the Rican's waiting hole. The Rican strokes me until my toes curl, while the goateed brutha fucks him like we're all on death row and there's no tomorrow.

T'Ray's plump cockhead enters me. His super-sized shaft feels like the Hubble telescope. I'm opening wider than I've ever opened before. But I'm in so much lust, I take it all. Soon he's thrusting in and out. My tongue reaches up and swipes at the goateed brutha's sweaty, musky ass crack. He moans and lowers his smooth chocolate cheeks while still pounding the Rican's hairy ass. My head bobs furiously. I need to taste them both. They comply. They keep fucking and I lick all the flesh I can: ass, balls, dick, more ass, sweaty, thighs, crack, hole, the area between the balls and the ass. All the while, my own ass is being rhythmically plowed by T'Ray's massive manhood. I've died and gone to jail. I never want to leave. I'm about to explode when the bullhorn goes off again.

"Day'am, I'm . . ." T'Ray yanks his already-shooting, one-eyed monster out of me. It baptizes me in boiling-hot cum. From the sounds of the Rican and the goateed brutha, I can tell they're well on their way, too.

I'm cumming! I hold my breath. With two asses hovering over my face, I can't see how far, but I can feel the burn as it lands all over my thighs and chest.

Paul, you fool. I love you cuz. Get drunk again any time. I love jail!

"Fucking A!" the Rican begins firing hot ropes of juice onto my chest. The goateed brutha must be coming, too—inside the Rican's brown hole—because he starts hollering like he's found religion.

"Just a minute!" T'Ray yells to the intercom high on the wall while hurriedly putting on his pants. "We're processing an inmate."

After a couple more bucks and spasms, the Rican and the goateed brutha dismount off my chest and T'Ray passes me a dirty towel and my clothes.

"Get dressed." T'Ray orders me. After I do, he hurries me towards a door and pushes me into a room. It's a small shower stall. I shower.

T'Ray watches me the whole time with hungry eyes. Like he's ready for more.

Enter the Fist

JXW1952

Upon seeing another male, many, if not most gay men focus on the package up front. But I go for the rear view. Over the years, I have taken note of asses of every imaginable shape and size: bubble butts, saddlebag butts, muscular butts, average Joe butts, smooth ones, hairy ones—it makes no difference. Each man's ass elicits a certain fascination within me. Of course, coming to terms with the fact that I am a buttman eventually led me to focus on my own ass. And so I have looked at my own rear from every angle. I have felt every square of my crack and hole.

Much like a fingerprint, each man's asshole is unique—like his signature. No two holes are the same. I should know: I take advantage of every opportunity to examine men's assholes. My fixation even forced me to become analytical. What was it about ass that captivated me? The feel of the skin? The wrinkles of the hole? The hair or lack of it? The smell? After much soul searching, a bubble-butted light bulb went on in my head and the answer became clear: a man's ass—especially the hole—is his most private area. It's a guarded place, hidden from the rest of the world.

Don't get me wrong. I truly love the feel and smell of a man's ass; but knowing I am tunneling into his most secretive realm is the ultimate turn-on. It was this realization that helped me come to terms with an unfulfilled fantasy: opening my ass to another man completely, without any embarrassment and hesitation.

Enter the fist.

I spent the better part of a year surfing the net for fisting websites and photos before I admitted that it was my turn to fulfill my destiny. Naturally, I had lots of questions. Will it hurt? Will I damage myself? Will my anus be tight enough for normal anal intercourse afterwards?

I couldn't answer these questions myself, but I met a man online that had twelve years of fisting experience, mostly as a top but also as a bottom. That was fourteen months ago. Do I have any regrets about taking the plunge and meeting him in person? You bet I do! I waited way too damned long and wasted too much of my life fantasizing rather than acting on my desires.

Hesitation and fear were key components during our first couple of play sessions. I had no reservation about my ass being exposed and vulnerable to another man but needed some time to reach a level of comfort and trust with my new trainer. Fortunately he knew what he doing and told me that taking a fist would take time and practice. We started with a few fingers, small toys and dildos, but progress was slow. My teacher was persistent but patient. He discovered my limits based on my body's responses rather than what was coming out of my mouth. The more trusting I became, the more I became an eager and willing student. We used digital photography and video to record our anal workout sessions and I soon discovered that I was an exhibitionist. I enjoyed being filmed and watched by others as I opened up myself and my asshole.

After a few sessions, we'd progressed to some rather healthy-sized toys, but at times I still fought against intrusions into my hole. Then, in an act of desperation—and with a certain taste for even

more kink, I suspect—my teacher stuffed a gag in my mouth and
restrained me stomach-down over an ottoman. I was a willing and
sober accomplice, mind you. We never trained under the influence
of booze or recreational drugs—not counting poppers, which were
critical in the name of relaxation and enjoyment.

With my body on the ottoman and my ass high in the air and
wide open, my teacher was about to give me what I craved. I was
still a little hesitant. After all, his hands were extremely large and I
am a small-boned, 163-pound man. But before I knew it, his fingers
had disappeared into my asshole all the way to his knuckles. The
sensation was at once wild and frightening. Moments later, his hand
was burrowed deep inside my ass, all the way to his wrist. What
went on in my mind at that instant is still somewhat of a blur, but
I remember feeling a sense of fullness unlike anything I had experienced before. I was oblivious to the room and my surroundings.
My mind was swimming, my vision engulfed by bright white light.
I had surrendered my entire being to another man and wasn't sure
I was still connected with my body. I was helpless to control my
destiny at that moment, left with no choice other than submitting
my inner self, both literally and figuratively, to another person. It
was almost spiritual.

Our training sessions continued, usually weekly, and I came to
love my role as a fisting bottom. My willing ass-chute became quite
familiar with the sensations involved and I craved more and more.
Sometimes we invited another top to join us and they'd take turns
exploring my anal depths. Amazingly, I could tell who was who by
the feelings rocketing through my ass.

We've moved on to new and larger toys that stretched my anal
canal even wider and enabled me to take fists more easily, permitting even deeper probing of my inner cavity. A recent session involved a large inflatable dildo, which expanded my second internal
muscle ring wide enough to let my top slide his fist through the

second opening. Depth levels have approached one half of his forearm and we continue to work toward the goal of me being able to take his fist to the elbow. We're also planning a professional photo shoot for possible use on an Internet pay site. I have often imagined how I want the scene to play out: I'm in a sling with a gag covering my mouth. My legs are secured and spread wide apart, my manhole exposed to the camera. My trainer . . .

I get excited thinking about the photo shoot, as well as the possibility of strangers coming onto the set and thrusting their arms up my hole—one after another. Scenes like that are the ultimate turn-on for me. They eliminate any shroud of embarrassment I might still have and give me a true feeling of self-worth. I now know that my life as a sexual being revolves around my ass and the pleasures it brings me. My desire is to continue to submit my asshole to a growing number of men in hopes of developing a large, gaping hole surrounded by engorged, swollen outer ass-lips that resemble a well-abused female vagina.

Why, you might ask, do I want my manhole to look like a part of the female anatomy? I have no answer for that question, but I am willing to accept my desire as a part of my being. It is also my desire that one day you will find me in a sling, legs spread, my begging ass-cunt calling out to you: "Take me!"

Boys and Pigs

P.P. REID

I first met Andy while walking down his seedy little street, a small oasis of GI Bill homes that had become a haven for hustlers, day-laborers and immigrant families looking for low-rent housing. My condo was a block away and I had traveled down the thoroughfare many times, be it for a convenience-store run or a trip to the neighborhood gay bar. As I passed the house where Andy lived, he mistook me for the john he was expecting and approached me. After we sorted out the misunderstanding, we both laughed. And then I took a good look at Andy. With his reddish-copper hair and those sinewy muscles on his tall frame, I was envious of that john and how he would soon be inside this delicious young man's pants.

That day we left it at "sorry for the mistake," but from then on, Andy waved when he saw me. Eventually I met his roommate, Rowdy, and the three of us would chat over cigarettes on the sidewalk or drinks when I saw them at the bar. Andy and Rowdy were both twenty-three and had been best friends since growing up in a little town in Texas hill country. After being kicked out of their respective homes in their late teens, they'd worked as ranch-hands, oilfield laborers and construction workers before discovering that some of the guys at the truck stop on the outskirts of town were interested in more than a good bowl of chili. Andy had begun hustling to supplement his pay and Rowdy got into it six months later when he saw what kind of money his friend was bringing in.

They'd moved to Dallas to get out of the sticks and had developed a steady clientele of johns which they saw individually or as a team. As a writer, I was fascinated by Andy and Rowdy. They talked openly about their profession, and unlike some of their competitors, were still sweet and good-natured. They knew I was gay but were never above a mischievous peck on the cheek and a wink when we parted company after a night out.

One day, six months into our friendship, I was heading to the store when I noticed Andy standing shirtless on the porch and looking even more sexy than usual: a cigarette burning between two knuckles held over his head; beautiful red downy-hair sprouting between his naked hard pecs; rubbery tits shrunken and nubby; his thick neck topped by the buzz-cut head cocked to one side as he casually regarded the activity on the street. A pair of onion-skin running shorts rode low on his hips and clung to his muscular thighs, the scar that ran down his knee struggling not to split from the muscles that it encased.

He noticed me and waved, very nonchalant. I approached and we chatted—not really about anything—while Andy smoked the cigarette to an ashy, burning cherry, crushed it out and snapped the waistband of his onion-skin running shorts. "Hey, why don't you come in for a second," he said, smirking as he led the way inside. I followed and immediately recognized the sounds of heated sex coming from the bedroom of the cramped little house.

"Harder!" a man pleaded. "Come on, fuck me!"

Andy shucked his running shorts so that he was completely naked now, and like someone returning from a break at work, said to me over his shoulder: "You can watch us work."

I wasn't new to the idea of watching a couple of guys screw, but I hesitated, not sure I shouldn't thank him and go on about my business. But Andy's self-assured, relaxed attitude and the fact that it was the first time I'd ever seen his jutting ass cheeks not covered by taut denim emboldened me. I followed Andy's hair-dusted cheeks, sparsely flecked with freckles and a tiny mole. The two raw, red balls that hung conspicuously low and could be seen clearly from behind didn't slow my progress either.

We entered the smoky back bedroom and I was greeted by the sight of Rowdy's lunging ass and swinging balls as he delivered a forceful pounding to the tightly-clenched asshole of a man who was on all fours atop a mattress and bedsprings on the floor. The john was a ripped young man in his thirties who looked as if he should be called "Muscles." Muscles, I learned later, was a criminal attorney who, in the next several hours, would prove to be an unstoppable cock-whore, the likes of which I have not met since. He was blond and about five-foot-eight with a deep tan covering all but the perfectly-rounded ass-cheeks that Rowdy was so methodically fucking. His hair was cut short—via an expensive salon, no doubt—and clung in cum-soaked wisps to his forehead and facial cheeks as sweat ran off his body, slicking his shaved thighs, soaking the sheets and dripping from pointy nipples he pinched and twisted.

Andy went to the front of the bed, and taking the man's drooping chin in his hand, tried to look into the john's lust-glazed eyes for some sign of consciousness. His face only inches from the ecstatic and grimacing animal, Andy said loudly, as if talking to someone who was deranged or slow: "Are you alright, man? Can you take it?"

"Yes!" heaved the man, angry at having been brought back from his reveries by a rational and ridiculous question. Just then, I was taken aback by the perfection of Andy's semi-hard prick. I had imagined in quieter moments what Andy's dick looked like and had assembled a picture in my head that only partially did justice to what was actually the prettiest cock I've ever seen. It was a pink-hued bat with an apricot-shaped crown concealed between quickly-disappearing folds of foreskin. Two baggy nuts dropped from its base, swinging heavily back and forth as Andy shook his cock to invigorate it for his next shift with Muscles. The two boys had been savaging the man for an hour already and Rowdy needed a break. Andy's thick-haired belly distended and contracted as he began to pant and motivate himself for another go-round, a bony, size-twelve foot proffered for the john's now-cramped mouth.

The stocky Rowdy had noticed me when we entered the room and had given me a shit-eatin' grin and a wink. Built like a tank, Rowdy had thighs as big around as my waist and a back made for heavy work. With dirty blond hair on his head and fine black hair everywhere else, the boy came from good Polish stock and had the body of a linebacker. Andy's return signaled that Rowdy could yank his very fat knob out of the john's ass. The man began to wail his displeasure until Rowdy groused "here, here" and made his demanding client scoot around and flip on his back so Rowdy could beat himself furiously to a gushing, spurting nut. Balling his face up and biting his lip—both boys had already come once—Rowdy flung his spunk onto the lawyer's face, after which the man rolled beneath the discharge and smeared himself with the jelly-thick spooge. I had been in the room less than a minute and had laid eyes upon one sizable dick and one copious amount of jizz. My head began to swim.

Stumbling back from his exertions, Rowdy flung the strings of cum that clung to his hand onto the floor and squeezed his hose clear of any semen still trapped in the tube. Then he thrust an arm behind himself and staggered backwards to me, his sweaty, hairy body seeking support from my outstretched arms as he threw an arm around my shoulder chummily, as if he'd just won a long-distance race. Then he flashed that winning, chipped-tooth smile I'd seen stretch across his face when he cracked wise at my expense or had beaten Andy at the video games they played constantly. Seemingly oblivious to the fact that Muscles lay on the bed two feet away, he said to me: "Whew! That guy grinds your dick like he's gonna rip it off!"

I was startled, but of course, he knew all too well that the man had heard him. In the several times they'd performed these services for Muscles, they had come to know that anything they said or did to their john was absorbed into the man's self-induced degradation and was the biggest turn-on the boys provided. Reveling in being the receptacle of their ample sperm, Muscles got off on being an impersonal fuck-object to two boys from this side of the economic divide. In turn, the boys found it helpful in their professional obligations that he didn't require them to play-act as they had to with other clients. This john didn't want some high-priced rent-boy fucking him with the practiced lasciviousness common in porn films. He was here for a mercenary fuck from the kind of boys who mowed his lawn. He liked to see their embarrassment for him as he worshipped their cocks. And their comic surprise when some new kink they'd invented only exhilarated him more and raised the bar for new experiments designed to stretch and prod his hungry mouth and ass.

"You got a cigarette?" Rowdy asked me, motioning me over to the dining-room chair he was sitting in against the wall. Andy took over with Muscles, grabbing a fistful of blond hair and admonishing him to "watch your teeth, man!" He rubbed his still-lengthening cock over the man's face and through his matted hair, tentatively letting him take the head into his mouth, ready to pull out at the first sign of pain.

"Sometimes," Rowdy explained in a low voice, "ya gotta sorta slap him a little to get the guy to back off your cock. We've never had to punch him or nothing, but I'm not sure we can keep seeing him if he keeps getting worse." As I proffered my almost-empty pack of smokes, he took one promising, "I'll take a break later and go get some."

While I took a long drag from the cigarette I'd retrieved and lighted, Rowdy rested and watched Andy, who was letting the now-conscientious cocksucker go all the way down on his hard dick. With all ten inches of creamy pink penis disappearing, Andy relaxed and let Muscles float off into ecstasy, occasionally encouraging, "Easy man. That's the way, easy."

We all drifted into a profound silence. I was entranced by the blowjob and the boys fell into a shorthand of gestures—Andy motioning for a sip of the beer Rowdy had fetched or signaling to put the cigarette between his lips. They also mouthed words to each other, stifling laughter and rolling their eyes when Muscles let loose a muffled moan, his eyes closed sleepily, his tongue and hands unconsciously exploring the textures and tastes of the oozing cock in his mouth. Forty-five minutes later, Andy alerted Rowdy that he was gonna shoot and proceeded to buck and swear as the john coughed and gagged, finally losing a long ropy strand of cum that swung from his chin and dropped. Not all but most of the load was secured down his throat.

As the man fell backwards on the bed, Rowdy roused himself and he and Andy began talking while the man lay there, his ass hanging over the edge of the bed with a twelve-inch dildo wedged inside. As the boys discussed what was next, Andy slowly drove the foot-long pole inside Muscles. Rowdy asked Andy if he was ready to "fuck the dude" again, but was interrupted as the attorney pulled Rowdy onto his face so hard and heavily, I wondered if the man could breathe. But breathe he did, as well as bury his face and tongue inside Rowdy's sweaty ass-cheeks. Then, as the boys continued to strategize, Rowdy jumped a little and exclaimed, "Oh, man, he's got a finger up my ass, dude!" This was followed by a glow of restrained pleasure which crept across his face. Andy laughed good-naturedly at what until now was his friend's private weak spot, then winked at me as Rowdy swiveled his hips and closed his eyes. Allowing Rowdy to enjoy the sensation but watching his friend's face, Andy softly reminded him, "Don't come yet, man," while fingering his own ass for the erection that would soon be required. After twenty minutes, Andy decided Rowdy was too close and declared they should both fuck the bitch at once—the suggestion of which brought an eager moan from the man between Rowdy's cheeks.

Muscles was turned lengthwise on the bed, his ass still full of dildo. Rowdy unseated himself and applied lube to his dick. Then—in an act that made me squirm—he lubed up his friend's swinging dick. The assist was seemingly old hat for the two. It was also necessary if Andy was to continue pacifying Muscles with faux cock while positioning him properly for the upcoming assault. Rowdy rubbed his friend's great pink pole with a thick layer of grease as he beat his own ass-eating-induced erection. The look of concentration on his face belied the extreme intimacy of the act, the technical nature of the lubing striking me as being more like diving partners who checked each other's tanks before submerging.

The boner in my pants became painful and I gave in to my excitement. My pants and underwear fell to my knees. I sat to the side of the bed against the wall and realized I had been invited because my presence added an additional thrill for Muscles. The random stranger who watched him get his ass stuffed with dick. For the first time, the john looked straight into my eyes while lowering himself onto Andy's towering dick. He impaled himself slowly, not a hint of exertion on his face, not a glimmer of emotion in his flinty blue eyes. Only sweat and short hard breathing revealed his intense pleasure as he squatted over Andy and slid the length of the boy's cock in and out of his ass, staring into my eyes, occasionally glancing at my cock. Once he even muttered "nice" as some sign of approval.

Rowdy added a finger to the gash that the man's asshole appeared to be after its prolonged use. Then, squatting on the bed, he got behind the lawyer and pushed his head forward to bring his ass to the right angle for the fat hard cock. Rowdy aimed to add to the john's already-full bowels. With a push, he was in and I watched as his dick crushed against Andy's, sliding into the depths until both of sets of balls bumped and tumbled against each other. The lawyer braced himself against the wall as he struggled for balance, Rowdy all but crushing his ribcage in the powerful embrace that steadied his methodically thrusting hips. The weight of Rowdy's body now borne by the thickly-muscled legs of the john, Andy flexed and thrust his hips off the bed as he and his friend slowly pounded the fist-tight hole.

Rowdy could be seen grimacing over the shoulder of the john as he crowed, "Yeah! You wanna get fucked, man, you came to the right house!"

Both boys laughed, proudly displaying the vigor their youth and strength possessed. The man on the receiving end began to wail as his overburdened ass smoked and burned under the increasingly furious assault. The boys actually began to show signs of real pleasure as what must have been a very tight fit squeezed and clutched their dicks, which certainly rubbed together in the recesses of the john's ass. For half an hour, the boys worked on him. When Rowdy became tired and needed to lie down, Muscles happily rode a now horizontal Rowdy as Andy, now at liberty to pound the john's ass with unbridled severity, balled the greedy attorney from behind with blows I feared might split the man in two. I imagined Andy relished the chance to avenge himself on the kind of man who'd always been around during the inevitable arrests. The superior but polite officer of the court who treated him as if he was too dumb to understand what was going on, who secretly wanted to taste the pleasures of their young clients. Rowdy simply rested beneath the sweating man, his arms folded behind his head as he squeezed his eyes shut and worked to control the boiling seed that threatened to fly from his fat, hard prick.

When the digital clock hit six in the evening and the sky began to turn from day into evening, the boys must have made the calculation that their john's time was almost up. They wordlessly agreed to release the pent-up spunk they'd both been controlling throughout the nearly hour-long fuck. Andy pulled out and Muscles, apparently also realizing the time had come, spun with Rowdy still seated inside him and milked the boy's cock. Coaxing the beautiful beast to burst and spit cum into his face and onto his chest, the lawyer was exultant. A few splashes landed on Rowdy, who, because he wasn't paying attention, had not been able to dodge them. Too close to climax to be concerned, he let his third nut go a few seconds later, the gooey white load running from the ass of the man onto his tightly constricted balls as he whooped and grinded himself into the boy's sputtering dick.

As the last of Rowdy's shots rocketed up his ass, the john waved me over demanding, "Come on me, come on, come *on!*" I tried to oblige, but only made it a couple of feet before I began shooting a stream of cum which flew through the air and landed on the man's chest and his thighs. My explosion earned an "oh, yeah!" from Andy, who beamed at my helplessness and applauded my performance.

As I shuddered and jerked, Muscles collapsed on top of Rowdy who held him close lest he flop off the bed. Andy ushered me out and muttered to Rowdy: "take him into the bathroom before you finish him off," a veiled reference, I learned, to the john's penchant for only getting off with a stream of piss raining down from above. The boys disliked it and took turns satisfying his kink. Today was Rowdy's turn. I heard him rouse the man with a resigned "come on, time to finish up" as Andy and I exited to the living room for a smoke and a beer.

As we downed the beers, Muscles was led to the bathroom, from where a few minutes later we heard a deafening roar as he finally orgasmed, immediately followed by the hissing of the showerhead, which signaled Rowdy's intention to see the john deposited back into the expensive suit that lay crumpled in a heap and sent on his way.

The twenty-five hundred dollars the john left was divided between the two boys after an envelope marked RENT was filled. Fifty dollars was then shoved at me by the two howling pranksters, who said it was my share for "all the work you did!" The three of us laughed and punched each other, then headed to the nearby bar where we played pool and drank beer on my fee. As always, the boys drew admiring stares and when they were eventually approached by a regular and his out-of-town guest, they'd dissolved into laughter after telling him: "We have to ask our new partner!" I laughed too. The boys bear-hugged me as they left, admonishing me: "Don't come by on your way home. We'll handle these two ourselves!"

A Good Spanking

JAY STARRE

Although I love ass and just about anything to do with it, I had never thought that spanking a butt could provide such an incredible sexual thrill. Then I met a sweet young twink named Grant. He had arrived two hours late for our dinner date, and when we went back to my place, he was still unrepentant, claiming I could have left had I not wanted to wait.

"Fuck you," I laughed, not really mad, but determined to teach him a lesson.

"How about a good spanking first?" the young blond giggled, waving his sexy ass in front of me as I sat on the living room couch. Without thinking, I reached out and smacked his butt with the palm of my hand.

"Oh yeah, baby." He wiggled his butt in my face. "More!"

I thought it was a joke and landed another good slap on one firm cheek. His squirming and giggling made me laugh, so and I offered his butt a few more whacks.

"Let me get naked so you can give me a proper spanking," Grant said. His face was flushed and his bright blue eyes sparkled. He was serious. He wanted me to spank his fucking butt! I wasn't quite sure what I thought of that, but he was already stripping, his clothes flying every which way, and before I could think of what to utter, he was—dare I say it?—butt naked. And Grant naked is quite a sight. Tall and lanky but with muscles in all the right places, his body is taut with athletic energy. A flat stomach and slim waist swells out at the hips to a rounded pair of melons that are impossible to say no to. I would spank that ass if that's what he wanted!

"Get naked." Grant tore at the fly of my shorts. "I want your cock to get hard and press up into my belly as you beat my butt." His own cock was stiff and bobbing.

"Alright, alright!" I said, already excited at the idea of playing with Grant's spectacular pair of buns. He had my shorts and underwear pulled off over my socks in seconds. "Get on my lap and spread your legs."

He plopped down submissively over my lap with his thighs wide open. His boner poked into my crotch and rubbed against my own growing erection. I gazed down at the lush melons being offered for my inspection. Grant has a big butt, which looks especially gigantic on his slim frame. It is sexy as hell. I couldn't just look. I began to feel it, reaching down with both hands, running them over the swell of his cheeks. His flesh was hot, and hard. There was a light coat of hair that was so blond, it was nearly invisible. The hair disappeared near the crack, and as Grant opened his thighs wider, I could see the slick skin of his entirely hairless butt-crevice.

"Come on, spank my ass. I need a good spanking, Jay." He lifted his butt and gyrated it. I was enjoying the fondling, but decided I may as well oblige him. I raised my hand. He raised his butt. *Whack*!

The smack was loud in the evening silence. The tingle on my palm was *vaguely exciting*. The pink mark I left on his ass was *very exciting*. The quivering of his big butt cheeks was *most exciting of all*.

"Yeah, spank me, Jay. Come on, spank my ass," Grant panted.

His ass fidgeted, eager for more. I raised my hand and repeated the action, this time landing a blow on the other cheek. The loud smack was answered by a twitching in my cock beneath Grant's belly. The jiggle of Grant's big butt cheek was so sexy, I raised my hand and smacked it again. And again. And again.

"Oh yeah!" Grant was caterwauling by then. "Please, spank me hard. Oh, yeah! Yeah, I've been so bad. Spank my poor butt, please!"

He was definitely play-acting. I wasn't spanking his ass *that* hard. But the vigorous slapping of my open palm against his naked flesh was leaving its mark. Both cheeks were flaming pink by the time I'd landed a good twenty or thirty whacks on each of them. I halted for a moment, breathing hard and staring down at my handiwork. My cock was throbbing and drooling, and so was Grant's, the two pieces of meat rubbing together as Grant writhed underneath under my hand's assault.

"More," Grant begged. "Give me at least a hundred." He had thrown his thighs wide and his puckered little asshole was visible between the reddened cheeks. As he shoved his ass in the air for more punishment, the slot quivered and gaped as if it too was hungry for more action. That's when I lost some of my control. It had been his game so far, but suddenly the sight of that vulnerable hole, sweaty, hairless and quivering, the beseeching whine of his voice, and the flushed trembling of his wriggling ass, all combined to drive me a bit mad. I slapped his ass again, much harder. He cried out, but his ass rose to meet my next blow with even more enthusiasm. His asshole spasmed, and gaped open. I rained down a steady stream of hard whacks, jammed my other hand between Grant's big heaving ass cheeks and pointing my index finger right at his hungry hole. I crammed that finger deep up the tight fuck-tunnel.

"Oh, god. Oh, god. Spank my poor butt. Finger my hot hole. I'm sorry I was so bad. Please don't stop."

Grant's blubbering was music to my ears. His writhing ass, now plugged and beet-red was a heady sight. My cock oozed pre-cum as it slid against his. I was getting higher and higher as Grant's heated ass grew redder and redder.

"Oh fuck! I'm cumming!" he shouted. His butt reared up and his jizz sprayed my lap. I crammed my finger farther up his steamy slot and held it there while he shot cum all over me, the last few smacks of my open palm on his sweaty butt resounding in the air.

That was enough for me. Wiggling my finger deeper, I thrust up into his gooey belly, rubbing my aching cock into the nut-cream he had just ejected. I ran my free hand all over his heated butt, the smooth flesh burning up from the powerful punishment it had just received. My cockhead swelled. Then, as I groaned out in rapture, it went off, adding my copious load to his. He lay in my lap afterwards, relaxed and half-asleep. I rubbed my hands all over his inflamed butt cheeks, and thought: I wouldn't mind a repeat performance sometime.

And Grant offered me that—in spades. The very next Friday night, he was late again for our date. While he dallied, I was left to fend off drunken men in the pub. And when he did arrive, just as before, he didn't apologize. But when we got to my place, he tore off his clothes the moment we entered the door.

"Spank my hot butt again. I was bad, very bad," he begged me. His passionate look galvanized me to action. I was stripped and on the couch before he had finished removing his own clothing.

"Get over here on my lap and spread your legs. I'm gonna beat your fat butt till you shoot your load," I promised with a leering grin.

Grant hopped on top of me eagerly, his sexy ass perched within easy reach. His bubble-butt wiggled and gyrated in my lap. He parted his muscular thighs, spreading his butt cheeks at the same time. Down in the crack, to my surprise, I couldn't help but notice the square flange of a butt-plug protruding from between his puckered ass-lips.

"I love doing it with a plug up my ass," Grant giggled. "If feels so fucking hot!"

I was shaking with lust as I began to beat his butt. The loud spanking was punctuated by his squeals of pain and pleasure. His crack rose and fell, the plug moving in and out as evidence of his lusty excitement. As I spanked him, I also pressed on the square flange, shoving it deep as Grant cried out and bucked upwards toward my hand. As his ass grew progressively more flushed and sweaty, we humped each other's bellies with increasing friction. I slammed my open palm down on his heaving ass cheeks. The big mounds grew more flushed, glistening with a sheen of sweat. Every time I landed a blow on a quivering cheek, I thrust my palm against the plug up his ass. Grant bucked and jerked, crying out with the power of his painful pleasure. His ass grew fiery red. My hand burned. My cock got harder and harder. I tore the plug from his butt and stared at the gaping hole, which was oozing lube and quivering with desire. I shoved three fingers inside him as both of our cocks exploded.

I held him in my lap, those three fingers deep in his steaming hot asshole, his ass-cheeks flaming pink. It took a good ten minutes for us to cool down. It didn't take too much longer for us to get hot all over again.

Since that night, I've been eagerly waiting for my next date with Grant. I have a sneaking suspicion that Grant's lessons in the art of pleasurable spanking have only just begun.

Fine with me. I can't help but wonder: what will he come up with next?

James, Dean

JOHN DOUGLAS

From: Rim Pig
To: Butthole
Subject: pics

Hey! GREAT ad and ass shot, man! HOT hole . . . love it, man.
I can really see my long wet tongue fucking your asshole. I'll get in
as deep as humanly possible as I LOVE a nice, hot, sweaty asshole in
my face. Like the aroma. Like it hairy. Am really into uncut cock as
well, and yours is mouth-watering. Love to be able to spend a night
with my tongue buried deep in your tight shithole. Wake you up in
the morning eating you out, too. That's a hole I could really make a
meal of. Up for meeting?

Dean

From: Butthole
To: Rim Pig
Subject: Re: pics

Definitely up for meeting. And soon! I'm a total pig
when it comes to getting my butt licked. It's gone beyond
a passion. Being rimmed is a fetish for me, could never do

without it! Great email. I think we could have lots of fun.
    James

From: Rim Pig
To: Butthole
Subject: facesitter—sit on me
    Then let's do it. Your ass is so HOT. I'd never wanna take my
tongue out of it. You have a nice round ass and great hole. I can see
just by looking at it, it's a hole I can really work on. Love to lick up
and down your crack, smell your sweaty ass, have you rub it on my
face. I love getting my tongue in as deep as it'll go, man, which is
pretty deep. Your shithole deserves a good tongue-fuck. In and outta that hole, man, fast, deep, hard, tasting it, licking it, sucking your
hole, fucking it with my tongue. Looking at your asshole makes me
hard. How about we start off with you sittin' on my face in a pair of
used, skid-marked briefs? I'd like to sniff your hole right through
them. Maybe even have you fart in my face. Hope that doesn't turn
you off, but I just wanna enjoy the total asshole. The Taste. The
Smell. Wanna have you blow a load in my mouth and all over my
face. Your cock and ass are both what I need. I KNOW I could make
a meal outta your ass man and never come up for air. When can we
meet? I'll be visiting my sister in July and she's only 30 miles from
you. Let's do it. I need ya.
    Dean

From: Butthole
To: Rim Pig
Subject: Damn shame
    I'll be in Seattle most of July, so we'll miss seeing each other.
I would love a good tongue workout. I've had enough tongues up
me to know who is a real rimmer and who just does it to get to
fucking, and while I enjoy all butt play, I LOVE being rimmed for

its own sake. If it were possible to breath through ass, I would have a tongue up me constantly. My last bf and I tried, but, damn . . . he needed air sometimes. Mind you, he could have died trying to live up inside my ass.

It was difficult shooting the attached butt shots—did best I could. When I was reaching around, I accidentally pushed out a fart as I took the pic. Made me laugh! So here they are—a fart photo and a non-fart photo! I like my butt being enjoyed totally, so I could get into farting for you. Nothing you wrote turns me off, skid-marks and all.

The bf I mentioned—he never let me wash my butthole. He liked to lick it clean for me. Shit is one thing that doesn't appeal to me. However he totally got off on it and I enjoyed having him love everything my ass does AND getting a great tongue fuck at the same time. Something very nurturing and infantile about him cleaning me: two men, one licking, the other being cleansed by him.

Haven't let my cock cum in last five days. I like the idea of being denied until a man decides to release me and wanks me or sucks me off without me being able to touch myself. Am always looking at men and checking out their mouths to see how long their tongue is, how wide their smile, the shape of their nose and face and how suitable they for riding. Sorry about July.

James

From: Rim Pig
To: Butthole
Subject: I wanna eat your shitty ass and taste that cheesy cock

Hey James! Too bad we're gonna miss each other. Just seeing an email from you showing an attachment gets my cock goin' before I even open it. I know it'll be HOT when we finally do meet. Love the fart pic. I can see my face in your ass and my nose in there when a fart escapes and savouring the aroma of your asshole stench.

I am not really into shit, but I do have fantasies. I could get off on seeing your shit caked on your ass hairs and around the hole and the idea of me giving you a hot cleaning session. Total asshole worship. Like to be kneeling in front of you while you're on the toilet taking a shit. Rubbing your balls between your legs and fingering your shitty hole. Lettin' my tongue be your toilet paper and servicing your asshole. I'd get off on licking your ass first through skid-marked briefs and smelling your ass juices. Putting my nose in your crack through your briefs. Mouth waiting. More and more it sounds as though even though you must be hot in bed, you sound like a nice person as well. All the more reason to wanna be in your ass. Any cum shots? I have a couple of butt plugs here I'd like to try out on your hole, too. Have a good day man. NEED YOU. :) When can we re-sked our hook-up?

From: Butthole
To: Rim Pig
Subject: Good morning to you!

Woke up with a real longing for your tongue—no need to say where!

Did extra sets of squats at the gym yesterday, so my ass is feeling especially tight. Was horny at the gym working out, seeing fit men (with very sittable faces), feeling my butt aching to jump on one. The change room was a sweet kinda torture, watching other muscular men undress, letting their cocks swing free while mine was trapped and aching for a wanking.

To be sucked off and not allowed to blow. How frustrating would it feel? And in meantime, keep the focus right where it should—smack on my butthole. Help me! My butt is a rimming radar, scanning for a friendly face. It's interesting having my cock unable to cum. It's demanding attention like my rear. Will never lose my first love though! I'm a rim-pig, ALWAYS will take a tongue fuck first. Not sure when we can meet. Will get back to you on that one.

James

From: Rim Pig

To: Butthole

Subject: wanna eat your nasty asshole and shit-stained . . .

Man, I wanna make you feel like I am eating your asshole like never before. You name it, I'd do it for you, man. You're everything I need and my tongue is longing to be in your shithole, reaching in there to its deepest depths. I won't kid you, if you give me a definite time to come visit you, I'll make the long drive (worth it, I'm sure) and work on your ass for hours. And yes, I wanna chew on your foreskin and suck you, too. I wanna taste your sweet juice and smelly cheese. Eat your ass, man, suck you off, then eat your ass again. While I suck you, I'll finger your tight asshole—maybe three fingers. Opening that shithole wider so my tongue gets in there even deeper.

I am an ass pig. I cannot get enough of a beautiful man's ass. Wanna have your hole rubbed in my face, have that ass smell all over my face, saliva dripping down your hairy ass crack while I lick up and down, all around and deep inside you man. Your cock screaming to get loose and explode as I eat you and you moan. Wanna have my cock in you, fucking you hard fast and deep like a jackhammer, cumming in your asshole, then sucking my juice outta your asshole and tonguing you the rest of the night into the morning, falling asleep with my tongue in your ass wakin' up still in your butthole. Wanna hold you, make love to you, and eat you out and make you happy.

It's cool seeing how far I can work my tongue in a butt and sometimes it feels like the little piece in my mouth beneath my tongue is gonna rip because I'm in too far. Have a good day, man. If you're this hot in email, I can only imagine the ass eating session I could have if only I had the opportunity to be in your ass for real. I am coming your way in the next week. How about we meet at that video store near you, the one I read about on the 'net? Say, 6pm on the 12th?

Dean

From: Butthole
To: Rim Pig
Subject: our butt needs your tongue

Dean, I want to have you take charge of my butt, write Property of Dean on it, then tongue-fuck it and make my butt a cum store. Anytime you want, you can eat your cum out of me. Or you can seal off my foreskin by squeezing it between two fingers, then milk me till I shoot in my skin. Then you finger my cum into my butt where I'll keep it for you for whenever you want it. Fit my foreskin with a tube and run it round to my butt so when I need to piss, I'll piss into my ass and hold it in there till you want me to let it out. Just to feel your tongue brush my cheeks as you explore around my/our butt, sleeping with you using my butt as a pillow, Property of Dean still written across it. Now, this does give me the shits! I am in San Fran on the 12th. Sorry, man. Not jerking you around like a cyber flake, I promise.

From: Rim Pig
To: Butthole
Subject: wish I coulda been there to smell your farts man

Thanks for the skid-marked Calvins! Oh, yeah, what treat for my hungry tongue! Thought about you farting in them and I blew 4 times. Whenever you fart, man, just imagine you are over my mouth and nose. And it's fucking hot if you go ahead and finger your hot hole for me. Shove it in deep and pretend it's my tongue. If my refrigerator was empty and all I had to eat was your asshole,

I'd be in heaven. It's totally cool if you explode a hot, smelly, loud fart in my face as my tongue is inside you. It's like a fantasy, man: I see you, I want you, I need you :) I can't have you. Gotta have you, man. In real life. You promise we're gonna meet someday soon? I'm praying you're for real.

From: Butthole
To: Rim Pig
Subject: Re: wish I coulda been there to smell your farts man
    Hey, been keeping well? Did these pix, hope you like them!
    James

From: Rim Pig
To: Butthole
Subject: lemme lick that shit outta your hole man
    Hey James! Missing you :) lately, but appreciate the pics man as usual, even if you didn't include any words with 'em. Jerked my cock looking at them and sniffing your rank undies. Did you get mine? When you get a good cheese load, smear it all over the crotch, please! I'm desperate for your man-stink. The shit coming outta your asshole is HOT and so is every ass shot you send me. Makes me want to be under your face sucking your hot butthole. I can only imagine how your hot ass tastes, man. Seein' it in pics gets me going. I'm desperate to see it in person. Like to get a whiff of that shit coming out of your hole. You sure are good with the camera! Your asshole photographs very well, and it's killing me that I can't have any. I know I could follow through and make my shit fantasies real with a man like you. Hungry for your hole, James. Get together this Wednesday? I'll be in town. Made an excuse to get away from work. All ready to cum.
    Dean

From: Butthole

To: Rim Pig

Subject: Re: lemme lick that shit outta your hole man

Sorry I couldn't see you last week. Was too busy to even answer email. But I was thinking of you using my butt as a place for you to store things so you don't forget them. Eat off it, put food up me and eat it out anytime you're hungry. Most of all, lemme sit on your face and do what comes naturally to us both. Can you come this way this weekend? Needing a big fat demanding tongue—yours. Now could be the time finally.

James

From: Rim Pig

To: Butthole

Subject: need a whiff of your smelly farts man

Can't do it this coming weekend. Working overtime. Damn. But like the idea of storing items in your ass man. Since I'll always be eating it, I'd never lose anything. Think of me every time you fart and how bad I wanna have my face under your ass. Wanna worship your shithole in every imaginable way, man. Want you satisfied, James. Your hot ass is MINE.

From: Butthole

To: Rim Pig

Subject: Re: need a whiff of your smelly farts man

Now who's flaking?! Just kidding. Cock still hasn't cum, though taken out a couple of times and wanked. Got me busting. My butt wants your tongue to take ownership.

From: Rim Pig

To: Butthole

Subject: my tongue is your toilet paper man, use it

Hey, James! More hot pics! Who is the lucky bastard you were showing off for man? :(Cheatin' on me man? Talking on the phone the other night was awesome. Hearing you wank and not cum for me was HOT HOT HOT. Your cock must stink, man. It's a hot cock. Your asshole though, man! Fuck! I wanna make love to your shit-hole, man, tease it, tongue the outside rim of it, poke into you. Lick up and down your dirty shit-caked crack. You in your pissed-in shorts, wanting to wank as I eat your ass sucking your hole licking madly. Lovin' the smell, the farts, the shit stains, the aroma of a tight manhole I need to be mine.

From: Butthole
To: Rim Pig
Subject: Re: my tongue is your toilet paper man, use it

Got a friend to help with the pix for you. No need to be jealous. He's not my type. You are. My butt is yours! He helped with those pix as I can only stretch around so far. Wanted to show you how my/our hole is wide and ready for your tongue. You standing over my butt ready to do what you want. All yours. When do you want it?

From: Rim Pig
To: Butthole
Subject: fun in the bathroom

I want it NOW! Wanna be in the bathroom with you, man, kneelin' between your legs, sucking your cheesy smelly cock as you take a shit. I can hear you grunting as it dives into the bowl, man. You shoot your load in my mouth and piss in my face. You go to wipe your ass and I grab the toilet paper outta your hand. I'm with you now, man, no need for toilet paper. You bend over, your ass in my face, and moan wildly as I do what I do best. Clean your hole out, lick it, love it. Want all of you, man. I love the thought of it being OUR ass, James. A LOT! I wanna do everything you show me in your pix and everything we talk about on the phone. But it's like shopping and seeing what I can't buy. I see you and want you and I can't have you. I'm gonna call tonight. We gotta stop flaking on each other. We cannot break this bond, man.

From: Butthole
To: Rim Pig
Subject: SHIT!

Sorry I was out when you called! Loved your message on the answering machine. Am thinking of not shitting ever again unless you are there, sucking or wanking me. Internet is great for making connections, but it's frustrating as hell. We gotta meet and do this soon. Want to have you lock my cock away, give you the key, sign a contract giving you my butt and have you put a chastity belt with a butt plug on me so no other men can get up in me and I have to ask you when I can take a shit. Damn, I hate distance sometimes. Can you meet me at the cheap motel near my place on the 30th?

From: Rim Pig
To: Butthole
Subject: my tongue IS your butt plug James

The thirtieth is IT! Man, I will be your butt plug. Take a shit, I will be there for you. Your arms tied, I decide when your cheesy cock cums and when you can shit and fart and where I wanna have you do it. My face is your face, man, use it. I love OUR hole man. It's MY hole man. I need it and wanna fuck it, cum in it, piss in it, eat it all out man. Tease your smelly sweaty cock. You're tied up man. At my mercy. You moan wildly. I'm ready. Finally. Yes. Yes.

From: Butthole
To: Rim Pig
Subject: Re: my tongue IS your buttplug James

We're on! FUCK. You're right. Your tongue should be the butt plug, more than adequate to keep other men out. I have to go out now, hard cock sticking up. Gotta walk down the street and as I wear no underwear, the thought of walking and my big hard dick sticking out of my pants and knowing it's yours makes me smile. If I have to shit again later, do you want me to photograph? Gotta go, but am thinking of you. Can't wait for the 30th.

James

From: Rim Pig
To: Butthole
Subject: yeah man take a nice shit for me tonight . . . I OWN you man

Hey James! Just a few more days until I taste your ass for real! Have a great day, but NOT too much fun. Yes, man, PLEASE, would love to wake up tomorrow, see my emails and see you and your shit. Think of me and my open mouth waiting and hungry. Remember, you're mine man. Keep 'em caged. My face is your butt plug man. You tied up and helpless. I do whatever I want to you. Have a great day man. Love, YOUR OWNER :)

From: Butthole
To: Rim Pig
Subject: Tucked

Dean, friends came around and went to lunch. While out, HAD to shit. Sorry. Will try and photograph it for you tomorrow, though this Friday is an exceptionally busy day for me. Farted earlier and smiled thinking of you. Sorry I missed your call again.

James

From: Rim Pig

To: Butthole

Subject: waiting for a smelly fart man

Mornin' man. 5:15 a.m., so I am sure MY hot ass and caged cock are sleepin' HOPEFULLY alone right now. Haven't heard from you in a while, but how could I help but think of MY man after seeing those last pics! Wish I could have been out with you for lunch when you took the shit. Truth be told, I was looking at your pics when I woke up and my cock was acting up. That did it man. Cum all over. But I had also loved the new pic with you starting a nice shit. I ran my tongue across my screen, lickin' your shitty hole, cleaning it for you and rubbing and teasing OUR caged cock, letting more cum build up in there. Nice knowing you think of MY face when you use our ass to fart or shit. What time on our fateful day? How about 7pm?

From: Butthole

To: Rim Pig

Subject: Re: waiting for a smelly fart man

Just a quick check of emails before running out the door. 7pm is ON! Haven't much time, wish my cock—sorry, YOUR cock—was loose and able to be wanked. Hope you don't mind, I did a quick finger-fuck before getting out of bed, not for long though. Would much rather get that exercise from your tongue ... grrrrrrrrrrr.

Better run, am late now. Got to go to doctors for test results.

James

From: Rim Pig

To: Butthole

Subject: HUMAN BUTTPLUG NEEDS HOT ASS TO OWN

Yeah, I know you said today was your busy day, so I appreciate sending pics. They were great as usual. Nice to see OUR cock still caged and being punished. Piss shot hot. The ass shot is a tease, man. I should bend that ass over and spank it real good long and hard. You are not supposed to be fingering yourself unless I say you can. My tongue is all you need. Wanna have your smelly, sweaty, hairy ass crack in my face. You will take out my cock and jerk it as I eat and taste your crack. Let a good fart go in my face and I will tease the outside of your hole, lickin' it, poking my tongue at it, teasing you and OUR asshole, tastin' your shit, your farts, your nasty hole. Your hands feel great on my cock and I explode all over your face, gushers of cum as I still eat you out. I wish you would phone me, but understand your troubles. Feel better. I will call you tonight. Have a good day, man! Get ready for 7pm on the thirtieth!

    Dean

From: Rim Pig
To: Butthole
Subject: owner needs willing whole

    Hope you've been ok, James? Miss you. The last time we talked on the phone was great, just keeps getting better and dirtier. Sorry for sounding mad at you for having to change our date. I was just frustrated is all. But the fifth of next month is fine. Just a few more days of waiting than the original date. No worries.

    You'd better not be getting naughty over there without me. Perhaps you need a spanking. Hope you are horny and frustrated. Have a great day, James! Can't wait for you to shit for me. In real life, I mean. Take care.

    Dean

From: Butthole
To: Rim Pig
Subject: Re: owner needs willing whole

    I did do a shit for you, not in person, but at least I took some quick pix; this one attached was the best as I missed the butt entirely in most shots! Did better with the dick ones. I may have to postpone our meeting on the 5th, but I'll let you know. Hold tight.

James

From: Rim Pig
To: Butthole
Subject: human buttplug misses you

Hey, James, you are very quiet these days. Hope someone isn't movin' in on MY cock and smelly hole, man. Those cigarette burn pix you sent were HOT!

From: Rim Pig
To: Butthole

Ok, 4 weeks and no reply. I can take a hint man. Have a good life.

from Behind

JONATHAN ASCHE

"Buy you a drink?"

I turned to look at the man who'd sidled next to me at the bar, giving him a five-second appraisal. He had the face of a bull terrier. The body wasn't much better. Broad shoulders and nice arms, but those were no abs of steel. His belly was just threatening to spill over the waist of his jeans.

Probably was a nice guy, but inner beauty isn't what I look for in a trick I meet at a bar. I was about to decline politely when another patron in the bar walked up, slapping the stranger beside me on the shoulder. "Eddie! How's it hangin'?"

"Excuse me," Eddie said with an apologetic smile, revealing his crooked teeth. He turned to chat with his acquaintance.

From behind, Eddie was a god!

Those broad shoulders tapered down to a waist that was surprisingly narrow from this view. And just below that waist was one of the most delectable asses I'd seen in recent memory. Full, firm and shapely, it commanded my full attention. My eyes riveted to Eddie's backside. I tried to picture that butt uncovered and imagined what I'd do with it when the jeans came off. My filthy musings quickly diverted much of my blood flow to my cock.

I traced my upper lip with the tip of my tongue as I marveled at Eddie's ass. I glanced up just in time to see his friend smile and wink at me. Blushing, I turned away. Eddie, no doubt tipped off by his friend that I'd been fixated on his ass, cut his conversation short and returned his attention to me. "Sorry about that. That was just a guy I know from work. So, about that drink . . ."

Okay, so I have my weaknesses. I accepted his offer. He ordered our drinks, then offered his hand. "By the way, I'm—"

"Eddie. I overheard. I'm Carl."

We shook hands, a business-like way to begin an evening we both hoped would end in carnal nastiness. When the drinks arrived I suggested we move to a quieter corner of the bar. What I meant, though, was a *darker* corner. If I needed to talk with his front to get to his backside, so be it, but that didn't mean I needed full illumination.

For what it was worth, Eddie was a nice guy, but fifteen minutes of conversation was enough. I scooted my chair closer to his, placed a hand on his knee and stroked his thigh. When I made contact with his hard-on, Eddie forgot what he was saying.

"Uh, where was I?" he asked, flushed.

I hadn't been listening. "I think this is where we decide if it's your place or mine."

We settled on mine. The door to my condo had barely shut behind us before we were rubbing against each other, our hands frantically groping. I closed my eyes and kissed him. My hands went straight for his butt, giving the rigid rump a hard squeeze. Eddie grunted, rubbing his bulging crotch against mine. He kneaded my ass as well, gripping my smaller, more compact butt with as much enthusiasm as I was gripping his. Briefly, I considered the possibility that Eddie might be a top, in which case our evening together would be fucked. I quickly dismissed this thought, though. With an ass that nice, Eddie had to be a pillow-biter.

We moved into my bedroom, shedding clothes as we went. I was just about to step out of my briefs when Eddie stopped me. "No, let me," he protested, pressing against me. He pinched my stiff nipples, first with his hands, then with his crooked teeth. As his mouth traveled over the ridges of my torso, I saw another possible problem: Eddie, it seemed, was primarily interested in my front. He pulled down my undies and started circling the head of my hard cock with his tongue. It felt pretty good, there's no denying that, but I had other plans.

"Wait," I said, pushing him away. "Uh, how 'bout I give you a back rub?"

Eddie gave me a curious glance. "I'm sucking your dick but you'd rather give me a massage?"

"I give very *thorough* massages," I said, raising my eyebrows suggestively, hoping he got the hint.

He shrugged. "Whatever."

I told Eddie to take off his underwear (plaid cotton boxers; no surprise there, somehow) and lie face-down on the bed. When the boxers came off, I saw that in addition to being blessed with a lick-your-lips ass, Eddie also was generously hung. Maybe later, I thought, admiring his long, fat cock before he climbed onto the bed and lay on his stomach.

I quickly joined Eddie on the bed, straddling the rise of his buttocks, my balls resting on the small of his back. Just feeling his butt cheeks beneath me made my dick quiver. Leaning forward, I gave Eddie a fairly perfunctory back rub. He made noises like he enjoyed what I was doing, but he had yet to experience my true skills. As I rubbed and kneaded the flesh of his back, I scooted down to the tops of Eddie's thighs. My stiff cock was now pressing against the groove of his ass. *That* got the pre-cum flowing. Eddie let out a low moan. He spread his legs a little bit, inviting me deeper.

A pool of my juices had collected at the beginning of his dark crevice. I dipped my fingers into my thick pre-cum and massaged it into the round hills of Eddie's ass. My fingers traced the crack of Eddie's voluptuous butt. I could feel the soft, downy hairs beneath my fingertips. I put a little more pressure against this dark divide, nestling my index finger between the warm cushions of Eddie's ass cheeks, tickling the coarser hairs that surrounded his hole. Just touching those hairs made my heart quicken.

I pulled his buttocks apart, letting the light shine in his hidden cavern. There was a thin brush of dark hair, and beneath that, barely visible, were the dark tan lips of Eddie's asshole. My thumb toyed with the slightly-puckered opening of his ass-lips. Slowly, Eddie gyrated his hips, letting out another moan. Under my breath, I sighed, "Oooh, *yes*."

Next thing I knew, my face was buried in Eddie's butt. So instinctual was my action that I couldn't attribute my decision to dig into Eddie's ass to conscious thought. Like breathing, I had to do it.

With my face pressed into his furry trench, I inhaled Eddie's scent. Smelled like he'd actually given his butt a spritz of cologne. Tell me he didn't know what his best physical feature was! Blending with this spicy fragrance was his own natural musk. Pulling my face away, I examined, close-up, the nuances of his sphincter—its darker hue, its tiny folds radiating out from a set of thin, tightly-pressed lips. They were lips I had to kiss.

I gently grazed Eddie's butthole with the tip of my tongue, moistening those closed lips. This elicited a few purrs from Eddie. I kept up this tender licking for a few minutes, letting Eddie enjoy the erotically relaxing sensation. But I was merely taming the wild beast before the kill. Without warning, I stabbed my tongue past the barrier of his sphincter and into the black cave within.

"Oh, my God!" Eddie howled, his body shuddering. His left leg kicked several times.

"Want me to stop?" I teased.

"Jesus Christ no," he sputtered, raising his ass up to my lips.

I tucked into his hole like it was a juicy cut of steak. My tongue swirled around the moistened petals of his rosebud, then plunged inside, reducing him to a quivering mass of Jell-O. Eddie burbled something about sucking my cock, so we got into the sixty-nine position, with him on top, his butt on my face. I curled my arms around his thighs and set to work, fucking his hole with my tongue. Eddie's tongue traced the veins of my dick. He licked my cockhead like it was an ice cream cone.

For a moment, the pleasure of his mouth on my cock paralyzed me—then turned me into a ravenous animal. As hungry as I was for his ass when I first tasted it, my appetite had now increased tenfold. I dove back into his furry channel, pulling at his ass-hairs with my teeth, gnawing at his tender bud, shoving my tongue into his juicy chute.

The noises in the bedroom filled the condo: Moans, groans, heavy breathing, slurping. I moved my fingers to Eddie's asshole, working the tip of my right index finger past his spit-lubed sphincter. Louder moans and groans. My left index finger joined the right one. His cock drooled pre-cum onto my chest. Carefully, I tugged his ass-lips apart. "Oh, god-*damn!*" Eddie howled before stuffing my cock back into his mouth.

It was my turn to howl. Eddie was trying to suck the cum right out of my balls, and was damn near succeeding. If I let him keep at it much longer he was going to get quite the healthy mouthful. Yet as appealing as that was, I had definite ideas about where I wanted my dick to be when I finally shot my load. I pushed him off me.

"Whatcha doing?" he giggled.

I wasn't as playful. "I want to fuck you," I said, my voice dead serious.

Eddie didn't question my intentions (thank God I didn't get any bullshit about him being a top). He rolled over onto his back. "Grease me up."

I grabbed a bottle of lube out of a drawer in the night stand. "Other way. On all fours."

He did as I said, pressing his face into a pillow and hoisting his smooth, round ass into the air. I crouched down to swab his twitching hole with my tongue, getting one last taste before I prepared to ram my dick into him. Eddie trembled. I could feel his butthole contracting against my tastebuds. "Fuck me," he gasped. I continued to tongue his asshole, torturing him with my slowness. "Shove your cock up my ass," he begged. This time I obliged; Eddie wasn't the only one being tortured.

Squirting lube onto my fingers, I got Eddie all "greased up," easily slipping my fingers inside his waiting butthole. I could feel his body twitch as I hooked three fingers into his chute. He made some noise that sounded like a cross between a moan and a sob. I couldn't deny him—or myself—any longer. With surprising agility I reached backward for the night stand drawer while still keeping my fingers plugged in Eddie's butt. Fumbling for condoms, I nearly knocked the lamp off the table before snagging three packets out of the box.

I pulled my fingers out of Eddie's ass long enough to get my dick covered and lubricated. That done, I moved against his ass, sandwiching the shaft of my cock between those warm, fleshy buns. Subtly rotating my hips, I ground my sheathed dick against his eager hole. Even with the rubber on, it felt pretty damn good, and it was driving Eddie crazy. "Fuck me," he pleaded desperately, pushing his ass back against my teasing prick.

Finally, I relented. The head of my cock nuzzled his slippery ass-opening. Though he'd been well primed, it took a little effort to get my tool inside Eddie's ass. Gripping the base of my dick, I leaned into him, forcing those succulent ass-lips apart. Eddie sucked in his breath as the tip of my cock poked into his hole. I hesitated, my cock just inside his hole, listening to our heavy breathing. At a deliberate pace I eased the rest of my cock inside him, savoring the feel of the walls of his ass as they pushed against my stiff dick.

When my cock was all the way in, with my pubes brushing against the groove of his ass-crack, I began to fuck him in slow, short strokes. Eddie groaned and gripped his pillow. He pushed backward, meeting my forward thrust. Clamping my hands onto the globes of Eddie's butt, I started to ride him a bit more forcefully, pulling my cock almost all the way out of his hole, then plunging back inside. Eddie bucked and jerked, babbling obscene nonsense into the pillow while I plowed into his ass.

I leaned forward, my torso resting on Eddie's back. We were both coated with sweat, our bodies creating the occasional farting noise when they rubbed together. It was almost funny, except both of us were too fucking horny to have much of a sense of humor. I started hammering Eddie's ass, brutally driving my cock into him. The mattress creaked loudly and the bed frame shook ominously. Eddie was all squeals, grunts and agonized groans. For a moment I eased up, afraid I might be hurting him. Reaching beneath him and gripping his dick proved otherwise: He was hard as steel and drooling pre-cum like a faucet with a worn washer. I cupped my hand beneath his cockhead, collecting a small puddle of his dew in my palm. My other hand tugged at his left shoulder, making him lift his face off the pillow long enough for me to roughly cup his ugly face with my other hand, the one full of Eddie's juice.

As Eddie slurped and nibbled at my hand, I slammed into his ass with all the tenderness of a rabid Rottweiler. My dick pounding against his prostate had him in such a state, he became unable to say whole words: "Fuh . . . shove eh uh muh ahhh! Fuh meh!" For a moment, I pictured his face as it must've appeared now—slick with his own pre-cum, the nostrils of that big, bent nose flared, those too-narrow eyes scrunched into wrinkled slits, those too-thin lips quivering to form coherent words. Strangely, that mental picture, for all its harshness, pushed me over the edge. My hand returned to his dick, stroking it as I bounced up and down on his ass

"Like that?" I hissed in his ear. "Like getting that sweet ass of yours fucked? Like it rough?"

Eddie's breathing became shallower, his moans more urgent. When he came, he cried out like he'd just been stabbed. Ropes of thick jism fired out of his cock, splattering the comforter. I managed to pump my cock into Eddie's sweet hole a few more times before coming with such force that for a moment my vision blurred. My dick, gripped by Eddie's sphincter, throbbed against his ass-lips as it pumped it's hefty load.

We collapsed in a heap on the bed. My cock stayed buried in Eddie's butt, lingering there until it started to go soft. Holding the base of the condom I carefully withdrew and went to the bathroom to throw it away. When I returned to the bedroom, Eddie was stepping into his shorts. "What're you doing?" I asked.

"S'pose you want the rest of the night to yourself," he said. Apparently experience had taught him not to expect to stay 'til sunrise.

When I first brought Eddie home, I'd hoped he'd leave this quickly and this quietly. Now I was asking myself if I wanted him to leave this soon. He was no fashion model, that's for sure, but was that really reason to discard one of the hottest asses I'd ever fucked? Was I that shallow?

I was, but my cock was blind.

"Wait," I said, stopping Eddie before he reached for his pants. "Stay."

The Sea in His Ass

DUANE WILLIAMS

In the travel agent's catalogue, Club Rio de Luna looked like a corner of heaven—an oasis of palm trees and pink azalea bushes, the white beach stretched against an endless turquoise sea. But it was the resort's swim-up pool that had sold them on the place. The pool was kidney-shaped with a bar you could wade up to and order margaritas from, which is what Scott and Zane were doing the first time they noticed Vladimir.

"Let me push you in the pool so he'll come over and scold me," Zane had said, licking salt off the rim of his glass. Vladimir, the lifeguard on duty, had been lecturing somebody's kid, a German boy, for shoving a smaller boy into the water.

"Or we could feign drowning," Scott had suggested.

The trip to Cuba had been booked months before Zane announced he was breaking up with Scott, but the ex-lovers decided to go anyhow. They were still friends and it was either go or lose their money. As it turned out, Club Rio de Luna was filled with retired couples, vacationing families and newlyweds who roamed up and down the beach all day, hand-in-hand, splashing each other in the waves. "Looks like we're the only fags in this entire resort," Zane had pointed out more than once.

Vladimir, his perfect round ass covered by a tight black swim-suit, was the best thing about the resort. Besides being a lifeguard, he took guests for catamaran rides in the Caribbean. Every morning Zane and Scott camped out on the beach in the hot tropical sun where they watched Vladimir working near the shore, his toned, naked torso shiny from a healthy sheen of sweat glistening on his bronzed skin.

After a few days of lounging around in the sun, Zane became convinced that a romp with Vladimir was a definite possibility. "I'm telling you, he checks out my basket every time I walk by," Zane said as they watched their hunky Latin dream fussing with the boats at the water's edge. "You never see any girls hanging off him, do you?" Zane shared his fantasies with Scott about going down on Vladimir's gorgeous ass, eating it until Vladimir was begging *en Español* to be fucked like a dog.

"I'm not so sure he's a fag," Scott said, turned on nonetheless by the image of his ex feasting on Vladimir's muscle-butt. "Gaydar doesn't work the same when you're in a foreign country."

"Then we'll have to find out some other way."

"It's not like being a homo is exactly a good idea in Cuba."

"It's a good idea if we've got a chance at sharing a piece of *that*," Zane said, looking over the top of his sunglasses to get a view of Vladimir's ass as he pushed a catamaran into the water, his glutes all flexed and powerful. After four days of Vladimir as Zane's only distraction—not that he was complaining—Zane was hornier than ever. He joked constantly about the three of them getting it on in their hotel room.

"I thought you didn't want to have sex together any more," Scott said, flipping a page in his novel. He wasn't sure if Zane was kidding, which made him realize how little he really knew his ex-boyfriend, even though they had been together for nearly a year. Maybe Zane was testing the waters.

"A three-way would be different."

"How?"

"I'm not sure, but it would."

Before leaving for Cuba, Scott had agreed with Zane that it was best to stop having sex with each other. "We're supposed to be broken up," Zane had said. They'd split up two months earlier, but Scott was still dropping by Zane's apartment once or twice a week, ostensibly to retrieve one of his forgotten belongings—a pair of Calvin briefs, any number of form-fitted shirts, his pen with the gold ink. Inevitably, Scott would be on his knees, milking Zane's beautiful cock before he was out the door with his belongings.

The next morning at Club Rio de Luna, Scott and Zane strolled down the beach, after their usual breakfast of papaya, scrambled eggs and coffee, but Vladimir wasn't there. They staked out their usual spot not far from the catamarans and Zane kept an eye out while flipping through the pages of *Men's Health*. Soon the buff bodies made his dick restless and he set down the magazine and closed his eyes. Soaking up the relentless sun, he daydreamed of eating Vladimir's ass, perhaps taking him down to the beach one night for a roll in the waves and slurping the salty water from his hole . . . .

"Hey. Wake up. You're missing our opportunity!"

Zane startled awake. He had fallen asleep in the sun. Scott was standing over him. Zane rubbed his eyes and squinted into the bright sunlight. "What's up?"

"Your dick, for one," Scott muttered. "And mine, too, soon. I hope."

A group of kids were burying a man on the beach nearby. Only the man's head was still visible above the sand. Zane turned onto his stomach to hide his erection, then saw Vladimir sitting alone in a chair near the catamarans, which were resting idly on the beach.

"You want to go for a boat ride?" asked Scott.

"Does it have to be a *boat* ride?"

Vladimir was a serious sailor. He hardly spoke as he flipped the sail back and forth from side to side, maximizing the catamaran's speed, each time gesturing for Zane and Scott to shift their positions to the other side of the boat. The wind challenged the sail's capacity as they moved farther and farther from the shore, but soon the sunbathers at Club Rio de Luna were just brightly-coloured specks on white sand.

Vladimir's forearms rippled as he pulled and fastened the ropes, fighting against the wind as the catamaran raced into the cold, explosive waves. Unlike them, Vladimir wasn't wearing a life jacket. In fact, he wasn't wearing anything but the black swim trunks, which were packed tight with his muscular ass. Vladimir had solid, hairy legs and taut, six-pack abs. Running from his crotch to his navel was a thick line of matted, black hair which became a soft trail that ran up his abdomen and spread out across his chest like dark, masculine down.

Zane and Scott made an attempt at subtlety, but Vladimir seemed to notice that they were more interested in him than the boat ride. Eventually, Zane decided the only view worth enjoying was the view of Vladimir's ass every time it shifted positions on the boat. This appeared to bring a smile to Vladimir's face. He'd catch them drooling, then glance off across the Caribbean, pushing back the wet black hair from his face as the cold seawater ran off his shoulders and over his chest in little streams, dripping from his large, hard nipples.

Scott was lying around in his underwear, playing with his dick, praying for a knock on the door, followed by the sight of Vladimir on the other side. At the beach, Zane had summoned the nerve to invite Vladimir to join them for a drink after he finished working for the day. "We bought a bottle of Cuban rum at the airport," Zane had said. "But we're not sure if it's the good stuff. We need a Cuban's opinion." Vladimir, who seemed to know what Zane really had in mind, had hesitated, expressing concerned that somebody from the hotel might see him entering their room. "Maybe" was all he offered in the end. When the knock came, Zane was coming out of the bathroom with a towel wrapped around his waist. "Come in," he said.

Vladimir looked up and down the hall outside their room.

"No worries," said Zane. "I'm just getting out of the shower."

Vladimir hesitated for a moment and stepped inside. He was wearing sandals, the black trunks and a white t-shirt. Right away he noticed Zane's cock, which was hanging loose and heavy behind the towel. Zane's cock, like the rest of his body, was impressive. He was a professional hockey player, an NHL hopeful, which explained why he was still closeted. In Canada, Zane avoided sex with strangers, fearing a trick might run to the media and his career would be ruined.

Scott was lying on the bed, watching music videos. His cock stirred inside his boxers. He was prepared for the possibility that something might happen but was doubtful. Even though it was supposed to be over with Zane, Scott wasn't about to refuse a three-way, especially one that involved Vladimir.

"Since we don't speak much Spanish and you don't speak much English," Zane said, "We'll have to find some other way of communicating."

Perfectly timed, his towel fell to the floor. Then he reached in the dresser drawer and pulled out an American fifty.

"Just a little something for your time," he said as he picked up the towel and wrapped it around his waist again, which did little to conceal his cock's growing interest.

"Thank you." Vladimir didn't hesitate taking the money. He turned the fifty-dollar bill over in his hand but didn't say anything else.

"Come in, hang out for a while." Zane said. Vladimir moved farther into the room but seemed tentative, as if he might bolt for the door any second now. "Have a seat," Zane added, gesturing to the bed where Scott was lying in his boxers and white socks. Vladimir sat on the edge of the bed and looked at the television. Janet Jackson was dancing with a crew of sexy, shirtless men.

"Sister of Michael Jackson, no?" Vladimir said.

Scott was surprised and curious. "You know American music?"

"Too close to *Estados Unidos*."

"Your name is Vladimir?" Zane sat beside Vladimir on the bed, the towel conveniently opened at the crotch.

"Yes. Vladimir Romero. Many Cubans with Russian names. My papa, he worked in Kiev two years."

"Really?" said Zane. "What did he do there?"

"Engineer," Vladimir said with a proud smile.

"But you grew up in Cuba?" asked Scott.

"Yes, my whole life. Havana." Vladimir slipped his feet out of his sandals and tucked the American fifty inside one of them. Zane reached out and ran a hand along Vladimir's hairy inner thighs while tugging on his own cock. Vladimir fixed his eyes on the floor as he reached over and took Zane's meat in his hand. Immediately, Scott shed his boxers and moved to the other side of Vladimir. He lifted Vladimir's T-shirt and his mouth went straight for his beautiful nipples, pinching and twisting them with his lips. At first, Vladimir didn't respond. His eyes were closed. He didn't make a sound. His bare feet were planted on the floor.

"We've been eyeing your ass all week," Zane said, enjoying the warm squeeze of Vladimir's hand on his balls.

"Yes. The beach." Vladimir stood up and pulled off his T-shirt.

Then he stepped out of the black trunks and tossed them on the bed. Zane was unabashedly eager. He got behind Vladimir, kneeled and opened the woolly crack of his ass, flicking his tongue on the moist, tight hole. Finally, Vladimir made some noise as he reached for his ass cheeks and held them open for Zane's lapping tongue.

Scott got on the floor in front of Vladimir's cock, then pulled at the loose foreskin with his lips, running his tongue under the hood of Vladimir's growing shaft. His mouth descended down to the base, hungry for Cuban jizz. Vladimir's hips rocked back and forth, relishing the pleasure on both sides of his body.

Vladimir's balls began pulsing in Scott's mouth. He could tell the Latin stud was getting close. He positioned himself underneath Vladimir's cheeks and worked on his ass instead. Vladimir's hole smelled clean but salty like the ocean. Scott's tongue began working in unison with Zane's, giving Vladimir's ass the royal attention it deserved. As they licked and sucked, their tongues pushed against one another and deeper into Vladimir's crack. For a fleeting moment, their tongues met in a spontaneous kiss, their mouths returning in a hurry to Vladimir's ass.

Vladimir was getting goose bumps on his back, moaning quietly as he pumped his hard-on and surrendered his ass to their tongues, fingers and roaming hands. Then, with a flurry of Spanish words, he sprayed a heavy, white load across the floor—and that was it. It was over. Vladimir needed to get back to work. He apologized hastily and put on his black trunks. Then he stepped into his sandals and squirmed into his tight T-shirt. Zane offered him more money to stay, but Vladimir was already disappearing from their room, the American fifty folded inside his hand. He made sure he wouldn't be seen in the hallway, then he was gone.

Zane looked at Scott, who was looking at Zane. Neither one of them had yet cum. "Well, I guess we'll have to finish each other off," said Zane.

"There goes our agreement."

Zane and Scott fucked most of the night, waking at sunrise against each other, naked and sticky. Scott was happy to give his ass to Zane for the rest of their time in Cuba, not caring what that might mean for the two of them down the road. Vladimir had changed something between them. Now it was Zane who was suggesting they give their relationship another try.

On their final day before leaving Club Rio de Luna, Scott snuck down to the beach while Zane was taking a short nap, tired from a second sleepless night of rum and Scott's ass. When Scott reached the catamarans, Vladimir was hard at work in the tropical sun, naked except for his blank trunks. Neither Scott nor Zane had spoken to Vladimir since the night in their room. When Vladimir was finally free for a moment, Scott approached him.

"I am busy today," Vladimir said immediately without taking his eyes off the sea.

"I'd like to buy your bathing suit," said Scott.

"Pardon?"

"Your trunks. I'll give you fifty dollars for them."

Vladimir smirked, puzzled but interested. Then he looked down at the front of his trunks and brushed the white grains of sand off his butt.

"To getting back together," Scott proposed, holding up his plastic wine glass. "Possibly."

"To Vladimir's excellent ass," Zane added, completing the toast with his own glass.

With the plane halfway between Havana and Toronto, Scott decided to pull the black trunks out of his carry-on bag, although they were supposed to be a gift for Zane's birthday, which was the following week.

"Those are not what I think they are," Zane said in disbelief.

"Yes," said Scott. "The real thing. For you."

"How the hell . . ."

"I'll never tell." Scott smiled. "Smell them."

Zane peered at the passengers nearby. They were all sleeping. He took a whiff of the trunks. "They still smell like his ass," he said, then sniffed again. "Or is that the smell of the sea?"

"It's the sea in his ass."

Zane held them to his face and took a deep breath. "Do you think they'd turn the plane around for us?"

In Blackhaven Forest

JAY O. DICKINGSON

Sir Gerard reigned in his mount and studied the clearing with an experienced eye. He did not like spending the night in the forest, especially during these direful times, but they had no choice. "It will be dark soon," he observed, trying not to let his concern show in his voice. "We had best make camp." He swung down off his steed—a powerful, black destrier from Ursikan—unbuckled the cinch and removed the saddle. Had he been stopping at an inn, or travelling with fellow knights, he would have left the responsibility of looking after the horses to his squire; but there being only the two of them, it was only right and proper that each looked after his own. Besides, they had been travelling hard since sunrise, and he knew his young squire, unaccustomed to being in the saddle all day, would be weary.

He glanced over at Francis, the young knight-aspirant who had been serving him now for three years, shortly after he'd turned fifteen. The young man had deep blue eyes, full cheeks, and a mane of thick black hair as dark as soot which he combed behind his ears and into a large floppy wave above his brow. The boy had been attracting the attention of young maidens wherever they went, and had brazenly begun to flaunt his assets if they did not notice him. As the youth bent over to lay his saddle on the ground, his shirt rode up and his breeches rode down, revealing the best of those assets: a strip of bare, white skin and the beginning of the crevice of his arse. He had a nice compact bottom with a slender waist and narrow hips, and the seasoned knight felt a stirring in his loins at just the sight. Over the years his love for the boy had grown, and lately so had his lust. From the glances he'd caught Francis returning, he also knew that the boy was aware of his carnal thoughts—thoughts that were becoming more and more difficult to dismiss—and he knew the young squire had similar thoughts about him.

Large triangular stains darkened the back and front of the boy's coarse, light green shirt and sweat beaded on his forehead as he rubbed down his mount. The farther south they travelled, the warmer the nights were becoming, and both men, accustomed to the northlands, were suffering more with each passing day. It did not stop them from doing their duty, of course, and as the youth groomed his horse, the muscles of his back rippled under his wet shirt and the muscles of his arms flexed and relaxed with each exertion. He had the body of a man now, hard and defined, the result of many hours of exercise and training; but he was still young and still possessed the sensual contours and smoothness of youth.

"You can finish off for me and get a fire started while I see to catching our supper," Sir Gerard advised as he picked up his bow and quiver.

He'd almost finished rubbing down his mount, and with dusk having arrived, it was the best time to seek their evening meal. Besides, standing there watching the boy was beginning to affect him, and if he waited too long, the lust welling up from his loins would flood his mind and he would be useless. As desirous and delightful as that state was, he had his duty, and besides, it was best that his young apprentice not see how easily he could arouse his tutor.

Young Francis Fabre, son of the wealthy and influential Lord Henri Fabre of Cabon, smiled as he finished rubbing down his tutor's large charger and then let the two horses seek out the longer and more tender grass in the small clearing. He had caught the look in Sir Gerard's eyes and for a moment, his mind could think of nothing else. It was a look young Francis was familiar with. Having always been a fine-looking boy with dark, handsome features, he was well aware of the prurient interest some men had in other men, and of his effect on them. With the others though, it had been a game of cat and mouse, of teasing and tempting, giving them a smile and a good feeling but nothing more. That was all it was, a merry pastime to wile away the long boring evenings at his father's manor.

With Sir Gerard it was different. Their relationship was a serious matter, the result of devotion and respect, but not the respect due a tutor from his apprentice, nor due a knight from his squire. Nor was it the respect demanded by age. It was a covenant based on the respect of one man for another. Sir Gerard was a man whose very nature commanded the respect of others. Demanding but expecting no more of others than he expected of himself: fiercely loyal but not with such blind faith as to be a fanatic. Sir Gerard was handsome as well, with hazel eyes, high cheekbones, dark, blue-black hair, and a narrow moustache that curled around the corners of his mouth to join his neatly trimmed goatee. He was skilled both in physical and intellectual pursuits, courageous and strong with a streak of brashness. He was everything that the young squire dreamed of becoming. Sir Gerard he would willingly allow in his bed if only such a thing was permitted. Over the past months those feelings had grown too strong to mask, especially as he'd come to realize deep down inside Sir Gerard was fighting the same desires.

With a shake of his head that caused his mop of black hair to bounce above his brow, the young squire began to pick up the dry twigs and litter on the forest floor to make a fire. Fortunately his tutor was not around or he would have given him a cuff on the back of the head for such foolish lollygagging.

At that moment, his tutor was stealing silently through the rapidly darkening woods, eyes sharp and ears alert, aware of every sound and movement. They had been travelling now for a fortnight, and with each village they had passed through, and with each traveller they had met, the more certain he'd become that something was terribly wrong in the Ten Lands. Although he found it difficult to accept that the demon swarm had somehow broken through the seal that the ancients had placed upon them—a tale that was the popular talk in the inns--he had to admit the evidence pointed to a reappearance of the old evil after all these years. The sheep he'd seen with their entrails ripped out had not been killed by ordinary predators, for it was clear that they'd been killed for the thrill of the slaughter, not for food. He had not yet seen any human corpses with his own eyes, but if what the villagers claimed about the nature of the deaths of neighbours and friends was true, this was also more than the work of a berserker.

Sir Gerard was not a suspicious man and he knew the horror of the tales multiplied with the telling, but he was not a careless man either. He knew that behind every myth was a bit of truth, and in the forests beyond the sight of man, there lurked many menaces, natural and supernatural. Last month he had celebrated his forty-fourth birth feast, and he fully intended on celebrating many more.

Returning to the clearing, his heart rose in his chest at the absence of his squire and his free hand instantly reached for his bow. He had not considered the danger of leaving the boy alone without at least a word of caution. To his relief, the youth stepped out of the shadows.

"I heard someone approach," Francis explained as he stepped forward, "but could not be sure it was you."

"You did right," Sir Gerard replied. He glanced at the horses and the fire confined in a ring of stones. Just as he had taught the boy. "And you've done well."

"I see you have done well also." The boy eyed the skinned and gutted carcass Sir Gerard was carrying. Not wishing to attract any wild animals to their campsite, he had cleaned the hare where he had killed it, and stuffed the hide in his pouch in the hopes of trading it at the next village.

While their supper roasted on the spit Francis had erected, they wiped the dust from the day's journey from their swords and scabbards and checked the straps of their packs and saddles for wear. It was a nightly drill Sir Gerard insisted on, and a practice that more than once had saved his life. Once finished, they consumed their meal while staring into the fire.

"Do you really think the Forces of Evil have escaped the holding spell that was placed upon them after the Battle of Morg and Guan?" the young squire asked, breaking one of the finer bones in half and sucking out the marrow.

"All I know is that something is amiss," replied his mentor. "I would not put it past some fool apprentice wizard to have tampered with the spell that was cast on them."

"I hear there is a wise and ancient wizard among the band seeking to fight the evil ones."

"And the evil ones are led by none other than the Druid Aberon," Sir Gerard added wryly. "All fantastic stories for all we know."

"You sound skeptical."

"The Druid would have to be hundreds of years old."

"Who knows how long the Dark Ones can live?"

"The Church says such legends are old wives' tales," said Sir Gerard. Frankly, he did not have much faith in churches or tales. A man's horse and his blade were all that a man could count on. The rapid spread of this new religion and the sudden disappearance of the druids was proof of that. He knew most knights across the Ten Lands sought the blessing of both Lord and Bishop before a quest and would find his thoughts blasphemous, but he was not like most knights. A knight of the Order of Occam needed the blessing of no one.

"There is talk of the Elves joining the humans in this battle," said Francis.

"The moon is more likely to turn and reverse its direction in the sky," Sir Gerard responded, looking up at the pale orb through the branches of the surrounding beech trees. The boy grimaced as he turned and followed the knight's gaze. "Stiff?"

"A little," the boy lied.

"Come here."

Sir Gerard wiped his greasy fingers on the grass, spread his legs and had the boy sit between them with his back to him. He grasped each of the boy's shoulders and squeezed, then released the muscles, slowly and methodically working his way down to the biceps and back again. Next he pulled up the back of boy's coarse hemp shirt and worked his fingers across the young man's shoulder blades, loosening the knotted muscles. After reaching around and untying the front laces of the coarse hemp shirt, Sir Gerard pulled it over the boy's head, then resumed kneading his shoulders, palpitating the tense deltoids until they began to relax.

As Sir Gerard continued downward, he bent forward, placing his head beside the boy's, and inhaled. The boy smelled of sweat and horse, of camp smoke and leather. He smelled like a man, but even more, he smelled of youth. Sir Gerard kissed his downy cheek and left a trail of kisses along his neck, gently brushing his moustache against the boy's tender skin as he did. The boy squirmed and began to turn, but the older and more patient man held him in place, sliding his hands down the boy's smooth torso to his narrow waist. Next Sir Gerard untied the cord holding up the boy's breeches, and after having the boy rise to his knees, drew them down. He removed the boy's new leather boots--which he'd ordered specifically from the cobbler--drew off the boy's thick woolen socks and slipped off his breeches, then his linen breeks.

The youth's delightful buttocks seemed even whiter now in the dark of night. Sir Gerard ran his fingers over them gently, almost reverently. They were warm, like fresh buns straight out of the baker's oven, and smoother than anything he had ever felt. He stroked them in concentric circles, starting on the outside and working inward toward the crack, each circle smaller than the one before it. He was in no hurry, and his touch was feather-light, just barely making contact, the caresses of a lover. The boy quivered with the pleasure, and in the flickering light of the campfire, his mentor could see the youth's delicate rosebud clench and relax with anticipation. There was a reason boys were made with narrow hips and smooth, compact buns, and that was to draw a man's attention to that delightful portal, just as a colourful flower attracts a bee to sample its nectar.

Sir Gerard slowly increased the diameters of his circles, slowly working back out to the edge of the boy's hips and his crack. The boy was trembling now, and he himself was beginning to breathe more heavily with arousal and anticipation. As he began to massage the boy's smooth ass more firmly, he felt his member beginning to swell in his breeks. He kneaded and caressed the youth's smooth cheeks, delighting in their feel and their sight until he could resist the temptation no longer. Removing his leather vest, he quickly untied and drew off his shirt, then undid the drawstring of his trousers and the ties of his underpants.

He ran his forefinger from the base of the boy's low-hanging testicles up along the crack to his portal of earthly delights, which immediately opened up to him. As Sir Gerard caressed the tender muscle surrounding that entrance, his manhood continued to swell in anticipation, and the memories of past pleasures hastened its transformation from a limp piss tube to a solid staff of manliness. He knew the boy's own member would be swelling in response to his caresses. Picking up a discarded bit of rib bone, the knight dug out the bit of fat still clinging to the cartilage and slipped the greasy fingertip of his probing finger into the boy's anus, twisting it before withdrawing it. Coating the tip of his finger with rabbit fat once again, he slipped it back in, this time to the first knuckle. By now his member was fully aroused and aching to replace his finger, and from the squirming of the youth, the boy was just as eager for the man's member.

Sir Gerard eagerly coated the helmet of his tumescent organ with bits of grease from their evening meal, then he eased first one, then another of his fingers up the boy's rectum, wiping the grease off inside him and loosening him for the much thicker digit to follow. He grasped his thick staff by the base and placed the tip against the boy's portal, and the boy eagerly opened it wide as he could. Grasping the boy's hips, Sir Gerard pushed forward, and the boy pushed out as he pressed back. Slowly the determined knight's greased helmet forced open the boy's sphincter, and slowly the young squire's asshole slid up his slopehead until his helmet was inside. The two paused for a moment, and then Sir Gerard continued, slowly but determinedly sinking his pike up the boy's rectum until at last his coarse black hairs were pressed against the boy's smooth arse.

He paused to savour the delight of being inside the boy's rectum and the joy of having his massive, thick pricke surrounded by hot, pulsating flesh. A fellow knight had once told him the reason a man's horn is curved as it is, is so that it can fit snugly up the curve inside another man's arse, and the reason a man's arse is so sensitive, is so that he can enjoy having it fucked by another man. Having been both the one doing the fucking and the one being fucked in his past, he could vouch for the accuracy of both statements.

He eased his member back out, and then slowly sank it in

again as he began to ride the boy. He had always been an ass man, right from his youth, and over the years no woman had ever been able to deter him from its pursuit. Let the minstrels and others proclaim the delights of the fair sex. Having the hot, moist asshole of another male enveloping your horn was, to him, the greatest pleasure a man could know, and he fucked the boy slowly so as to enjoy the pleasure to the fullest.

His breathing gradually grew heavier as he worked his body to and fro, and as he felt the approaching climax he held it back as long as he could, and then exhaled jaggedly as his seed erupted and filled the young squire's rectum. Having reached around and grasped the boy's own young, slender pricke, he was delighted to feel it throbbing as the boy began to pump out his own seed, shooting it out as fast as he was being filled.

Drained, the two sat back against a tree and the boy lay his head on the knight's hairy chest. Tomorrow they could die, and if they did, it would be with contentment, and if they did not, the morrow would bring another day in which they could delight in this forbidden sport once more.

How I Became a Butt Boy

MARTIN COX

Iwasn't always a butt slut. There was a time when I wouldn't let anyone touch my ass. But that all changed when I met Mr. Hughes.

Until then, I actually thought of myself as a straight boy—a straight muscle boy who used his hot body and big fat cock to make a few extra bucks on the side. That's right. I was selling it and making a ton of money. It was so easy, too. All I had to do was put an ad with a pic in the back of the local gay rag and soon my beeper was going off every damn minute of the day and night. I know I look hot and pics don't lie, either. The one I chose for my ad showed off my smooth, hairless muscles to their full advantage and was just barely legal for publication. I wore a tiny black g-string. My head was back, letting my long black locks dangle down my broad back.

Men called me all the time. I'd meet them in their hotel rooms or at their homes while their wives or lovers were away. Sometimes I'd let them suck off my fat eight inches in the back seats of their imported cars. I didn't care where they got their kicks, as long as I got my money. I never touched them—didn't ever have to—and none of them ever touched my ass. That is, before Mr. Hughes.

I could tell that he was different when I got his message. First of all, he didn't sound at all nervous, like a lot of my clients. Mr. Hughes sounded confident, his voice deep and a little hoarse. It reminded me of my gymnastics teacher in high school.

"Noon. The St. Martin hotel. Room 658. You got that, kid?" he asked in a growl when I returned his call.

"Yeah, I'll be there, man, no prob," I assured him in the cocky tone I reserved for my clients.

Click. He just hung up.

When I showed up at the St. Martin, a hotel near the beach on the sleazy side of town, I walked past the desk attendant without stopping. He stopped what he was doing, though, as his eyes hungrily assessed my body, clad in tight white athletic shirt and cutoff shorts. I knew how well I filled out this outfit and that was the point—wasn't it?—to get the client excited. I never wear underwear, either, and the head of my soft dick stopped at the fringed hem of the shorts. Part of my ass was visible through a hole in the back of the cutoffs, near a ragged pocket. I loved teasing men with my round, humpy butt, knowing they would never have it, no matter how much they might drool and beg. I headed for the elevator while the clerk tried to pick up his tongue from the front desk.

The elevator door popped open on the sixth floor with a ping. In no time I was standing in front of room 658. At this point, I usually just knocked, ready to get on with it. But somehow I knew this client was going to be different. Maybe it was the tone in Mr. Hughes's voice.

What the hell, I thought. He's probably just some old fart with a deep voice from too many years of drinking and smoking. I was getting spooked over nothing. As I knocked on the door, it swung open. The blinds were closed in the room, and it was very dark.

"Hello?" I asked tentatively. "Anyone here?"

"Get in here, boy," a familiar voice growled. This was definitely the place. I walked into the room, which smelled of hotel disinfectant and some sort of tropically-scented suntan oil.

"Where are you? I can't see anything," I said. My eyes hadn't adjusted from the bright sunny day I had just left behind.

"Over here, near the bed," rasped the voice. "Stand over there, on the other side."

I did as he asked, straining to make out the form on the opposite side of the bed. But all I could see was a dark shape. Was he using the darkness to hide a deformity? A missing leg? A third eye in the middle of the forehead?

"Take off your shirt," the disembodied voice commanded. I slowly pulled off the shirt like a stripper—a trick a friend had taught me—and tossed it on the floor.

"Nice tits. A little small," said the voice, "but nice. Play with them for me."

I fingered my brown nubbins lightly. My dick hardened in response. I wasn't sure where this was going, but so far, it wasn't so bad.

"That's good, now harder," he said.

"Like this?" I pinched my tits till they began to hurt.

"Better," he said. "I see you're starting to show."

My dick had lengthened so much that the head had dropped below the hem of the shorts, dangling alongside my hard muscled quads. A tiny droplet of pre-cum had come loose from the head, dripping to the floor, and its wetness glistened in a thin shaft of sunlight coming through the blinded windows.

"You're uncircumcised. Your ad didn't mention that. Nice plus."

I was beginning to wonder when we would get to the good part. My dick was already aching for release. My balls felt like they were weighted with lead.

"You can shuck off those shorts now," he said. "They're not doing you much good anyway."

I unzipped them and let them drop to the floor, my dick springing perpendicular as I did. It felt good to be free.

"Now get up on the bed on all fours, your butt facing me."

I hesitated. "I don't do that, man." No matter how horny I was, I wasn't giving up my cherry, especially to someone I couldn't even see.

"I won't touch you, I promise. I just want to see. Besides: you'll do it for me or no money."

Well, if that's all, I thought.

I climbed up onto the squeaky bed in the requested position. My dick was so hard it rose up and slapped against my hard belly. My balls dangled down low and heavy.

"You've got a fine ass, boy, pity you don't know how to use it. Now lower your head to the bed and reach around and pull those tight butt cheeks of yours apart. I can't see your bud."

I did as he asked. I could feel the air in the room caress my now-exposed asshole. I decided that as long as he kept his promise, everything was cool. If he touched me, though, I was out of there, money or not.

I looked back between my spread legs and saw Mr. Hughes for the first time. It was still dark, but my eyes were adjusting and I got a good glimpse of him. He sat in a chair beside the bed in a pair of white boxer shorts, his cock sticking out of the fly like a thick flagpole. It was huge—bigger than mine—and he was stroking away on it. He had pulled his balls through the fly, too, and they were so heavy that they rested on the fabric of the chair. His chest was broad and hairy, the chest of a mature athlete, and even in the dark, his nipples were a wonder: pink and ripe, like a woman's.

My dick got even harder.

"Now reach back and touch that beautiful hole for me, boy,

just run your fingers around it. You don't have to penetrate it."

Again, I followed his instructions. It felt good, as if had been doing it all my life. Of course I hadn't, but part of the thrill was being watched. I am an exhibitionist at heart.

"Here, use this." Mr. Hughes tossed a small bottle of lotion on the bed. I squirted some onto my finger and rubbed it into my tight virgin hole. As I rubbed, my asshole started to get warmer and warmer, and soon I felt like I was going to catch fire back there.

"What is the hell is this?" I asked.

"Just something to make you feel like a cat in heat. Feels good, doesn't it?"

"It's not bad, I guess," I said, but I suddenly felt like I needed a pail of water to soak my burning tail. It was a burning itch I couldn't scratch. Mr. Hughes's cock had gotten harder and he was still lazily stroking it.

"Now move your butt around. Show it off," he ordered. I gyrated my hips while my fingers teased the opening to my ass. My cock was drooling at this point. I could feel my juices dripping onto the cheap bedspread. I needed to cum, bad.

"That's it, boy . . . more . . . oh yeah. You're getting me so hot . . . yeah. God, your butt is beautiful." Mr. Hughes moaned. "C'mon, stick a finger in there. I want to see."

What the hell: I had gone this far. I slipped my index finger in my butt, in to the first knuckle. Surprisingly, it didn't hurt at all.

"Damn, boy. You've got me so hot, I'm about to explode. Keep going."

I didn't need any encouragement. I was starting to like the feeling of my own finger inside my butt. And the sight of Mr. Hughes jerking off his monstrous cock while fingering his bright pink nipples wasn't hurting either. I pushed in a second finger to go along with the first.

"Fuck, I'm cuming," Mr. Hughes growled. "Ahhh, shit!"

I watched between my legs as he shot a huge white load all the way up his chest, landing in the hairs between his pecs and dripping downward. Watching Mr. Hughes cum had gotten me so horny, I was about to cum without even getting sucked, but suddenly he got up from the chair and grabbed a hand towel for his cum-soaked chest.

"Here's your money, boy," he said then, taking money out of his wallet and handing it to me as my dick bobbed in the air, untouched and unsatisfied.

"You mean, you . . . that's it?"

"Yeah. This time."

"But I usually get off, too," I said.

"Go ahead, if that's what you want. I don't mind."

Suddenly I got ticked off at him, mostly because I was still horny and he wasn't the least bit interested in sucking my dick. Up until now, that had always been the main event.

"Forget it, man," I said, getting off the bed and gathering my shorts.

"I'm married," he said. "This is a way I can have fun and still be faithful to my wife. Get it?"

"Yeah, okay, whatever. See ya." I forced my painfully-hard dick inside my shorts, zipped up, grabbed my shirt and headed for the door, glad to be out of there.

About a week later, I got another call from Mr. Hughes. Same hotel, same room, same time. I was still pissed at him and almost didn't go. But something made me change my mind. The scene was the same, an exact repeat of the first time with one major difference.

"Here's a present for you," he said when we were finished. He handed me a small paper bag.

"What is it?" I opened the bag and pulled out an oddly-shaped piece of rubber.

"A butt plug," he said. "Have it in place before you get here next time."

"Maybe I will, maybe I won't," I said with a wry smile and left.

When I got home, I examined Mr. Hughes's present again. I had to admit, I had liked the sensations I gave myself playing with my hole while he watched. I had even started to play with my ass when I was alone and my butt was beginning to look forward to the attention. I still wasn't ready for anything else, mind you, but the gift intrigued me.

In a few short weeks, the butt plug and I became really good friends. I got off on the sensation of jerking off with it inside me. I came much harder, it seemed, and shot off gallons of spunk with my ass full. Once I even fantasized about Mr. Hughes's huge dick inside me when I came.

It took Mr. Hughes more a month to page me again, which made me more than a little pissed off. But I did show up with the butt plug firmly in place. I wore it often now, even to the gym and the supermarket. When I had the plug in my ass, my dick was always a little hard, if not fully erect, and I loved what his present did to my front and backside.

Feeling a little cocky and pissed at the same time, I walked into the darkened room, shed my clothes and propped myself on the bed, my back against the headboard. Mr. Hughes came to the foot of the bed as I raised my left leg insolently, knowing he could see the flange of the plug peeking out below my balls.

"I see you like your present." He licked his bottom lip. "Looks hot, too."

"Yeah, we've become buddies."

Mr. Hughes disrobed and sat on the edge of the bed. It was the closest we had ever been to each other. I lowered my body on the bed, giving him a great view of my tight butt now stuffed with his gift.

"Jerk yourself off for me," he ordered. It was the first time he had asked me to do that. I obliged gratefully since I was horny from walking all the way to the hotel with the plug bouncing around inside my ass. Just when I was starting to feel good, I felt Mr. Hughes's finger tap on the base of the plug. He tapped it hard, as if he was knocking at the door or something. It resonated inside me and felt incredible.

"You like that?" he asked.

"Yeah, yeah," I said, pulling my hard meat for all it was worth. "Do it again."

Mr. Hughes got between my legs and placed my feet on his broad muscular shoulders. The hairs there tickled the soles of my feet. I began to pull at my dick harder as Mr. Hughes reached down and played with the plug. I no longer cared whether another man was touching me down there. It was then that I knew I wanted more. Mr. Hughes's huge, fat dick throbbed in the air as he played with my butt plug. The head glistened with his juices. Damn his wife to hell, I thought, I want him in me.

I reached for his cock and stroked it, feeling the wetness emerging from the tiny piss slit.

"Fuck me," I said, staring into his eyes. "Please."

Mr. Hughes reached for the plug. "Push it out, baby."

I pushed and his gift popped out of me. Suddenly I felt emptier than ever before.

Then I felt Mr. Hughes's cock pressing against my hole. I pushed out, like I had done to get the plug in my ass, and he slipped effortlessly inside my wet silky walls. His head fell back in ecstasy as he slowly penetrated me for the first time. I couldn't wait. I grabbed his butt and pulled him all the way in. The feeling of being filled with a living cock, a man, not a piece of rubber, was incredible. It was as if I had always wanted it, but had just been too stupid to let myself believe it.

"Now fuck me hard," I moaned. "Be the first and the best."

My legs were still on his shoulders. He drove into me mercilessly. I felt his own ass muscles clench each time he pounded deep into my hole and it seemed as if the head of his dick was buried inside my belly, its fat tip glowing with an intense heat. My entire body shuddered in response. I used the new-found muscles inside my ass to milk his hot dick with each stroke.

"Damn, baby, you've got a hungry ass!" Mr. Hughes panted. "You've been starving it too long for hot cock!"

"God, yes, fuck me! Don't stop, don't ever stop! Fuck yes! I need it! I never knew I would love it this much!"

Mr. Hughes responded by pounding deeper and harder into my willing hot hole. "I can't hold out much longer," he said, thrusting deeper. "I need to cum!"

"Do it, baby, fill me up with that hot stuff!"

Mr. Hughes's cock christened my ass with jet after jet of hot white cum. I could feel it splashing in me as he shot. Then I felt his fingers tighten around my dick and he jerked me to an explosive orgasm that coated my chest with my own slick load.

We fucked three times that afternoon. Each time, after he shot his load in my hole, Mr. Hughes re-inserted the plug, keeping his cum inside me. After the third load, my ass was as juicy as an overripe mango.

While we were resting between lovemaking bouts, I asked Mr. Hughes why he had broken his rule and touched me, making him unfaithful to his wife.

"She left me three weeks ago," he said in that deep voice I had come to love. "We're getting a divorce."

"Her loss," I said, reaching for his fat cock one more time.

Licking LeRoy

RICHARD TRAYNER

L eRoy is a Nubian god—six feet, five inches of jet black sinewy
muscles on a classic dancer's body, complete with a strapping
bubble butt and a thick uncut cock that grows quite impressively.
We met in a chat room last week. As we swapped instant messages,
he emailed me a picture of his ass. He was on his hands and knees
in the photo, his asshole gaping open with a trickle of cum leaking
out. The stark contrasts of colors floored me: his glistening ebony
skin, his hot-pink and fuchsia fuck-chute, the creamy off-white jizz
oozing downward.

I imagined licking his ass crack and catching every drop of semen, then diving face first into his hole for a long, hot tongue-fuck
session. I alternated stroking my cock and typing steamy responses
to LeRoy, all the while fantasizing that we were sixty-nining while
some horse-hung stud pounded LeRoy's ass. I visualized him choking on my dick while I sucked his balls, milked his cock and rimmed
around his hole to taste the horse-hung stud's meat as he fucked
LeRoy's eager man-pussy. I was desperate to taste LeRoy's feverishly
hot asshole—the black pucker stretched tight by a thick slab of
man-meat sliding in and out.

After 30 minutes of chat, LeRoy abruptly typed: GOTTA GO, MAN. GOT A GUY CUMMING OVER IN A FEW MINUTES AND I NEED TO CLEAN UP.

The drooling cock in my palm gave me the courage to type: CAN I CUM TOO?"

The address he gave me was close enough to walk. I decided to drive, however, in case I got there and wanted to leave in a hurry. My precautions were unnecessary. When LeRoy answered the door wearing a pair of white silk boxers, I knew I was in for a treat. I stepped inside the small apartment and saw Scott, a skinny, pale blond boy who was maybe nineteen. He was naked, his enormous uncut cock standing tall and proud. It had to be a full nine inches long.

We didn't waste time with introductions. I stripped by the door and took what I could of Scott's cock in my mouth. The hooded head peeked out and the drop of pre-cum oozing out of his piss-slit tasted sweet and inviting. I let my tongue roam around the underside of his foreskin and savored his cheese while LeRoy pulled down his shorts and pushed two gorgeous mounds of chocolate flesh against my cheek. He wanted some attention, too, and I gave it to him. I laid on the bed with my head hanging over the edge and pulled LeRoy on top of me in a sixty-nine position. After sucking his cock and licking his balls, I pulled open his crack to reveal that hot hole I had worshiped in the photo. I rammed my tongue against his pucker, eagerly trying to force my way inside. His hole welcomed me and as I tongue-fucked him, Scott slapped LeRoy's butt-cheek with his drooling cock. Scott was oozing pre-cum like a faucet. I grabbed his cock and rubbed the head against LeRoy's hole, coating it with fuck-fluid. Then I ran my tongue across the silky folds to savor the flavor of the men.

My fantasy came true! I thought to myself.

Eager to have it all, I pulled LeRoy's cock backward and swallowed him whole while his big nut-sack draped my nose. Then I

took both hands and pulled his cheeks apart for Scott. Scott lubed
LeRoy's hole with his flowing pre-cum, then pushed his cock head
inside. I felt LeRoy flinch. The head of Scott's shaft eased past his
anal ring, then stopped, waiting for LeRoy to adjust to the monster
invading his hole. LeRoy's pre-cum flooded my mouth, filling my
throat with sweet, sticky man-juice. I pulled off his cock and sucked
his balls. I wanted him to know that I was prepared to service every
part of his hot fuck-machine. I could tell he wasn't used to having
his balls worked on, so I gave him a good workout.

When I looked up, I saw that Scott had almost buried his entire
cock inside LeRoy. I could see a couple of thick inches, and Scott's
hot shaved balls were dangling so close to my nose, I could smell his
warm moist scent. I grabbed his nuts and pulled him closer, sending shockwaves through LeRoy's stretched hole. I licked Scott's balls
and teased them with my tongue and teeth. He really seemed to like
having his balls worked on, so I pulled them into my mouth and
sucked and chewed on them as he began pumping away.

LeRoy was getting more into it. His sucking on my cock grew
more and more intense. He began moaning and sweating profusely.
I let Scott's balls slip out of my mouth and watched his enormous
cock piston in and out of LeRoy's hole. But I couldn't stay a specta-
tor for long. I reached upward with my tongue to lick LeRoy's crack
and Scott's cock. I almost shot my load when my taste buds first collided with Scott's meat ramming LeRoy's hole, so I concentrated on
serving these two studs and tried to forget the cum boiling inside
me. I gathered Scott's balls between my fingers and pulled down,
causing him to gasp. I could tell he liked rough ball-play, and I was
more than willing to indulge him. With his balls still in my grip, I
licked and chewed away, sending him into a frenzy.

"Aw fuck, man, I'm gonna cum!" he screamed. I held his balls
tighter and he pushed his cock deep inside LeRoy's ass. Scott's body
grew tense, then I felt him squirting cum deep inside LeRoy. As he

did, I took LeRoy's cock in my mouth just in time to receive the last of three hefty volleys of jizz. He bucked and writhed, pushing his cock deeper in my throat and choking me with his meat. Just as Leroy pulled out of my throat, Scott began easing his enormous cock out of the gaping black hole. I grabbed Scott's steaming meat and sucked it down, savoring the last few drops of his cum mixed with the taste of LeRoy's dark interior.

LeRoy had my cock buried deep in his throat when I shot my thick juice into his gut. He coughed and sputtered but never lost a drop. Satisfied for the moment, we lay in a sticky, sweaty pile of arms, legs and bodies. Eventually Scott broke the spell by saying, "Well, gotta go, dudes. Call me if you want to hook up again sometime."

I know I'm up for another workout with those two studs anytime, anywhere.

Razored Rear

JAY STARRE

"What do you think of that ass?" Carl grinned at the image of an anonymous, bent-over butt splayed across the computer screen. "It's been shaved, I'm sure of it. No hair at all. Real smooth."

"Hot, very hot," I said, my cock rising up. There wasn't a follicle to be seen on the entire expanse of luscious flesh. The ample cheeks were spread wide and the hole was peering up at us, every little wrinkle of the puckered slot visible.

"I've been thinking of shaving mine." Carl looked up at me, his soft grey eyes full of smouldering lust. "Wanna do it for me?"

My hard cock twitched at the thought. Shave my short blond bud's ass? That would be a novel experience. "I like your ass any way I can get it," I said. "Shaved should be more than fuckable. Go for it."

Carl and I were just friends—friends who did the nasty when we were either drunk or very horny. The raunchy-sounding experiment was exactly the right mood-enhancer that had us both ready for action. He rose from the computer eagerly and led me in a race to the bathroom, shedding clothes as he bounded down the stairs. I followed his example and by the time I reached the bathroom, he was on his knees beside the tub with his legs spread, his naked butt bouncing sexily before my eyes while my own hard cock lurched in front of me. The look of passion in his eyes had me shaking.

"Shave it," Carl said laughingly, wiggling his delectable can. "Make my ass smooth as a baby's bum!"

My buddy had a great ass. It flared out from a narrow waist with chunky roundness, the two large dimples on either cheek adding to its sexy appeal. I'd never paid much attention to the fuzzy coating covering Carl's ass—a scant pelt of swirling brown hair that thickened as it ran down and into his crack—but now that we were talking about it, and now that he was on his knees and his deep butt-crevice was wide open, I realized I could barely detect the pucker of his ass-slot beneath the coating of light brown hair disguising it. It would definitely be interesting seeing that sexy ass naked, free of all hair, I thought.

"Okay, I'll do it," I said aloud. "I guess it'll grow back if you don't like it."

My cock was so hard I wanted to fuck that spread ass right then and there, but I controlled my passion and searched the cabinet for a razor and shaving cream. When I knelt on the bathroom floor with the shaving can in hand, Carl turned on the faucets in the tub. That way I could wipe the razor clean as I shaved, he said. For some reason it seemed as if he knew exactly what to do.

First I rubbed a generous palm-full of light blue shaving cream all over his big, sexy ass. He sighed under my touch, raising his butt as my fingers slid into his parted crack with the silky shaving cream. I took a momentary side-tour as I massaged the foam around his tight butthole and listened to his appreciative moans. He was very excited, which had me even more worked up.

"Get to work, man," Carl moaned.

Reluctantly I abandoned the crinkled folds of his quivering slot and began to shave his ass. It was a very erotic act, sliding the razor over the hard yet yielding flesh, watching the lather disappear only to leave behind a pinkish white trail of clean, hairless skin. I took my time, wiping off the razor in the running water, then returning to slowly travel over every inch of each of Carl's big, sexy ass-cheeks. As I worked, I imagined my own naked ass becoming razor-clean. After I had both massive cheeks naked of hair, I wiped them clean with a warm washcloth.

What a sexy sight! The large mounds looked even larger without their hairy pelt. The skin was glowing with a sexy flushness and was without a single blemish or disfiguring mark. I had to bite my lip to control my passion or I would have shoved my stiff boner right up between those hairless cheeks and fucked that shaving cream-coated—

"Don't forget the crack," Carl murmured, "and the hole. I want to be totally hairless."

I quelled the trembling in my hands and bent down to the task. Carl was cooperative, raising one thigh up and holding his ass cheeks apart with both hands. I shuddered at the sight of the sexual position he presented, his dark butthole pulsating and pouting underneath its foamy coating of cream. The razor swiped over the length of the crack, leaving behind flesh without disguise. I was fascinated by the sudden appearance of his hot little hairless slot, but I managed to finish the job, working the razor down toward his dangling ball sack, around the perineum and over his upper thighs.

After wiping him clean with the warm washcloth, I was presented with a totally new ass. Carl's muscular thighs were hairy, and the stark demarcation between his thick legs and his creamy white ass-flesh was now obvious, making his big butt swell with added, sexy proportion. I found myself unable to resist that ass. I ran my hands over it, turned on by the feel of his smooth, hairless skin. I pulled the cheeks apart and stared at the pouting butthole, totally revealed now. The slot seemed so much more sexy now, unprotected, available.

I buried my face in Carl's hairless butt. His moans increased as he squirmed halfway into the tub, bending over with his head down and his ass higher in the air. I rubbed my cheeks all over his, feeling the silky smooth flesh quivering under my caress. I stuck out my tongue and licked and sucked on his hairless skin as my face roamed all over his upturned ass. I burrowed my nose into his crack, pulling it open with my hands, licking up and down it, revelling in the satiny feel of baby-smooth, hairless skin. The hole shuddered and gaped under my roving tongue, and again I was struck by the unprotected nature of that suddenly-bald butt-opening. Now nothing stood between his steamy ass-pit and my eager passion.

I had to fondle it. I pulled up from my butt-feast with saliva coating my face. His pale ass was flushed with excitement. Frantically I rummaged in the cabinet below the sink to my right until I found what I was searching for: baby oil. I sprayed the transparent lubricant all over that expansive butt. Carl was so far gone in his lust that he merely encouraged me with a sexy wiggle and a desperate yes. When his shiny butt was coated with oil, I ran my hands over the mounds. Fuck! It was so damn smooth. I kneaded the chunky flesh of his cheeks, watching as his crack spread open and his snug little asshole gaped and pouted in response.

I dove in with my fingers, teasing the opening, tickling the puckered rim and quivering ass-lips that glistened with slippery liquid. I rubbed my fingertips over his slot, causing Carl to shove upwards with his hips in an effort to capture a digit or two with his twitching butt-lips. I almost laughed, but I too was far gone with lust. Finally I inserted a lone finger between the puckered rim.

"Oh yeah! Yeah!" Carl nearly shouted when I penetrated his tight sphincter. "Finger my hairless hole!"

I slid in deeper, enveloped by the slick heat of his insides. I added a second oiled finger and worked them both in circles as I used my other hand to run over the hairless expanse of his pink butt. The sight of my big hand caressing his bald ass made me even hotter. I poked and prodded eagerly, and soon I wanted more. Sliding my fingers from his hungry, oiled hole, I turned again to the nearby cabinet. I found a big dildo, then squirted a liberal amount of baby oil over all ten inches of it. Carl's face was still down in the tub and he had no idea what was coming. I grinned as I placed the oiled dildo on his ass crack. The rubber cock looked obscene against his pink, shaved butt. I rubbed it up and down, watching as Carl groaned in response.

"I'm going to shove this big dildo up your razored ass," I warned him in a shaking voice.

"Oh, man, that is hot! Go ahead, fuck my hairless butt with that big hard dildo!"

Carl was obviously not going to challenge any of my decisions. That turned me on even more. I held his butt open with one hand and with the other, rubbed the fat dildo along his crack. The hole pouted and gaped. Nothing was stopping me from shoving the fat dildo up that oiled butthole!

I did it. Carl's sudden squeal did little to stop the steady sinking of fat rubber up his gaping hole. His tight lips stretched wide around the dildo's shaft, every crinkle and crevice of his ass now visible. I plugged Carl with the whole length, burying it to the fake balls and holding it deep inside him. He squirmed and bucked and fucked himself, his ass dripping oil and sweat and becoming redder and redder. I suddenly realized I could no longer hold back from satisfying my own passion a moment longer and wrenched the dildo out of Carl's clamping hole. He cried out, but his ass rose higher in anticipation. The small ass-slot was a gaping pit, dripping oil and rosy and raunchy.

I threw the dildo on the floor and rammed my cock deep into the fuck-tunnel in front of me. The hot hole spasmed around my penetrating cock. In the part of my mind that was still thinking, I realized that Carl was grunting encouragement, but the rest of me was focussed on one thing—that smooth hairless ass and my ramming cock. I fucked it. In and out, faster and faster. The oiled-up asshole was slippery and yielding. The hairless lips gaped and protruded as I pulled out, and expanded and parted as I drove in. I slapped the big hairless cheeks, watching as they grew pinker with every smack and as droplets glistened atop the hairless mounds.

Sometime during that relentless fuck, Carl creamed. I didn't give a shit. I was too immersed in my own imminent orgasm. Pounding his slippery fuck-channel was driving me to the brink. The heated friction of that hot freshly-shaved hole finally did me in. I cried out as I yanked my cock from Carl's battered butthole and sprayed his ass with jizz. The sight of that pristine smooth butt coated with sticky cum was the icing on the cakes. What a raunchy scene!

After that, every time Carl and I got together, he bent over the tub and offered me his ass. I shaved it smooth and had my way with it. I could not get enough of that hairless can. One night when Carl couldn't make it over, and I was extremely horny, I went into the bathroom and began to check my own ass out in the mirror. What would it look like without the light down of blond hair obscuring its fleshy curves? I wondered.

The decision was made without a moment's hesitation. Half an hour later, my butt was devoid of any trace of hair, and I was grunting happily around the ten-inch dildo prodding my deepest pleasure spots. I watched in the mirror as my own hairless butt writhed and squirmed around the fat rubber tubing. My own vulnerable asshole, now hairless and smooth, was revealed in its every fold and crevice. I fucked my smooth, hairless ass in the mirror to a gut-wrenching orgasm.

Now I'm addicted to razored rears, including my own!

Buddy's Fine Behind

TROY STORM

I ran up the stairs to Buddy's small garage apartment.

"Hey, Buddy, good buddy, can I borrow a cup a ... a ..."

My mouth froze as I stared through the screen. Buddy was on the bed, on his stomach, bare-assed. Which meant I was seeing the glory of the man unveiled for the first time. Which meant I was speechless.

Now, my next-door neighbor is nice enough looking in a broad-shouldered, woodsman-stud sort of way, though the dimples and the devilish grins tend to blunt his butch persona and render him merely cute as hell. However, his mouth-watering good looks are nothing compared to his soul-wrenching butt. I had already known that Buddy's snow-white tighties could barely contain his thick beefy mounds of solid flesh, mounds that were sculpted with such definition that the center seam of his undershorts sank from sight deep into his crack. I had already known that all Buddy had to do was take a couple of steps and his flexing buttocks gobbled up cotton. (Oh, how I desperately wanted to put my loving lips in the same vulnerable position as his briefs and get sucked under in the same satisfying way. While down there I would perform a search-

and-rescue for what I figured had to be an equally-matchless butthole to end all buttholes.)

But up until this moment, I had never seen Buddy's bottom
in all his glory. Now, before my eyes, was almost more than I could
handle. Buddy was deeply tanned. (I'd even had the privilege of
slathering sunblock deep into the pores of his rippling back.) His
butt, however, was where the sun didn't shine under his boxer swim
trunks, and his glutes glowed like twin pale moons. The taut skin
on the surface of those moons had the look of shiny porcelain polish—probably from the sheen of late-afternoon sweat since neither
Buddy nor I could afford air conditioning. His smooth back flowed
into his flawless butt. Body hair appeared, first as a pale shadow underneath his chunky buttocks, and then thickened into a dark veil
cast over his bulging thighs and calves. Between the deep color and
broad expanse of his back and the dark massive underpinnings of
his legs, his ass was like a lighthouse beacon of succulent, inviting
flesh pulling me into its safe harbor. My dick jumped to attention in
my sweats, full-blown and solid, punching out the lightweight fleece
into a full-masted sail that homed in on the beckoning beacon.

He began to stir. Somewhere deep in his subconscious, he must
have heard my unfinished yell. His short-cropped head turned on
the pillow. His thick dark lashes blinked against the light.

"Unh. Martin, come in, little buddy." He yawned and pushed
himself up, sitting on the edge of the bed with his legs wide open.
"Oh, man, I am so fucking wiped."

The air drained out of my lungs. He had a hard-on that stuck
straight up from his crotch, seemingly within inches of his drooping chin. He could have pole-vaulted with that boner. He scratched
his nuts and with a deep groan, hoisted himself up and stumbled
for the door. Halfway across the room he paused to look down,
appearing to try to determine if the massive pendulum swaying
between his beefy thighs might be responsible for his tentative bal-

ance. With a series of slow blinks, Buddy seemed to realize he was
waving his hard-on at his next-door neighbor. He looked around,
noticed something on the floor and turned to pick it up. Which
meant he mooned me with those perfect pale porcelain bowls.

His glutes tightened and shifted as he retrieved a crumpled
T-shirt. I held tight to the doorframe. He spread his legs to give
himself more solid footing and his ass opened, revealing a dark,
shrouded asshole peeping from the depths of his protective crack.

Pre-lube pumped into my sweats.

Buddy pulled the T-shirt over his head and settled it over his
chest, which seemed to satisfy his sense of propriety. He opened the
screen door, grinned groggily, and pulled me in. His dick waved
hello and drooled a trickle of thick pre-cum onto the bare floor.

"Aw, man—ah, man." He put his big hands heavily on my
shoulders. "She dumped me, Matt. She fucking dumped me." He
staggered back to the bed and flopped down on his stomach again,
quickly hiking his hips to rearrange the pole that had jammed into
his pubes. He twisted his head and smiled wanly at me. "You said I
deserved better than that unappreciative bitch." His grin faded into
a thoughtful distant stare. After a moment, his dark eyes narrowed
as he refocused and watched me watching his bare butt. The angles
of the slope and elevation of Buddy's ass formed a championship
course. I could imagine my tongue going for the gold over those
pale precipitous mounds. His lids lowered to half-mast. His lower
lip stuck out and he nodded sagely. "I could use a little hands-on
comforting, man."

I stood frozen in the middle of the room.

"C'mon, Matt," he begged, "gimme a little rubdown." His ass
wiggled as he snuggled the manly log on which he was lying deeper
into the mattress. The T-shirt covered his massive back. His butt
was bare. It only made sense that his butt was the part he wanted me
to rub. I gulped. Buddy contemplated my tented crotch. His gaze

drifted up. "You've been wanting to get hold of my ass for a long time. Well, now's your chance. Take my mind off my troubles, man." He turned his head to face the wall.

With such an offer, I found my legs could move. I crossed to Buddy and stared down at his butt, hitching my hips back to see past the pronging tent of my sweatpants, the apex of which was already covered with a thick muck oozing through the fabric. I shucked my sneaks, peeled down my sweatpants and used the balled-up fabric to wipe myself as clean as I could, but the lube was pouring. Finally, I just let it drizzle onto Buddy's ass.

He turned when he felt the hot liquid sizzling on his buns and noted my state. He nodded and shrugged appreciatively. "You got a big one, man. I kinda figured you might have, even if you are a little pip squeak." He reached up and fondly squeezed the end of my draining bone, getting a handful of goo that he rubbed into the glossy skin of his butt.

"Take care of me, Matt." He turned his head away.

I dropped to my knees, opened my mouth and pressed it against his ass. The feel of his warm, moist flesh against my lips, the aroma of his crack and his crotch, the musty smell of the sweaty sheets underneath rose to fill my nostrils with a savory headiness.

He chuckled. "So that's what they *really* mean by 'kiss my ass.' Ummmm."

After a couple of lungfuls of scented testosterone, I raised up to knead Buddy's big muscular mounds, digging my fingers into the powerful tensed glutes and plowing deep with the heels of my hands. The crescent-shaped packs of muscle relaxed.

"Shit! That feels great, Matt."

I bent down to bite at the tight skin. I began to moan, the reality of what I was finally getting to do beginning to sink into my brain. I munched on his hard-packed globes, pulling at the tiny hairs with my teeth and feeling him pimple under my dragging teeth. "You have the most beautiful butt . . . on any man I've ever seen, Buddy . . . I am such a butt lover . . . a connoisseur, man . . . um . . . of fine asses . . . I *know*. You are prime meat."

My tongue dragged out long and wet to soothe the red trails I had laid down.

Buddy's half-hooded eyes looked back at me slyly. "There's, uh, stuff in the drawer." His big head inclined toward the small table next to the bed.

Stuff? Heavy-duty condoms—colored and textured. Tubes of flavored lube. Toys! A small nubby ass probe and a couple of battery-operated deep massagers.

"You've got a whole playpen in here."

"I thought it'd turn her on. She says I've got a dirty mind. Guess I do. Maybe I've been just working on the wrong sex."

"Well, you have found Mr. Right," I said, happily rolling on a bright cherry-red rubber. Squeezing a couple of handfuls of lube over his ass-cheeks, I rubbed the quickly-melting gel in hard circles. My hands worked closer and closer to his crack, then started an alternating pattern of spreading the cheeks outward, opening the slick mounds to let in air and light and allow the moist lubricating fluid to puddle into the dark recess. I leaned in. His butthole was a dark target, a mocha latte of rich puckered red-browns, the tightly-fluted flesh of his entranceway giving way to a smooth circle of surrounding curling protective hairs, damp and shining. A field of shorter, softer hairs fanned out to a pale tan oval of surrounding flesh that quickly faded into the surrounding un-sunned buttocks.

I puckered my lips, mirroring the tight o-ring, and blew against the steaming entrance. The surrounding flesh goosebumped as the entrance to his hole did a little twitching dance and the tight folds relaxed. Buddy moaned. I licked, stroking my nubby tongue over the quivering hole until it sighed open and my insistent organ slipped inside.

"That is fucking awesome." I could hardly hear Buddy's fervent whisper.

He arched his hips to give me more access and to give him room to shove his hand under his crotch. From the way his hips ground against my mouth, I imagined his dick was doing a similar grind in his grip. My chin sandpapered its afternoon stubble against his fat perineum. Buddy writhed, his whole body grinding against the sheets. I pressed a blob of lube—strawberry parfait—against his open butthole and massaged the grease in with the pads of my fingers. They slid in easily and the hot, wet interior closed hungrily over them. Sawing in and out, I shoved in more. The digits pried his hole wider and wider.

"Damn, man . . . do it!" Buddy's deep voice begged.

I smeared a handful of the slick, scented goo up and down my bone, straddled Buddy's thick thighs, arched my hips forward and drove my dick all the way up his ass. With a gasp, he cursed mightily, howling and humping his torso. "Oh, fucking shit! Keep it in there!" he barked. His ass bucked up and down like a unbroken bronc. "Whoo, boy!" He pounded his fists against the mattress. I hooked my thighs around his waist and fucked for all I was worth. His ass was hot and tight. The thrashing colon muscles deep inside writhed around my pistoning bone. My pubes pounded against his bruised butt.

Buddy's bucking butt began to settle down. He pushed his hips up to meet my downward thrusts. My dick seemed to dig itself deeper and deeper. The solid hills of flesh smacked against my hips, rebounding from the impact. The clutching butt-lips curled around my thrusting ramrod, sucking it deeper and dragging against its withdrawals.

"Fucking A, I'm gonna hit a homer. Let it go, man, let's make it a double."

I shot a load into Buddy's butt like I had never shot before.

Over and over the thick cream pumped out of me. Buddy's body jerked with wracking spasms as he blew his load into his hands and over the sweat-soaked sheets.

"Well, I'll be damned," he purred over his shoulder as I snuggled against his broad back, exhausted, rubbing my chest into his sweat-wet T-shirt, our bare bottoms locked together. "Who would've thought my queer next-door neighbor would've been able to make me feel so fucking ... fine."

He stuck out his tongue and I pushed myself up to greedily suck on it.

A few minutes later I needed to breathe. Buddy revolved under me and lifted me to position his big body under mine. His fat, soft sausage nestled against mine, both still oozing gooey drops.

"Do I get the pleasure now?" he asked, beginning to slowly undulate his hips.

"You want to fuck my poor li'l ass? It's been so beat up it might not be worth sticking your prize pole into."

"I'll take my chances, cute butt," Buddy grinned, his dimples digging deep enough to bury a dick in. "Y'know, us straight guys know how to appreciate a hot-looking ass, too. You got a hot-looking ass, Matt. Fuckable."

"If I'd had the slightest idea you were interested in tucking into my sweet tush, I sure would've made it available long before now."

With a raucous laugh he pushed himself upward, toppling me onto my back. He grabbed my legs and hoisted my ass high. His mouth smacked against my butthole and he began to lick and ram his tongue into the already-yawning anal opening. He rolled me back and spread my cheeks with his big hands. He peered at my hole, wide, wet and waiting. Buddy stretched his mouth wide and suctioned onto it.

I yelped. The man's tongue stabbed deep, drumming in and out, swabbing around the rim until there was no rim. My asshole melted. His hands were all over my butt, grabbing, slapping, and briskly rubbing. Lube poured in, instantly melted by the steaming heat. He drove his thumbs in deep and stretched me wide. My sphincter screamed but the pleasure searing my insides soon overwhelmed the pain.

Buddy stood on the bed and aimed his dick. It was shod in silver blue plastic. There was a lightning blue streak followed by a red-hot stab of heated pressure that split me wide. He stuffed his huge tool into me, the massive cap popping through my ravaged o-ring, followed by a bloated rock-hard shaft that tunneled deeper and deeper. My ass gobbled up the invading meat, chewed it, masticated it and swallowed it whole.

"Yeeehaw!" Buddy bellowed, squatting above my rolled-back torso. His massive thighs, stretched wide, flexed and strained as he pumped fiercely, pile-driving his huge pole in and out of my ass. My butt-cheeks sizzled with the slap of his pubes. Tingling waves of pleasure erupted from every nerve-ending.

"Oh, baby, yeah!" Buddy yanked his dick out of my butt, ripped off the condom and let fly with a fountain of white streaks that splattered over my chest, into my hair and onto the floor. He continued to shoot, his hips bolting forward with each explosive discharge. I let loose another load onto my chest and the sheets. The scent of sweet and sour cum filled the air.

It was Buddy's turn to lean heavily onto me, his emptied hose next to mine.

"I'm feeling a lot better," he said. "Thank you for your attention to my needs."

I stuck my tongue in his dimple and headed for his mouth.

Lucky Night

SIMON SHEPPARD

A piece of ass. Warm piece of ass in the bitter cold.

I'd just killed somebody—maybe two hours before, maybe less—when I saw the guy in the alley's shrouded darkness, big, vacant eyes catching green/white/green neon. "You a Mullah Assassin?" he asked, and grabbed his crotch.

"Yeah, me," I said. Even through the gloom, he'd been able to recognize my uniform.

"Fuck. Killer. Turns me on." He walked closer, hand on hardening dick. "You want?"

I pulled down my night-visor for a better look, everything clearer now, though tinged with lurid dark red. Short, Jesus— maybe only five-two, but handsome, a shock of dark hair, scraggly beard, little punk. From what I could see, his compact body would be worth a fucking. He took his jack-off hand from his dick: meat pleasingly small, even on a man as short he was.

"You one of the Benway Gang?" I asked, walking right up, grabbing his shaft in my gloved hand.

"Hell no. Lousy junkies."

When I squeezed down hard, he squirmed.

"You fucking piece of lying shit," I said. He spit in my face, a big gob. The back of my leather-clad hand across his face lifted him damn near off his feet, only my grip on his dick anchoring him to Earth.

"Suck your cock," he said, blood trickling. "You want?" Somewhere there were sirens, far enough away.

"Your ass instead." I took my hand off his cock. Hungry little snake. "Drop your pants."

"Make me."

I made him. The trickle became a little red river. He had nice, meaty thighs, powerful. But he'd shaved his pubes. I hated that.

"I hate that, shaving. You want to look like a little boy?"

"Why care what you think?" Taunting, asking for trouble. He'd reached down, started stroking himself, foreskin darting back and forth over shiny infidel head.

"I kill people. You forget that?"

As if to say "no" he turned around. Nice ass, really nice ass, smooth, sculptural, though with a telltale red rash on one cheek. Not that I wouldn't fuck him regardless. I grabbed hold of his shirt with both hands and ripped at the cheesy nylon.

"Hands on the wall."

He just stood there.

"Hands on the fucking wall, cunt." I was getting angry.

His smooth, muscled arms stretched up to rough brick. Big, ugly tracks stretched from the crooks of his elbows all the way to his thick wrists, dark even in the dark.

"The Drug, huh? Fucking pathetic," I said, peeling off my gloves, "but the fucking usual for a Benwayboy gangbanger. Shit." My right hand shot between his spread thighs, grabbed a big handful of balls, and tugged. He squirmed, shifting his fucked-up little body. I pulled down harder. He moaned, pulled away, his sac even tighter. I was beginning to enjoy this.

He moaned something.

"What's that, fucker? Can't hear you."

"Fuck me," he said. I could see his breath.

My hand still grabbing his nuts, I angled my forearm upward, up between his meaty, sullied ass-cheeks. His hole was hot and moist, a little sticky. He probably needed a bath. My cock was good and hard.

As I pressed into him, my gun jammed against his hot, starving butt. A searchlight, erratic but insistent, swept across the alley's mouth. The Mullah's patrol? Maybe. Probably. Fuck, I didn't want to be caught out. But like any good leader, the Mullah cared more about efficiency than morality. I'd capped the shit I'd been hired to kill, so didn't I deserve a little fun? I pulled off the little punk, grabbed, shoved him farther into the dark. His feet hit something with a soft *plouf*. He looked down. I did, too. A body.

"I killed him," I said. I hadn't, had no fucking idea who he was, but I enjoyed the Benwayboy's resultant gasp. Those fucking moral hypocrites with their drug-soaked opposition to *jihad*. Fuck 'em, let 'em gasp. Let their meaty asses be fucked. Fucked.

The body in the alleyway stirred, sighed. I looked down again; a hypo was in one arm. Fuck. If I hadn't just killed somebody on the job, I'd have done away with the scum. Just because. Just because.

The Benwayboy was against the wall, slumping, sort of. "Fuck me fuck," he drooled out. I looked down at his ass, all night-vision red. My gloves were in my right hand. I spun them out, brought them hard against his behind, metal studs against firm, shapely, Drugged-out flesh. He pushed his butt toward me, ready. It was too easy. A lot of the worst things in life are. Too easy.

I reached down and pulled out my cock, stroking at it hard. He was looking over his shoulder at me, smiling. A missing tooth. Two.

"Get down on all fours," I said.

"Facing East?" There was a Drug-fuzzed smirk in his voice.

"Just do it, asshole. Leaving behind another dead boy won't make a shitload of difference to me." The pants around his ankles made it tough. But he managed. I dropped to my knees behind him, grabbed at his ass, spread the two cheeks, one with the rash, the other perfect. Half-perfect butt. Not bad. *If I could take a bite out of that ass, a big chunk . . . .*

It was drizzling now and everything was slick. I got the dispenser from my pocket, shoved it up his hole, squirted out HyGel. I'd be damned if I was going to catch anything. Hell, I'll be damned anyway, to hear the fucking Mullah speak. But boys' assholes makes damnation easier to bear. Easier.

"Uh!" I wasn't about to take my time; I'd shoved the head of my dick in his semi-lubed hole, and then the rest of my I-hoped-brutal shaft followed, eeling right up the fuck's guts. Sudden hesitation: I should have reported back by now, let the Mullah know the deed was done, but the flesh is weak, right? And the hole is hot.

I reached around him, him on all fours like the little bitch we both knew he was. He had a bit of a belly, so maybe he hadn't been doing the Drug long. Who the fuck cares, really? One damn gangbanger from Benway's troops is pretty much like another, all drugs and hungers and eventual stupor. I slammed in hard, and he gave a little shudder, then an "Oh, yeah." Whatever smell there was floated into the general stench of the alleyway, lost. I slapped a cheek, the one with the rash. Through the night visor, red got redder. I rocked back and forth, in and out. Sodomy for sure. Even with the uniform's kneepads, the asphalt hurt.

"Yeah, fuck that ass." Did he really have to say that? I felt like pulling out, leaving him there with his shit hole gaping in the midnight breeze. But, hell, I was already in, might as well finish. I lifted the metal tube around my neck up to my nostrils. Inhale. A sudden rush into him, his hole, his stupid need.

Something. A hand grabbed at my ankle. The Drugged-out not-corpse. I kicked it away, clipped its head with my boot, I think. Almost lost balance. Another noseful. With renewed ferocity I rammed my hard-on into now-sloppy hole, gritting out, "*This* is for Benway killing the only man I ever loved." In the Stadium, after what passed for a trial. Nick. And when I thought of him, dead Nick, I came. Couldn't help myself, it was like a collision, car accident, angular crashes of sex, just sex. Breathe. Breathe. I pulled out from the punk's sunset of an ass, my slit still dripping. Reaching over for the shreds of the Benwayboy's shirt, I wiped his traces off me. He was still whimpering and moaning, though if it was for me or for another dose of Drug or just for the whole general disaster, who knows?

I stood up, rearranged my clothes, and walked out of the alley, not looking back, not like Lot's wife, not like Orpheus, not even a little. I did hear, though, as I strode out of the alley, back into the contested city, a shout above the roar of cold-late-night traffic, rumbles of hover tanks and maybe bombs. "I fucking hate you," the boy called. I kept going, boots on wet concrete. "We're going to fucking kill all of you." Then fainter: "Come back. Please." And finally, maybe plaintive in the distance, something that sounded like "I'm as much of a man as you."

Whatever. The Earth spun on its meaningless axis in the big, freezing void. The sun would rise again soon. There'd be, no doubt, another show trial in the Stadium. More war. Even more war. And I'd probably get another job to do, another killing. Whatever the Mullah told me to do. Paid me to do. Oh well, fuck, I'd gotten me some ass. I looked down at my red right hand.

The Storm

JERRY METKO

The temperature hovered near the three-digit mark and the humidity was just as high. I sat on a bench in a small, park-like area, watching my fellow students traversing the university's main thoroughfare. It was my last year of post-grad and the scene was all too familiar: patrons entering and exiting the cafés and shops along the street, people lounging on the green lawn surrounding the Tower of Education, kids getting their kicks in makeshift games of football and Frisbee in this, the center of campus. Despite the brilliant sun, the air was hazy and in the distant sky, a growing darkness approached. Gusts of wind swirled bits of trash and tree branches swayed in the breeze. It was refreshing and I could see the cooling effect it had on the students who passed. Still, I didn't see *him* until he crossed the lawn, running and laughing while tossing a Frisbee to a buddy. Tod. Two hundred thirty pounds of toned, bulky muscle with deeply-tanned skin and wavy dark hair. He was wearing a T-shirt emblazoned with the university seal and the word WRESTLING. His buddy was equally tanned, much thinner, yet no less defined.

Never were two people more incompatible than Tod and me.

He was a member of the wrestling team while my own athletic prowess was limited to walking. That thing called Fate had brought us together when I was a senior and he a sophomore. We were in the same class and one day, the professor asked me to tutor him. Tod and I met several times that semester. I tried to be professional, but Tod didn't. Conversations often shifted to off-topics and one evening, with finals approaching, he told me to meet him in his dorm room for an impromptu study session.

His room was larger than most, thanks to his athletic scholarship. Near the end of the session—as we sat on the floor—he reached over me to turn on the television. As he did, he leaned on me, his hand resting on my shoulder for support. I had gotten used to his playful slaps and squeezes, and his placing his arm around my shoulder. I was too introverted to return the gestures, but that didn't seem to bother him. As he pressed against me that night, I could smell the aromatic scent of his masculinity.

When the TV came to life, pro wrestling was on. Tod rolled over to a small refrigerator, pulled out two cans of beer and handed one to me. We discussed wrestling, but there wasn't much I could offer to the conversation. Time passed, more beers were consumed and when Tod had a slight buzz, he asked me if I had ever wrestled. Before I could answer, he bum-rushed me, our bodies collided and I fell back onto the carpet. Then he landed on my chest, driving the air out of my lungs, his hands securing my arms over my head. He laughed and slid forward, not stopping until his hairy, muscular legs framed my head and his package was thrust against my face. Instinctively I struggled, causing him to snicker as he positioned my arms under his legs, freeing up his hands. He brought his bulbous crotch further across my face until only my eyes were exposed. Then he rumpled my hair and tapped the top of my head. I realized that I was stimulated and hoped he wouldn't notice. I'd only had sex—if you can call it that—with one other guy, a roommate a few years ago, and that alcohol-induced experience had resulted in nothing but awkwardness and a friendship that quickly faded and eventually ended. I wasn't about to suffer a similar embarrassment with this prime-of-his-life jock. But to my own stupefaction, Tod was also stimulated; his denim-covered bulge was growing.

Finally he rolled off, laughing and asking me if I was all right. I nodded and gave a nervous chuckle. The rest of my stay was short, the lateness of the hour serving as my excuse for a hasty departure. Two days later, I saw Tod at the final exam. He approached me after class, telling me that he did well, that he might even get an A. We wished each other a merry Christmas and departed. That was the last I saw of him. Until now.

He and his buddy were twenty yards away, throwing the Frisbee over their heads with precision, weaving through the pedestrians with ease. Tod dashed ahead; his buddy threw the disc high in the air. An unexpected gust of wind sent it straight towards me. I raised my arm to protect myself, but the flying projectile grazed the side of my face and bounced on my chest before landing in my lap. I didn't move. My arm remained frozen in the air, my eyes fixed on the plastic dish.

"Hey!" Tod ran towards me, a smile on his rugged face. "You okay, buddy?"

I lowered my arm, then nodded. "Oh, yeah. Sure."

"Sorry about that," he said, his defined pecs heaving under his tight T-shirt. "The wind and all."

"It's all right." I shrugged nervously. *He doesn't remember,* I thought, almost grateful.

His eyes suddenly lit up in recognition. "Hey . . . buddy . . . how're you doing?"

"I'm fine. And you?"

"Pretty good, pretty good."

"What's up?" his friend asked as he joined us.

"Didn't you see me brain him?" said Tod.

"Sure." His friend eyed the Frisbee, which was still in my lap. I picked it up and handed it to Tod.

"It's all right," I said. "No damage."

"This guy tutored me, like, years ago," said Tod. The two young men eyed one another with some kind of mutual understanding, eyebrows raised, grins on their faces. "Ryan here's on the track team," Tod said of his buddy.

"Hmm," was all I could offer, averting my eyes. The wind picked up and the sky was dark, even though it was only mid-afternoon. The students around us hurried about, as if in a rush to finish their errands and find shelter. I wanted to get back to my apartment before the tempest struck, but Tod sat down next to me, his body rubbing against mine. He leaned forward, his face close to mine, eyes squinting.

"No Frisbee wound on your head." He turned his attention to my arm. "But you've got one here."

On my forearm was a small, already-fading red mark. "It's nothing," I shrugged.

"My fault," said Tod. "Sorry, buddy."

"Really, it's nothing. I'd better be going."

"Ever toss a Frisbee?" he asked, flipping the disc in the air.

"Not for quite a while," I paused, "and not like you guys."

"So you were watching us," Ryan surmised.

"Yes. I mean, no. I mean, I . . . just noticed you over there. I saw . . . the Frisbee."

Tod and Ryan looked at each other, almost smirking as if confirming some shared thought.

"Well," Tod sighed dramatically, "looks like we're not going to be tossing it around anymore today."

The wind rushed down the street, the leaves rustling in the

gale. I moved to stand up, but Tod's hand grabbed my shoulder and gently forced me back down.

"So, you still live in a dorm?" he asked.

"No." I wanted to leave. The storm was almost upon us. The sky was black with boiling clouds, illuminated by distant flashes of lightning, followed by thunder. "I'd better go." I stood, this time with determination. "The storm."

"Where do you live?" Tod arose.

I pointed in the general direction.

"How far?"

"Six blocks or so." I don't know why I told them. *Yes, I do.*

"You're never gonna make it, buddy." Tod laughed. A bright flash of lightning caused us to flinch, followed by an exploding crack of thunder. The wind stopped, the air deathly still. "We live a block away," he said. "Wait it out with us, have a couple beers. Our way of saying sorry for having brained you."

Ryan broke into a soft chuckle. Tod slammed an elbow into his friend.

"That's not necessary," I said nervously. "If I get stuck, I can wait it out in . . ."

"You ain't gonna make it, man," said Ryan. The sky was almost as dark as night. The street lights snapped on, casting an eerie, yellowish pall.

"Let's go." Tod wrapped an arm around my shoulder and began walking.

"Really, fellas, I . . ." My protests faded. They weren't going to leave me alone. As I got a whiff of his sweaty, musky scent, an unexpected rush passed through my body.

"Whooh!" he said as he shoved me inside the lobby of his apartment building seconds after the rain came pouring in torrents. "See? You never would've made it."

"I guess you're right," I said softly.

It was dim inside their apartment, but neither Tod nor Ryan turned on the lights. The only illumination came from the haze of the window, occasionally heightened by fierce flashes of lightning. It was a small unit furnished with an old sofa, a table with a couple folding chairs, a lopsided recliner with upholstery that had long seen better days, and mismatched end tables with equally mismatched lamps, one missing its shade. Decorating one wall was a poster of two men wrestling, the caption reading: No wimps need apply.

"Have a seat." Ryan pointed to the couch. "We'll get some beers."

I sank into the sofa. Tod fell onto the cushion next to me and stretched out, one arm resting on the back of the couch behind me. Ryan could be heard moving about in the kitchen. Soon he reappeared, handed us our beers and sat on the floor. I took a large sip, hoping it would calm me.

"You do any sports these days?" asked Tod. "I remember you saying you weren't that really involved in them."

"Not really." I took another sip, stalling. "Tennis once. But that was a long time ago."

Tod nodded. "Done any more wrestling? Remember when I whipped your ass in my old dorm room?"

I lowered my head. "Kind of. That was a long time ago."

Ryan got up and went back into the kitchen.

"Have you started working out?" Tod asked.

"What?" I was already feeling light-headed, the effect exaggerated by my anxiety.

"Work out at all?"

"I walk a lot. I suppose I should do more. Don't have the time." I explained that not only was I attending grad school, I had to work three part-time jobs. Ryan returned from the kitchen with three more beers and said:

"You should find the time." He handed us our second round and returned to the floor.

"It makes a big difference." Tod rubbed his hand against his pecs. "Pumps you up." He raised his muscular, hirsute leg and dropped it in my lap, pinning me to the sofa and giving me a start. "It won't bite," Tod said laughingly. "Feel how toned it is."

I stared at his thigh, then his shorts and the very obvious bulge of his crotch.

"Squeeze it," Tod grabbed my wrist and forced my hand onto his leg. An electrical sensation pulsated through me. "I've bulked out quite a bit since way back then." He rubbed my palm back and forth. It felt like I was pressing against rock. "What did I tell you?" He led my hand up his thigh until it made contact with his Lycra bike shorts. Out of the corner of my eye, I could see Ryan leaning back on his arms, his legs spread out, the package in his own gym shorts growing and filling. Suddenly, Tod put my hand over his crotch. "Feel how hard *this* is."

His erection throbbed under the Lycra. It was impossible for my trapped hand to engulf it. He moaned and I tried to free myself, but he maintained his hold, kneading my fingers over his bulge. Then he abruptly released me. Hastily I reclaimed my hand but my body remained trapped beneath his leg.

"You should work out." Tod stared into my eyes.

"You think you're such hot shit," Ryan scoffed. I turned towards him, not sure who he was addressing until he added: "Just because you wrestle."

Tod leaped off the sofa and dove onto Ryan's chest. Both jocks fell to the carpet and in seconds Ryan found himself in a headlock, struggling and clawing underneath his larger opponent.

"And *you're* such hot shit?" Tod said, balancing himself on his knees. "Do I hafta teach you who's the man again?"

I was mesmerized. Holding the headlock, Tod pressed his

enormous pec into the gangly runner's face, the mound of flesh filling Ryan's mouth and gagging him. Ryan fought to buck his buddy off, but the disparity in weight made it impossible. They thrashed around a bit—the track jock gaining advantage when the wrestler broke out in laughter—until Tod mounted Ryan's chest in a schoolboy pin. Tod laughed as he slid forward and Ryan fought harder, twisting and turning, as if he knew what to expect. Tod bounced up and down, driving the air out of his buddy's lungs. Ryan gasped and kicked, but my eyes zeroed in on Tod's huge, solid ass, his two buttocks perfectly outlined in the Lycra. He straddled Ryan's head with his massive legs, his pronounced package covering his friend's mouth and muffling his protests.

Adding to Ryan's humiliation, Tod slapped his hands on his vanquished opponent's head like a bongo. Then, while watching me, Tod lifted up Ryan's head and pushed his buddy's face into his bulging crotch, rubbing it up and down and humping in rhythm. When the wrestler released his grip, Ryan's head fell to the carpet, his mouth still gagged by the victor's package. Tod laughed again, but this time it was more devious-sounding, prompting fear in Ryan's eyes. The wrestler lifted himself up and slid forward until his ass was directly over his buddy's face.

"No, man, come on." Ryan pleaded, but Tod sat on his friend's head, smothering the ear that wasn't pressed against the floor.

"Yeah. Oh, yeah. Do you give?"

"Yes!" Ryan murmured.

"You're not gonna give me any more shit?"

"No!"

"All right, then." Tod didn't release him immediately. He settled down hard, rubbing and humping one final time. Then he pulled back and settled on his opponent's chest. Ryan was red, both from blushing and the friction of the shorts against his face. He was gasping for air as Tod gave him one brisk and playful slap on the cheek. "I can wipe the floor with you," he said as he stood up. "See," he then said to me, "It pays to work out."

The storm pounded the window behind me. The wind had subsided, but the heavy rains continued, lightning flashing, thunder rolling. Ryan got up and rubbed his hand over his face. Tod stood before me, his T-shirt damp with sweat, and nodded at a door. "We've got some equipment in there. Come and see it."

I hesitated.

"Come on." Tod pulled me up and led me across the room. "Maybe it'll give you some ideas."

Their bedroom was as dim and gloomy as the living room. There were no decorations on the walls, and in the center of the room was a large, king-sized mattress, partially covered by an unfitted sheet and a few pillows. Plastic crates lined the perimeter and were filled with clothing, books and CDs. In one corner stood a workout machine, consisting of a seat, bows and pulleys.

Before I knew it, Ryan had me in a hammerlock, bending me and rendering me immovable.

"What the . . ."

"We're going to teach you how to wrestle," said Ryan.

"No, man." I tried to shake free. "Not interested."

"Sure you are," Tod insisted. "We had fun wrestling a couple years ago, didn't we?"

Ryan relinquished his hold long enough for Tod to yank off my shirt. Once I was topless, he nodded at the mattress and Ryan forced me towards it.

"Come on, guys, joke's over. This isn't fun."

Tod wrapped one arm around me and Ryan tripped my ankle. The three of us toppled onto the mattress, the bulk of their weight exploding the air from my lungs. Next they flipped me onto my back and Tod mounted me, his muscular chest smothering my face.

"Suck it real good." He forced a nipple into my mouth. "I said suck it!"

I did as I was told, tasting sweat and dark hairs against my lips. Ryan was on the mattress moving about. He was pulling Tod's Lycra shorts off, I realized. I felt Tod's erection pressed against my stomach. He swayed back and forth, his nipple slipping out my mouth, his chest rubbing over my face. "See how easy it is to pin your ass when you don't work out?" he said sarcastically. It was difficult to breath with his weight pressing down on my lungs.

"Yes. All right," I gasped. "Now let me up."

He slid forward until he was straddling my head, his thick, hard cock and enormous ball-sack near my face. I kicked with my legs, but Ryan crawled on top of them. Trapped beneath them, my mind was reeling, but my senses were aware of everything in minute detail, the crunching of the mattress as they shifted their weight, the pattering of rain against the distant window. I saw Tod's enormous cock looming over my face, pulsing and throbbing, his chest rising and falling, covered with perspiration, his mouth partially open, the bottom row of teeth intensely chewing at the upper lip. I wanted to be away from there, even in the fury of the storm, and yet electricity jolted through my body. And while I shivered with trepidation, I could not deny that it *was* pleasurable, and more than anything, I hated that I could not deny it. I wanted *more*.

"Lick my balls," Tod told me. "Suck them. Service them." He placed a hand behind my head and forced my face upward. I could smell his musky scent and I breathed it in. I did as he ordered, flicking my tongue over the silky skin. "That's it." he said. "Take them in, suck 'em."

I serviced them for awhile, then he moved forward. His balls went onto my forehead and the area between his ball-sack and his ass covered the rest of my face. Coarse black hair and an even stronger musk took over my senses. "Lick it," he said, his voice distant. "Lick there."

I moaned in protest—not wanting to appear as if I was enjoying it—but both jocks increased their grip on me until I relaxed. Tod began rocking back and forth. His movements became short, sharp and quick. He grabbed my wrists and forced them onto the mattress as he lifted up, holding his ass over my face, hovering there, allowing me to see his muscled buttocks and deep crack, the rosebud barely visible through a thick matting of hair. I shook my head from side to side in a futile effort to avoid what I knew was going to happen.

He lowered his butt and smothered my face, momentarily cutting off my air. Then he rose up slightly, his asshole over my nose. He spread his cheeks, revealing his butthole, and pressed downward, over and around my nose, thick fur rubbing against my tightly-closed eyes. I felt him squeezing and contracting his buttocks as he slid back and forth, his asshole rubbing up and down over my eyes, nose and mouth. My face was burning and I wanted it to end. I struggled again, finding escape just as impossible as before.

Eventually, Tod released a long, loud groan, then rested there for a minute before sitting back a bit while maintaining his straddle. His dick grew limp, the enormous head covered with semen. I felt a dampness on the pillow behind my head and smelled the bittersweet aroma of his cum. Ryan was hidden by Tod's bulk, but I heard him slap his buddy on the shoulder.

"My turn," he said with a laugh.

My body quivered almost uncontrollably and I began to squirm, but Tod maintained his mount as Ryan pulled off his gym shorts, his own hard cock pointing up into the air, slapping against his slim, chiseled abs. His shirt was already off, exposing a lean chest and a fine line of light, brown hair leading from his pubes to his navel. Facing Tod, he positioned his ass above my face, and as if to torment me, spread his cheeks to reveal his hole. Musk and sweat invaded my nostrils, but the moment I tried to kick my legs free, Ryan sat on me in a reverse schoolboy-pin.

I moved my head to one side to avoid contact with his butt, but he reached behind and gave my head a swift shove upwards, burying my face firmly in his crack. I offered loud and incessant protests. Ryan raised up slightly, permitting me to breath, exposing his rosebud which he positioned over my mouth. "Lick it," he ordered, but I resisted. He smashed his weight down, asphyxiating me. "Lick me, then. Do it."

I opened my mouth and stuck out my tongue, touching the soft, sweaty flesh.

"That's it," he said. "Stick your tongue way in there. Rim it all around."

I swirled my tongue in a circle and I could hear him moan. As he continued to grind into my face, I felt a strange sensation and I realized that Tod was jacking off his buddy. Ryan's thrusts became rapid and powerful, his balls bouncing against my chin. Soon he released a cry and I felt wet globs of cum landing on my lower chest and stomach. He sighed loudly and relaxed, ceasing his humping of my face, resting his ass against my chin.

"Shit," he said. "I came too goddamn fast."

Tod laughed. I remained still and silent. Ryan fell to one side, the dim light from the window filling my eyes. Both men climbed off me and collapsed on either side of me on the mattress. Tod wiped sweat from his forehead. Ryan rubbed his eyes and chuckled. I didn't move, my arms at my sides, my legs stiff and straight. Tod leaned forward and slapped me playfully on my arm.

"You okay, buddy?"

I couldn't answer at first. Eventually, I was able to nod.

"Good." He got up and pointed at my chest. "You've got cum all over you." Stepping over me, he went into the bathroom.

Ryan gave me a friendly slap on my belly. "You did great."

I was numb, my mind racing with thoughts and emotions. Tod returned with a wad of toilet paper and dropped it on my chest. "There you go."

I wiped off as he sat back down, Indian-style, wrapping his arms around his legs.

"Did you like it?" he asked.

Again, my mind swirled. I concentrated on getting the cum off of me, and when I finished, I held the soaked tissue until Ryan grabbed it out of my hand and tossed it onto the floor. Slowly, I sat up, leaning against my elbows.

"Well, did you?" Tod insisted.

I looked at him, then at Ryan, pursing my lips. Finally, I answered.

"Yes."

It was almost inaudible.

"Huh?" Tod grinned.

"Yes," I repeated. "I . . . did."

"Cool," said Ryan. "And we can keep this just between us, can't we?"

"Yes," I replied.

"Great." said Tod. "You want to take a shower?"

"No, I've got to leave. I'll take one back at my place."

"You can't go out in that storm," said Ryan.

"The storm's over," I said.

"Shit, you're right." Tod rose and went to the window. "Still sprinkling though. You can wait."

"It won't hurt me. I can go." I stood up and retrieved my shirt from the corner. My sandals were still on my feet. I made my way through the bedroom door. Tod and Ryan followed. In the living room, Tod stopped me, wrapping his arm around my shoulder, his other hand pressing against my chest.

"It's just between us, right?" he asked.

"I said it was." I pulled away and headed for the front door. I opened it, then stopped. They were both standing there, watching me. "I want to do it again. If you do."

Their cocky smiles served as their answer.

I closed the door behind me. For a moment, my hand stayed on the knob. I still could smell them on me, the scent of their musk, the odor of their sweat, and I liked it.

Outside, the sky was still gray. The clouds had passed, but the epilogue of the storm was still playing out, the air cool, the humidity tamed. Rivulets of water ran down the streets into the drains. I walked quickly, then ran, heading back to the small park where I first saw them, not looking back at the apartment building, not wanting to know if they were watching me, just wanting to be out of their sight.

In the far distance, there was a final roll of thunder. The storm was moving on. But, as if to reassert itself, it released a new fall of rain, not heavy like the initial deluge, but light and warm. I spread my arms, the rain washing over my face, the cool water embracing me.

I will be back. We will do it again.

Posterior Power

MARC JAMES

I have lived most of my life as a straight man, but whenever I'm put on the spot about my orientation, I usually end up saying I am bisexual. I've had my share of relationships and encounters with women (and men) and I definitely find the female body attractive—just not as attractive as a man's body. Especially a man's ass.

In my early teens, I began looking at the male buttocks in a whole new, highly sexual light. And that was before I saw them naked! At fifteen, all hell broke loose when I finally summoned up the courage to walk inside an adult bookstore. (I was big and mature for my age.) I can still remember trembling at my first glimpse of naked male ass. It was as if a mysterious current of energy soared upward from the magazine in front of me, coursing through my arms and sending shockwaves into my heart and my brain—and, of course, certain lower regions.

The next big step was actually grabbing and feeling another man's butt, a pleasure I didn't get to experience until I was in my mid-twenties. The sensation was amazing, the electrical jolt ten thousand times more powerful than the feeling that came from ogling a mere magazine layout. The owner of that butt laughed because I took forever to take my virgins hands off his incredible posterior. But I didn't care.

Eventually, I learned that only one thing surpasses touching a fantastic butt: breaking and entering. I guess by now you can tell I am a top and an extremely visual man. For the past five years I have lived an exclusively gay life, and thanks to the Internet, I have found other men who share my affinity for male butts. It's been great meeting other men like me and realizing that in a world that is clearly more driven by dick, there are guys who prefer to see what's behind a man instead of what's in front.

I've also come to accept the fact that there are certain butts that drive me crazy more than others. I love smooth butt over hairy, white butt over black (I'm black, by the way). A nice smooth butt is like a tongue-magnet to me. And here's an odd one for ya: I like a defined tan line, but I go gaga for a pale white butt with no defining features except for bulbous curvature. I also love light brown-skinned booties, be they on fair-skinned black men or hot Latinos. And if you really want to see me tremble—though it's rare—put a smooth Asian ass in my face. Seriously guys, how often do you see some lil' Asian bottom cutie hanging out with a big burly black top? It's more of a delicacy.

Because I prefer smooth butts, you might assume I despise hairy butts. Not true. There's a distinct difference between hairy butt and downright furry ass. No, I don't like furry ass, but I do like a cute fuzzy butt, and that's just what my boyfriend has: a cute fuzzy butt.

I also love big masculine dimples on butt-cheeks that are so round and firm, you'd swear you could bounce a quarter off of them. At the same time I go crazy for perfectly round, soft butt. Talk about melting in your mouth.

There are so many possibilities nature has given the male butt: long curvaceous butt-cracks flowing from the small of the back to the base of the balls; cute little derrières with the short and simple slits. It's hard to say which I like the most: firm muscle butts with no give, or butts that have just the right amount of Jell-O jiggle. On second thought, I think I prefer the latter. Butts with more meat than muscle look better when quivering from a spontaneous slap of the hand. Don't confuse this with spanking, mind you. No red marks on my smooth bottom boy butts.

You can slap it, you can eat it, you can caress it. You can grab it, you can probe it, you can fuck it. The male posterior encompasses masculinity and submission in the same package. Seeing a handsome man walking down the street with a defined butt in a tight-fitting pair of jeans or slacks is the epitome of masculinity. Yet there is nothing more submissive and beautiful than a gorgeous butt bent over in front of me, ready for our mutual enjoyment.

Hungry Bum

JAY STARRE

Up here in Canada, those who know me call me Hungry Bum. Not because I'm some kind of famished tramp, but because my hot bum is always hungry. Hungry for fulfillment. Hungry for just about any attention possible, be it fingers, dildos and toys, dicks or tongues. Even slaps, pinches and the odd whipping serve to stimulate and eventually (albeit temporarily) satisfy my hungry bum. I spend my free time searching out those who would service my ravenous ass, and adequately adore it, or perhaps even punish it. There is a thin line between pleasure and pain as far as my ass goes. It merely craves attention, almost any kind at all.

Tall and well-built with direct blue eyes and a charming smile surrounded by a neat goatee, I do not exactly look like the typical bottom. Although I am quiet and reserved, when I see what I want, I usually make the move. And I make sure the object of my attention understands what I want. Like Dean, whom I was immediately attracted to when I bumped into him late one Friday night.

"I like my ass played with," I told him as he groped me in the dark corner of the music-filled nightclub.

"You like to get fucked?" he asked as his eyes searched mine in the dim light.

"I've got a hungry ass that'll take just about anything up it or in it. Care to oblige me?"

We were about equal in height, build and age. His blond hair was only a bit paler than my light brown hair, and his eyes were as direct and blue as mine. We could have been brothers. But did we want the same thing? His lusty grin was answer enough.

Dean took me to his place. We barely got in the door before he was tugging down my jeans and plunging his fingers into my underwear to explore the cheeks of my ass. "Ahh, ample and sexy!" Dean whispered in my ear. "And although hard, very pliable and smooth as silk! Let's take a look in the light."

He moved to the centre of the living room to switch on a lamp. I took the opportunity to kick off my shoes and get out of my pants. When he turned back to me, I was already on the floor on my knees. My ass was in the air, facing him.

"It's all for you," I murmured. "Do whatever you like with it. Get creative. Anything you've ever wanted to do to a willing ass, go for it."

Dean's smile was appreciative as he took in the sight of my thickly muscled thighs, large biceps and broad shoulders. I was wearing a tight green T-shirt, and an equally tight pair of white cotton undershorts that clung to the cheeks of my ass. It was up to Dean to remove my remaining clothing. I had become the passive bottom, and was merely his willing butt-toy from that point on. He stood in front of me and stripped off all his clothes while I waited in breathless anticipation. In moments, his nude body hovered over me. His thick, hairy calves were at face level, and as I looked up-wards, I was treated to the sight of his powerful thighs, also covered with swirling blond hair. Then there were his fat, full balls dangling down beneath a curved, throbbing erection. My asshole twitched hungrily at the sight of that lengthy piece of man-meat. I was certain I would have that thick thing up my ass sometime that night.

Dean leaned over to cop a feel of my butt. A loud smack resounded in the air and I felt a stinging wallop against one cotton-covered cheek of my ass. I jerked forward so that my face was against Dean's hairy calf. Another strong but playful slap landed on my other cheek. The pain sent shivers up my spine and caused my butthole to quiver with pouting pleasure. In that position, my asshole was wide open, although my underwear still hid it from view.

"Nice tight butt! I think I'll take a look," Dean gruffly announced as he landed yet another blow across my quaking ass.

He tore away my underwear, literally. The material ripped under his fingers like paper. I felt air on my stinging ass-cheeks, then another smack on my naked flesh. My underwear hung in tatters around my thighs, the waistband still clinging to my waist. My crack was wide open, my twittering asshole was alive with little eager spasms. His deep sigh of enjoyment was followed by more stinging slaps across my butt-cheeks.

"Your cheeks are nice and pink now," he murmured as he bent over me to inspect my butt. "Just like the pink little slot between them."

Instead of the blow I was braced for, I felt a delicate sensation against the lips of my asshole. Fingers grazed the entrance, gently stroking the sensitive flesh. I shivered from head to toe. His tantalizing digits ran up and down my crack slowly and deliberately, pausing every time they ran across my butthole, teasing me with agonizingly pleasurable caresses. I was moaning by that time, my butt on fire from the spanking, my crack alive with sensitivity and anticipation. My asshole gaped open, eager and willing. He toyed with the rim and lips and fingered the puckered and extremely sensitive inner flesh protruding so hungrily. I felt as if I was coming inside out in my eagerness to get that hole touched and pleasured.

Dean chuckled deep in his throat as he teased my spasming rectum. I realized I must have been creating quite a spectacle as I lay there moaning with my butthole fluttering in and out like a living thing, my ass rising up in an attempt to capture Dean's torturing fingers. I was drooling against his calf, and biting my lip when he abruptly rose and stepped around me. I shuddered with anticipation as I wondered what would come next. I could not see him with my head down on my folded arms. I felt him drop down and kneel between my spread thighs. His hairy legs pressed mine outwards, splaying me in two halves, my ass-crack wide open and my hole palpitating madly with hungry desire.

"Sweet butt, so very sweet! You have to shave it to make it so smooth and silky. There's not a hair to be seen. And white as cream."

Then I felt the oddest sensation. Air was blowing across my gaping, nervous asshole. His face was down there in my crack! The feel of warm, moist air sent shivers along my spine. I awaited the lips or tongue that might come next. The hot air tormented my asshole. I raised my ass up in an attempt to connect with that hovering face.

"Now there's a hungry bum!" Dean chuckled from behind. "Eager for action, eh?"

I hadn't succeeded in my quest to rub my butt against his blowing mouth. He had moved away enough to frustrate my attempt, but he was still close enough to blow hot air all over my quivering slot. It was almost cruel. Then suddenly I felt fingers digging against my hole, pulling it wide apart. A moment later a thick, wet tongue dove into my parted gap. I squealed. That hot, wet appendage delving into my inner flesh felt like lava being poured inside me. I wiggled and squealed and muttered in my hands as I closed my eyes and concentrated on the sensation of getting my asshole tongued. Dean used his fingers to stretch me open and his tongue to explore inside my gaping butt-pit. The loud smacking of his lips was a lewd stimulus to my already-vibrating lust. I was shivering, I was so excited. My cock was dripping pre-cum between my spread legs and jerking constantly. I was close to cumming already.

Dean tongued my hole for some time while I grovelled with moaning submission in front of him. I loved every moment of it, but after a while I began to crave more. Getting my ass eaten was something I undeniably loved, but it was also a vaguely unsatisfying experience. My asshole was moist and hot and gaping open. The tongue lapping over it and stabbing into it was amazing, but not enough. I wanted more. Dean must have read my mind, or more likely my body language. He rose from his butt-feast and laughed out loud. While I knelt there and moaned, he rubbed several fingers teasingly over my spit-slick slot.

"What a nice wet hole! I think I'll feel it out. First some lube, though."

He rose and disappeared for a few minutes. I attempted to catch my breath. Air against my wet hole sent more shivers up my spine. I was wide open for Dean in that position, waiting and expectant. That thought made me hotter than ever. Then I heard him moving behind me on the carpet and lifted my head to look back at him. He had a bottle of lube in his hands, and an armful of sex toys!

"Oh yeah, fill my hungry hole with something, anything."

"Don't worry, I intend to stuff you full."

I dropped my head and waited. What would come first? I heard the sound of lube squirting, then felt it dribbling down over my crack in a gooey stream. Next fingers slid up and down my crack. At first they were gentle, grazing my pouting hole and tickling my perineum. I had become accustomed to his light touch, and was taken by surprise when the two fingers softly rubbing the rim of my asshole suddenly plunged into the gaping centre.

"Fuck!" I bleated. The two fingers had sunk past the knuckles up my heated, wet hole. There was no pain, only exquisite, delicious pleasure. The ache inside was finally being satisfied.

"You like two big fingers up your hot little ass?" Dean grunted behind me as he rammed his digits inside me and twisted them at the same time. Gone was his gentle fondling. Replacing it was rough and forceful reaming that had me squirming and squealing.

"I love it! I love it! I love it!"

He added a third finger before I finished my reply. He stretched open my aching butt-rim and dug deep into my squishy insides. Those fingers turned as they poked and prodded. My prostate was banged and rubbed as Dean frigged in and out while twisting and stretching. I was gasping for him not to stop.

"You're still kind of tight up there. It's going to take some more work to turn you into a sloppy cunt. I'll have to use something bigger and longer."

I shuddered, but I had no time to prepare myself for the reality as he abruptly ripped his fingers from my stretched slot and replaced them with the blunt head of fat dildo. I bit my lip and willed my ass-rim to open for the flared head. It slammed inside me. I grunted as it savagely ploughed into my guts. Dean fed me more and more. I raised my ass and spread my thighs even wider. It was awesome. I felt the head sliding past my prostate, then, as I relaxed my inner butt-channel, the dildo found its way deeper and deeper. Finally it felt as if it was resting against the bottom of my lungs.

"Yeah, you took it all," Dean said, a hint of awe in his voice. "What a hungry hole. There's nothing left of it but the base."

I felt like a stuffed pig. I was trembling all over. Then Dean pulled the dildo out, which had me gasping. Immediately he rammed it home again. I screamed. He did it again. I screamed again. He poked me with the dildo over and over. I squealed and writhed and took it all. My ass was on fire. My prostate was aching.

The friction against my sensitive butt-lips and inner butt-tunnel was suddenly too powerful to resist. I was shooting.

"Good laddie, spray the rug like a fucked pig," Dean was laughing from behind me.

He yanked the dildo from my ass while I shivered in the throes of my orgasm. My empty butthole convulsed wildly. I felt as if I was an open pit. Jizz drooled down on my thighs. Then I felt something pressing against my spasming butt-lips.

"Take this plug up there."

I was dizzy and weak. The plug was huge. I felt the tapered peak slide inside me easily, my defenceless asshole no match for Dean's insistent shoving. I exhaled and relaxed as I felt the increasing girth of the butt-plug stretch my sphincter. Wider and wider. And wider. Jizz spurted from my limp cock as the plug finally rode right up my ass and my asshole clamped around the narrower end. I felt the square base nestle inside my lubed crack.

"That looks so hot, the big black base against your white, glistening crack!"

Then the spanking began again. I knelt there and gasped with a mixture of shocked pain and pleasure while Dean slapped my ass-cheeks over and over with his open hand. He laughed, teasing me, calling me a hole and a pig. The flaming heat emanating over the expanse of my ass-cheeks radiated into my plugged hole and up my spine to my head. I was floating in butt sensation. Dean was still laughing when he ceased his brutal spanking and began to tug on the base of the plug. It did not want to exit. My ass-rim had clamped over the narrow base and was resisting. Dean slapped one of my butt-cheeks and yanked on the plug. I groaned and relaxed my sphincter. He pulled it out. I shook and groaned as the fat thing ever so slowly exited. Finally it squirted out with a loud plop. I was once more a gaping, empty hole. The strange thing was, my cock had gotten hard again. And my asshole was far from feeling overworked. In fact, the pouting gap was spasming in and out like a hungry mouth. I wanted more!

"We'll try these anal beads."

I had had a glimpse of them and they were not exactly beads. They had seemed as big as baseballs. Again I had little time to contemplate what was in store for me. Dean was already stuffing the first bead up my ass. I squeezed my eyes shut and concentrated on my sphincter. The ball was well-lubed and entered me without too much trouble. But suddenly it seemed too large. Dean shoved. My asshole collapsed and the thing popped inside me. It felt fantastic! Then the second ball was being pressed against my clamped butt-rim. I could feel Dean holding it against my ass with the palm of his hand. He shoved and my hole once more opened up for him.

"Now we're getting somewhere," he said. "Relax that little nasty rim."

He fed me three more, one after the other. I felt them rolling around in my guts, my cock rigid and jerking at the sensation. Then Dean was pulling on the string. The last to go in was suddenly the first to want out. My asshole clamped against it, not willing to let the greasy object escape. I rose up on my knees and cried out as I felt the huge ball pressing outward from inside me. It was awesome. When the first one finally spurted out of me, I shot my second load. The next four were just icing on the cake as my cock pumped jizz all over Dean's carpet. I was a moaning mess by then. When the last of the beads was out of me, I felt Dean fingering my sloppy butt-entrance.

"Nice and loose. Time to fuck it good and hard."

Without waiting for my reply, his fat cock plunged deep into my sloppy orifice. I was totally out of it by then. My asshole welcomed his hard poker without any resistance. He lifted me up and carried me to the couch, his cock still deep in my hole. I was limp in his arms. He lay me on my back and raised my legs up in the air.

Then he pummelled my ass. His hairy hips slammed against my sweaty butt. His long cock rammed way up inside me. He turned me on my side and fucked me that way. He turned me back on my belly and lay over me, his heavy weight pinning me to the cushions of the couch as he rammed steadily into my ass from above. He shoved my thighs together so my ass-cheeks were tight, and still he rammed into me with his big cock.

My own cock was limp, no longer important. Only my ass mattered. My hungry hole was being fed, and fed, and fed. I sucked in Dean's cock with my anal muscles like it was the most precious gift my ass had ever had. Dean had stamina. He fucked me a good hour, in every position he could think of. I was on the carpet on my hands and knees when he finally rammed his cock home and filled me with his cum. My hungry bum drank it all.

Afterwards Dean shoved the butt-plug up my ass to keep his jizz in there. "You're my hole now. I've marked my territory with cum. Later we'll start all over."

My ass was already growing hungry again.

Traveling Salesman Rim

TOM G. TONGUE

Howdy, y'all! Name's Tommy Lee Garrison. I'm nineteen and live with my Paw on our farm in Bugswallow. Maw ran off with some travelin' salesman about ten years ago and we ain't set eyes on her since. We stay so busy tendin' to the animals and crops and such that we ain't got time to miss nobody, much less some woman who didn't care about us none to begin with.

With all the chores I have to do around the farm, I've built me a right nice body, and all the girls at the Church of the Redeemers seem to like how I look. I ain't never had sex with nobody, but that don't mean I didn't want to! Me and my buddies skinny-dip in the crick sometimes and we've pounded our puds together, but I'd never touched anybody, much less some man, till Matt came along.

It was about 9:30 in the evening and Paw had already turned in for the night. I was sittin' on the front porch with my dog Blue, watchin' the fireflies, when a man comes walkin' up our drive, purty as you please. I was surprised, but not scared none, 'cause thar weren't no reason to be. Blue t'weren't even growlin' or nothin'. He just walked up to the stranger and got his ears scratched. Some watchdog, huh?

I spoke first. "Evenin', sir, what brings you 'round here?"

"My car broke down up the road just after I passed your place. Can I use your phone to call a tow truck?"

He was tall, blond and good lookin'. I liked him right away. He had a sorta "aw shucks" smile on his face that made my dick tingle fer some strange reason.

"Sorry, Mister," I replied, "but we ain't got no phone, but if you want, you can sleep in the barn and I'll take you to town in the mornin'. Name's Tommy Lee."

His lips turned up to a full-fledged smile and his pearly whites shined in the moonlight. He reached out his hand to shake. "Thanks, Tommy Lee. I'm Matt. You don't know how much I appreciate this."

"You ain't from around here ere ya?"

"I'm from Atlanta, heading toward Birmingham. I got lost on these back roads that my boss told me would save time. I'm a salesman for a clothing manufacturer." It was then that I noticed the satchel he was a-carryin'. It was big and black with zippered compartments all over it.

"Paw is asleep in the back bedroom and he don't like no travelin' salesmen, but if you keep quiet, I'll go get you some blankets and we'll head out in the mornin' afore he wakes up."

I gave him a lantern and pointed him towards the barn, then me and Blue went inside the house and got some blankets, quick like, from the cedar chest in the main room. All I was wearin' was my long johns, but I went around dressed all the time and I wasn't gonna put on my pants for no travelin' salesman.

I walked into the barn to see Matt takin' off his shirt. Damn! He had a lots a muscles all over the place. That tinglin' in my prick was stronger this time. I'll be switched if he didn't take off his pants too. He was already barefoot and was wearin' these real neat-lookin' shorts, white and tight, but like boxers. They didn't hide much and

I wisht that I coulda seed what he looked like without 'em. I didn't really get why I was feeling that way, but it didn't matter. Matt turned and faced me with another one of them big ole smiles on his face.

"Thought I'd make myself comfortable. Hope you don't mind, Tommy Lee."

"Hell, no, mister, I mean, Matt. I ain't never seed shorts like those you got on. They look like they would be neat to wear. I just have these here ole long johns."

"They're called boxer briefs. I sell underwear to stores in the Southeast. I've got my sample case here. I didn't want to leave it in the car. You want to try on a pair, see what they feel like?"

To answer him, I threw the blankets to the side and unbuttoned the 'johns, then pulled them off my shoulders and down my hips until I stood there buckass naked. Matt heaved his case atop a hay bale, opened it and reached inside. He gave me the once-over, eyes stayin' awhile on my big whang, then pulled out a handful of undies and spread them across the top of the bag. There were about five or six pairs, different colored. One that looked like a jock but didn't have no leg straps.

"Hey, Matt, what're those?" I asked.

"You like those? They're called the Cup. Wanna try 'em on?"

I shrugged.

"Here," he said. "I'll put on a pair and show you how to wear 'em."

He grabbed his boxer briefs and pulled 'em down. I couldn't help but look at his dick—I mean, it was there, weren't it? I noticed somthin' different about him. First of all his dick was big, almost as big as my nine-incher. But what made him different was that he didn't have no pubes! I guess he noticed my staring and said, "Oh, I shave off all the hair on my body. I like my skin smooth."

I'll hafta admit, it did look a might interestin'. I'd never touched any of my buddies' cranks, but for some reason, I wanted to do it to Matt. My own dick started to grow and I had to try thinkin' 'bout other stuff to keep it down.

He grabbed a black pair of the Cup, stepped into the elastic band and pulled it up his legs. His prick disappeared from sight, but it made a huge bulge in that pouch. Next he grabbed a white pair and threw 'em at me. I caught 'em, smiled and turned and bent to step into 'em. I heard Matt take a long suckin' breath. Still bendin' I glanced back and saw he was starin' at my lily-white butt with a strange look on his face. I moved quick and pulled them up but had one hellava time trying to cram my John Henry into the pouch.

"Man, you look great in those," Matt said. "Let's see how they fit."

He knelt in front a me and ran his hands up my thighs, real friendly-like, and, boing, I was hard as a rock! My balls were pulled tight against my shaft and everything was pointed right at Matt's face. My face was burnin' red. He looked up and grinned at me. I sputtered, "I-I-I don't know . . ."

He interrupted me as his hands reached my hips.

"Don't worry about it, Tommy Lee. Happens to men all the time. You should be proud." His hands got closer and closer to my cock. His thumbs were running up and down along the space twixt my balls and my thighs, making me shudder in pleasure. "Turn around," he said. "Let's see how the back looks."

I did what he asked. I could feel his breath on my bare skin.

"Oh, Tommy Lee, you should never cover this backside of yours. It's incredible." He was rubbin' my butt and it felt mighty good, I'll tell you what!

He pulled my cheeks apart and I could actually feel him blowing cool air across my poop-hole! Before I knew what wuz a-happenin', he drove his face forward and started kissin' my ass—that fancy French kind. His tongue was everywhere. He was lickin' and lappin' and makin' gruntin' noises. I couldn't believe that in less than ten minutes after I'd set eyes on him, this guy was tongue-fuckin' my asshole. I'll tell ya somethin' else: I fuckin' loved it!

"Oh, Matt! I didn't know you could do that, but don't stop. Kiss my butt, man. Lick it out."

Matt pulled away and I groaned at the loss. But he wasn't done, not by a long shot. He grabbed a blanket and put it on top of the hay bale, then he got down on his back with his head on the edge and said, "You taste great, Tommy Lee, but I want to dig deeper with my tongue. Sit on my face."

I turned around so I was facin' away from him and did jest what he asked. I sat my hole right on his lickin', suckin' mouth. I bounced up and down and we were both havin' a good ole time. I kept saying "eat it!" over and over. I was real close to spurtin' my load and wondered if he was one a those cocksuckers, too. I was kinda curious about what he tasted like, too! I stood up and turned around fast, sittin' on his lovin' mouth one more time. His prick was standin' straight up against his belly, throbbin' with lust, and still covered with black underwear. His smooth balls had worked themselves free and I decided that was as good a place as any to start my own taste-testin'.

I leaned forward, without lettin' my hole get away from his tongue, and put my face alongside his big ole dick. It was hotter'n hell and smelled good—real good. Kinda musky and sweaty and sweet, all rolled up into one. I stuck out my taster and took a lick. It was a hot night and, at first, all I tasted was salty sweat. But I realized I liked it. Turnin' my head to the left, I took one of his balls in my mouth and spun my tongue all around it. He groaned so loud, I could feel his tongue vibratin' deep inside me. It felt fan-fuckin'-tastic, and I was startin' to wonder what he tasted like between his cheeks, too.

But first, I wanted to be one them thar cocksuckers myself. I reached down and grabbed his underwear pouch and tried to pull his big ole joint free. But it wouldn't come loose, so I thought, "fuck it!" and just started licking away on his covered cock. He'd been leakin', and the taste came right through the fabric. And I liked it! In no time 't'all, I had half his hard-on in my mouth, suckin' and lickin'.

"Oh, you wanna suck my dick, huh? Good boy, Tommy Lee!" Matt said and grabbed the waistband of his underwear and pulled it upward, towards his chest until his big ole penis popped free. Not even stoppin' to look too long, I dropped my head again, and sucked my first dick into my hungry craw. I was movin' my face back and forth, tryin' to get more of him into my throat, and even though I was chokin', I was not gonna stop. I wanted his cum and I jest knowed it'd taste right good.

Somethin' strange was going on with my butt hole, too. I lifted off Matt's sweet joint and looked between my legs to see that he was pushin' his fingers, two of 'em, straight up my chute! Strange thing is, it didn't hurt none. I guess he'd sucked and licked and slobbered it up so much, I was wide open. Then he touched somethin' deep in there that made my whole body shake. I thought I was gonna shoot off fer sure.

Throwin' back my head, I wailed, "Oh, Matt, I don't know what yer doing, but don't stop. I'm gonna squirt!"

He had other ideas. He pulled hisself away from me and started blowing cool air on my hiney hole again. "No, Tommy Lee, not yet. Let's have some more fun first, okay?"

"Whatever you say, Matt, whatever you say." I wuz ready for anything. His fingers had felt so good inside me that I wuz beginnin' to wonder 'bout that cornholin' stuff my best buddy, Billy Joe, had tol' me about. I thought, if Matt's tongue and fingers felt so good, his big ole salami would feel even better.

He rolled out from under me, and said, "Here, Tommy Lee, get up on your knees on the hay and let me rim you some more. You taste soooo good."

I did it: put all my weight on my chest and reached my hands back and spread my butt open wide. Matt started lickin' slow circles around my hole, not yet goin' in. He was drivin' me looney.

"Come on, Matt! I want your big ole tongue inside me! Give it to me!"

And he did just that. We were both moanin' and groanin' and I could hear and feel him suckin' air outta my hole, makin' it open up even more. I was gettin' close again and Matt knew it. He ripped the cup off the Cup and threw it to the side. He grabbed my freed cock and pulled it ass-backwards towards his wide open mouth. The second my dick-head reached his hotter 'n hell mouth and tongue, I blasted off. Matt was suckin' away and pullin' my love-lava outta me. I couldn't even talk, it felt so great. I jest made noises deep in my throat that sounded like I was havin' a seizure or somethin'. As I calmed down, he dropped my John Henry—causing it to *twack* back up against my rippled belly—and dove back at my rectum, pushin' my own juices back into me at the other end. I realized what he had in mind, and I was all for it.

"Plannin' on puttin' somethin' else up my hole, Matt?"

"Sure am, buddy. Roll over on your back. I wanna watch your face while I fuck your sweet ass."

I followed orders, and, afore I knew it, my legs were on his shoulders, and his fat drippin' dick was touchin' my nether hole, ready to take my virtue. I stayed relaxed as I could, and, you know what, he was buried inside me lickity split—no pain whatsoever. I was still hard as a rock and as his head brushed over that "spot" again, I thought I'd go a-squirtin' again way too soon. His face was real close-like to mine and I could feel and smell his breath against my lips. He smiled, and stayed real still. I think he wuz nearly ready to spurt hisself.

"Oh, Tommy Lee, your hole is so tight. It's trying to suck a load outta me and I haven't even started fucking you yet."

Lookin' me right in the eyes, he started rockin' his hips back-ward and forwards, Every time he rubbed that nubbin inside of me, I made a "ungh" noise. I was in heaven.

"Matt! Come on, man. Fuck my hole. It feels so good."

Pickin' up speed, he leaned forward a little, and just like that, his lips were planted against mine and his tongue was halfway down my throat. I tasted my cum, my butt and Matt's spit. It was all good. My first real kiss. It was enough to send me right near over the edge and I started moanin' real loud-like. Matt was fuckin' so fast by then, I could hear and feel his hairless crotch slappin' over and over against my hairless butt. Then he did somethin' that surprised the shit outta me. He leaned forward some more and sucked the head of my dick and the first few inches of the shaft into his mouth hole. I threw back my head and screamed, "Cumming!" And I did jest that.

Matt made a gruntin' sound as the first of my spurts hit his throat. Then he started hosin' down the insides of my asshole with his own white gravy. We were both so busy gettin' off, neither one of us noticed the figure standin' at the barn door for a good long while. I was still twisting my head from side to side in pleasure, and on one pass, I saw him.

"Paw!"

I was scared as hell. Paw's a big man, lookin' younger than his thirty-six years. I'd never really noticed before, but my daddy is a good lookin' man, too. I pulled myself away from Matt fast-like and my hole snapped shut, tighter'n last year's clothes, already missin' its new friend. Getting over the shock in a hurry, I saw that not only was Paw smilin', he was buck-ass naked. His John Henry was up and smilin' too, pointin' at least ten inches out in front of him.

"So, Matthew," Paw said. As he spoke he moved over to where we were, "I'd be guessin' your plan worked out jest fine. Tommy Lee, don't worry, son. Me and Matt's ole friends."

Paw dropped on his knees in front of Matt, and afore I knowed it, Matt's big ole slimy thang disappeared down Paw's throat. A battleship could've dropped outta the sky and I wouldn't have been more surprised. Suckin' on it for a minute or two, eyes locked to mine, Paw backed off and said, "Oh, son, that thar hole of yorn is mighty tasty. Let me get it, first hand." Afore I knew it, Paw was between my still-spread thighs and his face was right there where Matt's prod had just been. He was sucking Matt's cum right outta me!

Realizin' I'd been had, I decided to wait'n worry about things later.

"Paw, my hole is empty now! Why don't you fill it up again for me, pleeeeaase?" Taking one more suck-kiss at my hole and lickin' his lips to get some more of my taste, he straightened up, lined up his massive man-pole and drove hisself into me in one powerful shove.

Matt moved around and, facin' Paw, straddled my face, planting his smooth butthole right on my mouth. My tongue reached out for him afore he even made it all the way down. His shaved crack wuz smooth as silk and tasted better'n any food I'd had in a long time. I reached up with both hands to pull his cheeks apart to get in there deeper. I knew I wanted to taste somebody else's—Paw's—hole this way too, and knowin' he'd let me made me hotter'n hell.

As Paw began deep thrustin' in my now-stretched-to-the-limit hole, Matt leaned forward, and for the third time, began suckin' away on my still-hard prick. We were one big ole fuckin' and suckin' and ass-lickin' machine. Paw was the ringleader, fuckin' me harder than a prize bull, babblin' a stream of cuss words like, "fuck, shit, sweet boy pussy" over and over. In jest a few minutes we were all on the brink! Matt pulled his hole away from my hungry tongue and pushed his big ole dick, still kinda assy-flavored, deep into my mouth and throat. He began fucking my throat at the same pace Paw was fuckin' my happy hiney.

With big groanin' noises comin' outta the three of us, we all started shootin' our fireworks nearly at the same time—Paw in my ass, and me and Matt swapping loads into our hungry mouths. Our big blasts musta lasted a few minutes. I was feeling better'n I'd ever felt before and shootin' even more than I did the first time. Paw pulled free, and my ass missed him, but I knew he'd be back. He lay next to me, grabbed the back of my head and shared a spit-and cum-swappin' kiss with me. My dick throbbed in Matt's mouth, squirtin' out a few more drops of sperm for him to enjoy. After Matt lifted hisself off of me, I smiled at Paw, kissin' him one more time.

"Okay, Paw, when did ya meet this here city slicker, and why did y'all wait so long to include me?"

Paw just grinned, leaned over to kiss Matt, then said, "I guess you could say I changed my mind about travelin' salesmen when I met Matthew here."

We all laughed, and as Matt moved 'round to suck Paw's load from my drippin' hole, my sexed-up brain started plottin' a plan to introduce my buddy, Billy Joe, to the fun stuff I'd jest learnt.

Life in Bugswallow had jest got loads better. Thank God for travelin' salesmen!

The Groom's Virgin Ass

J. SCOTT NEWMAN

Gordon rolled over and eyed his alarm clock. It was 6 a.m. In five hours, he was scheduled to marry the girl of his dreams. That meant he had five hours to make the biggest decision of his life: go through with the wedding or abandon it altogether. He glanced at the man lying next to him, the man who had completely possessed him last night, the man who had changed everything. It all seemed like a dream, but the ache in his ass reminded him it was real.

Gordon thought back to yesterday. He had been in the garage working out in his home gym, desperately trying to avoid the frenzy in the den where his fiancée was busy with last minute wedding plans. (Gordon himself had little to do; his family refused to attend the ceremony because he was marrying a black woman.)

As usual, Gordon exercised in nothing but a jockstrap. He enjoyed watching himself lifting weights and had shaved his entire body—all the better appreciate his muscles in the mirrors he'd set up all over the garage. He also liked looking at his butt which was firm yet bubbly, especially for a white man.

After working out, Gordon made his way to the master bedroom. The shower was running and he assumed his fiancée was getting ready to spend their last night as an unmarried couple at her parents' house. To pass the time, he decided to do a few extra crunches on the floor. He wanted to look his best for his wedding photos. After all, they would remain with him forever. He imagined the snapshots as he worked on his abs, barely noticing that the shower had stopped until a manly voice said from behind: "Looking good."

Gordon startled and spun around on his ass to find a tall black stranger towering over him. A towel was wrapped around his otherwise naked body and his caramel-colored physique rivaled Gordon's in both smoothness and perfection. His shaved head only added to his beauty and sleekness. There was a tattoo of a panther on his bulbous left pec. Gordon couldn't help noticing both the artwork and the muscle.

"Don't stop crunching on my account," the stranger said, peering down at him with a wry smile. "Those are some mad sexy abs."

"Who are you?" asked a flustered Gordon.

"Hello? You're marrying my sister. She did tell you she said I could stay here, didn't she? I'm Jerome."

"Fuck, right." Gordon swallowed the lump in his throat and made sure his heart was beating normally again. Then he leaped to his feet and thought: *Jerome. Travels a lot. Outcast of the family. Honey, he can stay here for one night, okay?* "Sorry about that. You completely startled me."

"It's cool," Jerome grinned mischievously. "Seeing you in that jockstrap completely startled *me*. My sister definitely has good taste in fiancées."

Gordon blanched. Was Sharon's brother flirting with him?

"So what has my sister told you about me?" Jerome walked over to his suitcase at the foot of the bed, then removed the towel from his waist and began drying off.

"Oh ... uh ... not much." Gordon, despite his best efforts, could feel his mouth drop at the sight of Jerome's enormous black cock. It was at least 8 inches completely flaccid and thick as a baby's wrist. "Just . . . that . . . you move around . . . all over the world."

"Did she tell you why?" Jerome said laughingly as he toweled off his pecs while admiring his body in the large mirror on the chest of drawers.

"Uh, nah," said Gordon. *That cock. So fucking huge. So fucking black and huge.*

"Well," Jerome said, making eye contact with Gordon through the mirror, "you might as well know why I'm the recipient of stares and whispers at the rare family gathering I show up at. I am an escort. I provide very wealthy men services in exchange for money, presents and globetrotting. The family sees me as the black sheep, but I think of myself more as a wolf."

"You're homo . . . sexual?" Gordon said in disbelief. "I didn't know. You're so masculine. And well-built."

"Thank you for noticing, bro-in-law, but I yep, I'm one of *those*." Jerome let his towel fall to the floor and bent over to fumble around in his suitcase.

Gordon was mesmerized by the naked, caramel-colored ass a few feet in front of him. So soft and smooth, yet so muscular. The little hole in the center almost appeared to be winking at him.

"I'm okay with gay," Gordon said absently. "Not phobic or anything."

"Are you staring at me, Gordon?" Jerome asked slyly from his bent-over position.

"No." Gordon turned away. "I mean, I'm sorry. I don't know . . . I'm sorry."

"It's cool." Jerome stood upright. "I don't mind if you don't." He moved across the room until he was inches away from Gordon. "Does my sister know about this side of you?"

"What side of me?" Gordon said sharply. "I'm not like that. Not like you . . . not that I have a problem . . ."

"... with what, checking out big dicks?" Jerome swayed his hips so that his dick moved back and forth against the cotton pouch of Gordon's jockstrap, which expanded and tightened. "I meet all kinds of men in my travels: married, straight, bi, whatever."

"I'm not bi and definitely not 'whatever.'" Gordon tried to back away but couldn't move his legs. "I've only been with women. Period."

"And tomorrow, you'll never be free to explore anything other than pussy ever again." Jerome's face was so close, their breathes collided. "What a shame. What a damn shame."

Their eyes locked on one another as they stood there, hard pecs brushing against hard pecs, throbbing cock pulsating against throbbing cock. The sweat from Gordon's forehead warmed Jerome's face. Jerome leaned in a little closer, close enough to kiss. Gordon could have turned away but didn't. Finally Jerome broke the stalemate and their tongues collided. A lifetime of censors in Gordon's brain suddenly went blank, out of order, on vacation, gone fishin'.

"Nice." Jerome said when they came up for air. He grabbed the pouch of Gordon's jock, then sunk to his knees and reached inside. He took Gordon's dick in his mouth and began to tongue his brother-in-law-to-be. Gordon threw his head back and thought: *what the hell, last night of freedom, love the one you're with* and a dozen other clichés that helped him let go. Blame it on being pumped up after the workout. Chalk it up to pre-wedding night jitters. Say it was the gay guy's fault. Whatever.

Jerome sucked as good as any girl, if not better. He knew just how to use his hand as a jack-off tool, too. *Damn, you have to teach girls how to do that.* Jerome's other hand slid around to Gordon's backside and caressed his buns. Gordon spread his legs wider. Jerome stroked and caressed and eventually his middle finger found Gordon's pucker. He plunged inside, prompting a soft moan from Gordon.

I could never get her to do this.

Soon one finger was joined by another. Jerome probed in and out, massaging deep inside Gordon. This brand new feeling sent shockwaves over Gordon's body. He never knew how much pleasure his ass could give him. He had always curious but never knew.

"How does it feel?" Jerome's fingers slipped out of Gordon's ass, causing a plopping sound. "Want more?"

"Show me everything. Do it all."

"Get on the bed. Facedown, ass up."

Gordon practically leaped on the bed. No turning back now. He had to know just how good sex between two men could be. He lay there with Jerome's hands quietly kneading the roundness of his butt. Then all of a sudden, he felt Jerome's warm breath on his ass. Gordon quaked at the tingling sensation but welcomed it. Without warning Jerome's tongue was completely inside of Gordon's ass, plunging him to depths he hadn't even dreamed of. Jerome tongue-fucked Gordon until he wanted to scream, but just as he felt an orgasm building in his balls, Jerome withdrew his tongue and kissed Gordon's butt cheeks. Jerome was a pro.

"No!" Gordon begged. "More! Come on, more!"

"Wait." Jerome retrieved a small dildo and a bottle of lube from his suitcase. He lubed the rubber projectile, then rubbed some on Gordon's crack. The cool sensation caused Gordon to gasp. Jerome placed the dildo against Gordon's hole and gently pushed. Gordon let out a yelp as it pressed past his pink ring. "Breathe, baby," said Jerome. "Let yourself go."

Once Gordon relaxed enough to take the entire dildo, Jerome began a slow fuck.

"How does that feel, baby?" asked Jerome.

"Fuck, yeah," Gordon said as the initial discomfort turned into unbelievable gratification. "Amazing!"

"You ready for more? You want the genuine article?"

"Yes, please yes. I want it in me."

Jerome slid the fake dick out of Gordon's ass and put a condom on the real thing. Gordon's hole was hot, wet and quivering, but he still flinched and tightened in pain at the first feel of Jerome's thick black shaft.

"I don't know if I can do this," Gordon wailed.

"Don't know or don't want, baby?" Jerome dove into that ass again with his tongue, practically shoving his entire mouth up Gordon's silky smooth hole. Gordon moaned with delight again and gyrated his ass in an attempt to get that tongue to go deeper. His wet ass became wetter from his future brother-in-law's spit. His heated anal walls became even hotter. Tongue was good. Dildo great. He was now ready for the whole nine yards.

"The dick. I want the dick. Let me try it again."

Jerome lined up his cock and gave one steady push. His mushroom head disappeared. The shaft sank deeper and deeper. Gordon tried to relax, but it felt as if his insides were being torn apart.

"That's it, baby," Jerome assured him. "You've got all of me now. Just breathe."

Gordon did as he was told. He felt himself loosening up and the pain began to diminish, replaced with a sense of euphoria. Jerome began maneuvering in and out, pulling back so that just the head was inside, then ramming his cock back in until his black-haired pubs met Gordon's smooth white ass. Before long Gordon couldn't get enough of Jerome. "Come on, give me more," he ordered, greedily pushing his ass backward to get as much of Jerome inside of him as possible. Jerome plowed that ass, his balls slapping against the mounds of Gordon's insatiable ass, until the "straight" man began blubbering:

"I ... love ... this ... been ... missing ... out ... whole ... fucking ... life ... fucking ... fuck ... me ... me ... fuck ... me ... fuck me, fuck me, fuck me."

The cum inside Gordon's balls was near the boiling point. His ass was on fire, his body one big hole in need of plowing. He buried his head into the pillows to muffle his scream and spurted all over the bed sheets beneath him. As he shot, his sphincter gripped Jerome's dick like a vise, causing Jerome to blast a hot load of cum into the rubber, all while Gordon's untouched cocked kept bucking and spurting and spitting and spraying.

Exhausted, Jerome collapsed onto Gordon's back and they segued into a spooning position, Jerome's front to Gordon's back.

"That was the most incredible thing that has ever happened to me," said a blissful Gordon.

"It was great for me too, baby," Jerome said, then kissed Gordon and they both fell asleep . . . .

Gordon turned away from Jerome and looked at the clock again. Six something in the morning. Wedding day.

How can I possibly get married after what I found out about myself last night?

"You okay there, baby?" asked a groggy Jerome.

"Just things on my mind is all," said Gordon.

"Would one of those things on your mind happen to be me?" Jerome started stroking Gordon's back.

"Actually, I've got you stuck inside my head."

"I know. Suppose I put my head inside you." Jerome placed the tip of his dick against Gordon's shuddering ass.

At that moment, Gordon knew.

No wedding today. Maybe not ever.

Collaboration

THOM WOLF

Thom gazed at the reflection of his arse and wondered what Kevin would think. There was no reason for him not to like it. But would he love it and cherish it? Would he want to fuck the hell out of it? Kevin was getting on a bit. Was he still interested in men under thirty? Probably. What sane man isn't?

A straight one.

Kevin's not straight.

But he's married.

I can still take him.

Thom turned, examining his arse from various angles. He took the mirror off the wall because he loved to see himself from below—the furry stretch up the back of his thighs, the sweep of his buttocks. It was a fine arse, full and meaty. It was a real man's arse. He habitually wondered what it would be like to see himself from the perspective of a lover. To kneel on the floor and stare in awe. He would love to press his lips against the plum-coloured birthmark, high on his left thigh, just below the fold of his cheek. What did he taste like? His come tasted different to other men's, often stronger. Would the flavour of his arse be different too? Headier? Richer?

He wanted to pursue the line of his butt with his own tongue, curving up from the birthmark, following the freckles like dot to dot, until he reached the rose tattoo on his left cheek. The tattoo was a present to himself for his seventeenth birthday, a focus point for the men who fucked him. They would remember the boy with the purple rose.

In twelve years hardly anyone had mentioned it.

He squatted over the mirror, opening the dark crack. He loved the look of it. For years he had resented the natural brown tone of his anus. It worried him that men would think he was dirty when he was meticulously clean. Time had taught him to love the dusty hue. Its colour was rich, like dark honey. He used to shave his crack but hadn't bothered for a long time. He preferred his bud encompassed by a swirl of dark brown curls. It looked more mysterious that way.

He used to emulate his favourite porn stars, aping their tanned and shaved physiques and resenting the fact that he didn't have a perfect pink butthole like Derek Cameron. It was only when he discovered men like Matt Bradshaw and Paul Carrigan that he accepted brown could be beautiful, too.

In *Ricky's Romance* by Kevin Killian, the hero gets trapped in a broken photocopier while making sneaky copies of his Faye Dunaway fanzine. The janitor comes along and, mistaking Ricky for the boss, rapes his snared arse. It was Thom's favourite story and he read it again and again.

Thom had an idea that he hoped Kevin would appreciate. He wanted to share with the author his most precious asset. To send his arse from Durham UK to San Francisco USA. Thom had dozens of photographs that he shared with men on AOL: explicit, florid images, designed to make them want him. More often than not, they did.

But he wanted something different. He didn't want to show

Kevin, novelist, poet and playwright, the same tired shots that he had emailed a hundred times before.

The idea struck one Saturday afternoon while masturbating again to *Ricky's Romance.* Thom didn't have a Xerox machine but he did have a flatbed scanner.

His arsehole had been loosened by his favourite dildo and its inner passage gapped in a deep pink pout. He removed the lid from the flatbed and positioned his buttocks over the scanner. The bright white light slipped below his cock and balls, moving across his sloppy cherry.

He splattered the lens with come as the explicit image emerged on his PC monitor. He emailed the image, cropped and sharpened, to Kevin later that afternoon. He included a message: "Come and see me soon."

Kevin was staying in Thom's spare room for three nights. Thom planned to take him into Durham, sightseeing. He would show him the castle and the cathedral. Americans loved all that historical stuff.

Thom pulled on a pair a clean white briefs that did nothing to hide his state of arousal. He crossed the landing, tapped once on Kevin's door and entered without waiting.

Kevin was in bed, the covers pulled up to just below his big nipples. The lights were off but the television was on, tuned to the BBC late news. Two large posters of Kylie Minogue looked over the bed. Her image shimmered in the light from the telly.

"I wasn't sure if you would be able to sleep," Thom said, "being in a strange bed in a foreign country."

Kevin spread his body beneath the covers, pressing his limbs into the cool corners of the bed. "I'm used to sleeping in strange beds."

"Right," said Thom, putting a porn tape in the video. Sam

Crockett hammered the hell out of Kyle McKenna's grateful arse. "Are you naked under there?" he asked, having already noticed Kevin's clothes folded neatly over the chair. "I could do with a cuddle."

Kevin raised the cover, moving over to make room. Thom kicked off his briefs and slipped into the warm space. He lay against Kevin's side, pressing all down his body. His cock was on the older man's hip. He put his head on his chest and his hand on his meat, which was soft, and they gazed at the television. Kyle McKenna was giving a career best performance.

"He's dead now," Kevin said. "He killed himself."

"I know. Dramatic to the end. He was beautiful."

"He has the prettiest asshole. It's like a rose."

"You haven't seen mine yet."

"I've seen your pictures."

"They don't do me justice."

He nuzzled his mouth in Thom's hair. "Show me."

"I might."

"Isn't that why you're here?"

Thom kissed his shoulder. He had always been attracted to middle-aged men. Their bodies were wider, softer than men his own age, less attractive. It was true what they said about experience—it made for a better lover. Older men were consistently better at fucking than the twinks he picked up in nightclubs. There had been a few disappointments but the majority of his older lovers had been well above average.

Kevin's bio said he was born in 1952. He looked about right for a man in his fifties, from the wise lines around his eyes to the flecks of grey in his short hair.

His cock hadn't been hard when Thom first climbed into bed, but as he stroked the hairy curve between Kevin's belly and his groin he felt the lengthening twitch of an erection against the back of his hand.

On the television, Kyle was thanking Sam for the merciless treatment of his asshole. They say he took an overdose. Thom once tried to research his death on the Internet but information was scarce. The first he knew of the suicide was an off-topic posting in a Kylie Minogue forum.

"I think I'm frightened to have sex with you," Thom said, rolling his finger tips over Kevin's nipples.

"Why?"

"I've read your stories. They're like horror movies, aren't they? Something bad always happens to the characters who have sex. I don't want to die for the sake of an orgasm. *I Cry Like a Baby* is one of the sexiest books I've ever read. And it scared the hell out of me."

"That's why it's so exciting."

"For all I know you could be like Catherine Tramell, acting out your stories."

"And I could be the fuck of the century."

Thom kicked the covers onto the floor. "I don't like having my cock sucked."

"Let me see your ass then." Kevin turned on the lamp.

Thom got on his hands and knees in the middle of the bed. He spread his thighs and lowered his head to the mattress. With his arse raised high for Kevin to look right in, he felt exposed and bare.

"You do like it, don't you?"

Kevin was touched by his vulnerability. He leaned in close, putting his mouth inside the crack, feeling the soft hair on his face. Thom's arsehole twitched as Kevin put his lips on top of it and pressed a moist kiss. His mouth felt like wet satin on Thom's hole. His back arched, pushing his arse back further.

Kevin ranged between Thom's legs, curling his fingers around his dry cock-head. Thom gasped. It was uncomfortable but he didn't complain. Kevin squeezed the head, wringing out a gluey tear and smearing it down the shaft with his thumb. He followed the vein down the underside to Thom's fuzzy balls. As he did this, his mouth worked over the arsehole, poking, forcing the orifice to yield.

Using a mix of saliva and Thom's own pre-cum, Kevin slid a finger into him. The boy gasped and spread his legs a little wider. Kevin slid deeper, pressing his finger all the way inside the warm, brown hole, into its red interior. He wriggled around, pushing backwards and forwards, applying more pressure.

"You are going to fuck me, aren't you, Kevin?" Thom was hopeful and desperate. He hadn't been fucked by a married man before. Or an American. Let alone one he admired, a writer who thrilled and frightened him. "There are rubbers and stuff in the cabinet there."

Kevin withdrew his fingers from the eager hole and watched the ring contract. He found condoms and lube in the top drawer. "Lie on your back," he said. "I want to see your face when I fuck you."

Thom rolled over and shoved a pillow beneath his hips. He hugged his knees to his chest while Kevin stretched a rubber over his dick. He was larger than Thom, and it was difficult to breath with the full weight of him on top. He felt Kevin's sticky cock between his legs, making a successful jab at his arsehole. The writer's cock entered his apprentice's impatient orifice.

Kevin bore more of his weight on his elbows, getting some leverage for his hips. Thom clung to him, binding his limbs around the older man's back, craving his body. He kissed Kevin's neck.

"I fuck myself to your stories," Thom cried gratefully. Kevin thrust. "With a dildo." Harder. "I squat." Tighter. "I ride it while I'm reading."

Kevin put his hand over Thom's mouth. He fucked the boy harder, giving the little bastard what he wanted. Thom's brow furrowed with each thrust of his dick. Kevin didn't care if he hurt him. Neither did Thom. He fucked a load into his arse.

Kevin pulled out of the sloppy hole straight afterwards. He ripped off the condom and poured his gooey semen over the boy's face, smearing it across his nose and mouth, pushing it into his hair.

Thom licked his lips and wrung out his own milky torrent, shooting into the gullies of his stomach.

The Kyle McKenna scene had finished. Some beefy blond was chewing out Logan Reed's arse.

Thom rolled onto his side and Kevin spooned him, resting a finger in the younger man's loose arsehole. Kevin talked about his *Duets* book and the other collaborators he had fucked. Sliding in a second finger, he talked, excited by the project that had taken years to compile, until without realising, the whole of his writing hand was inside Thom's arse.

He didn't mention the tattoo.

Chow Down: Confessions of an Ass Muncher

JAY STARRE

I love to eat ass. My personal nirvana involves my face being perpetually buried between a hot stud's steamy butt-cheeks. My roommate Tony and I share that special taste for male asshole. In fact, he upstaged me recently in an ass-licking bout that had to be my most awesome sexual experience to date.

Tony and I are physical opposites. I'm tall, blond and lean. He is short, raven-haired and stocky. His Italian features are rough and rugged while my Germanic ancestors handed down a broad, placid visage. Yet we both love the same thing: some dude with his cheeks spread and his inviting asshole gaping open for our mouths, lips and tongues.

The first time we discovered our mutual love for ass-eating was by accident. Tony walked in on me while I was tonguing a trick's snapping little slot, the young jock's thighs shoved back to his chest and his spit-slick ass wide open.

"Do you mind if I join you?" Tony had asked with a bright grin.

We had licked that poor fucker's hole 'til he was squirming in his own pool of jizz. Tony and I had enjoyed the pucker meal so much, we made a pact to share all the hot butts we came across if the circumstances were right.

Tony brought home our most recent banquet. Roberto or maybe Ernesto. The guy did have a name, but it was of no consequence. His sexy bubble butt was all we were after. He was handsome though, Italian like Tony. In fact, their looks were so similar, he could have been a brother or cousin. Only Roberto (I'll call him) possessed a more refined, square face, with a touch of stubble that made him appear older than he was.

"Want me on my back or on my face?" Roberto grinned mischievously as he rapidly discarded his clothing.

He was sexy! A few inches under six feet tall, with short curly auburn hair, his body was jock-perfect. Broad shoulders, nice pecs and abs, well-defined arms, a cock that was already arcing out in a stiff erection, and shapely, muscular thighs were revealed as the young jock paraded himself around our living room with an immodest smirk.

"We'll start you on your stomach with your legs wide open. Get on the floor so I can see your ass," Tony enthusiastically ordered.

"I agree. Show us your cheeks. And your hole while you're at it," I added. I was already down to my jockey shorts. Tony was stripping as he spoke.

Roberto giggled as he sprawled facedown in the plush carpet that covered the living room. He spread his thighs apart and wiggled his ass in the air seductively. "How do you like my ass? Tony claims you two can eat it out 'til I shoot my load. Well, it's all yours. Munch away."

We all laughed at Roberto's brazen suggestion. But Tony and I also shared a look of passionate awe. Roberto's ass was fantastic! His lower back curved upwards to the swell of his buttocks, the deep crack beginning at a narrow waist and splitting two big mounds of muscular flesh in half. The cheeks were covered in a light coating of auburn hair, which blended sexily with the olive tint of his skin. Roberto rolled the cheeks in lascivious circles as he lifted his hips and shoved his thighs wider apart. The crack was revealed, paler, less hairy, and with a puckered slot in its centre, seemingly just waiting for our mouths.

I was salivating at the sight. I noticed Tony was licking his plump, juicy lips with equal greediness. Both of us were completely naked by then, and with stiff cocks protruding from our hips and wagging tongues, we were like two animals in heat. Fortunately we didn't have to fight over our prey.

"You go first. I'll spread him open for you," I offered magnanimously. The truth was, I loved watching Tony eat butt almost as much—*almost!*—as I enjoyed licking butt myself.

Tony winked at me, his golden amber orbs flashing with lust. He dove for the prize even as I was in the act of kneeling down beside our spread-eagled victim. Tony was down between those parted hairy thighs in the blink of an eye, his face crammed up into the deep crack a nanosecond later.

My cock twitched at the sound of slurping lips and tongue. I always found the lapping and sucking noises associated with a good butt-kissing to be incredibly sexy. So did Roberto.

"Yeah, stud," he crowed with delight. "Chow down on my steamy pucker-hole. Eat my ass."

I was kneeling beside the sprawled young jock. His head was thrown back and the look of bliss on his face was as much a turn-on as the noisy butt-munching going on down below. But I was too excited to merely observe. I reached down and parted those plump butt mounds with both hands, revealing Tony's busy mouth at work. Roberto's crack was almost hairless, and much paler than the golden flesh of his butt. The skin was flushed and wet with spit. Tony's big tongue swiped up and down the deep crevice as Roberto thrust up with his hips to meet it. While I watched, Tony's mouth settled on Roberto's hole, his tongue darting out to stab and tickle the reddened opening. The little slot quivered under the assault, gaping open with desire as Tony drilled it rapidly with his tongue. I pulled the cheeks even wider apart, which opened up the hole as well. Tony jabbed his fat tongue right in the centre of the slot and dug in.

"Oh, fuck. That is so sweet. Get your tongue up my hole!" Roberto blurted out.

"Get up on your knees," I told him, "so he can go deeper."

He obeyed instantly, pulling his knees up under him while remaining down on his elbows with his head pillowed on his folded arms. Tony was too busy eating ass to say anything, but his louder slurps sounded appreciative. He shoved his face into the upraised crack and went to work on Roberto's gaping orifice.

Tony's mouth was clamped over the hole, and I could see little of what was going on. But I could imagine his tongue delving deep to tickle the tender inner walls and jab at the sensitive steamy flesh within that hot asshole. My cock was so hard I began to stroke it as I massaged Roberto's pliant butt-cheeks. The hairy mounds were jock-hard beneath my fingers, yet plushly yielding at the same time. To the smacking sounds of Tony's busy mouth, I got my fingers down in Roberto's hot crack and stretched open the hole Tony was tongue-fucking.

"Oh yeah," Tony managed to mumble. "So tasty . . . ummh . . . unghh . . . yeah . . . ohhh."

The sight of Tony's handsome face covered in sweat and spit as he ate Roberto's ass was too exciting. I released one cheek of

Roberto's ass and grabbed hold of my hard cock. Rapidly whipping it up and down, I pulled myself to orgasm in seconds.

"Look out, hot load coming your way," I cried out just in time.

Tony's red face rose just as cum rocketed out of my stiff boner. And right on target, the gooey stuff rained down on Roberto's wide-open crack. In fact, gobs of pale cream splattered his swollen, gaping asshole.

I was gasping for air, staring down at my own cum coating Roberto's amazing asshole. The little pucker quivered and pouted as warm spunk drooled down over it. He was moaning and rolling his hips with desire. He wanted more.

"I gotta taste that," Tony muttered.

My heart was still pounding, and my cock leaking the last dribbles of jizz as Tony began to lap up my gooey spunk. His big tongue swiped at the sticky stuff coating Roberto's olive skin. He licked it off the sides of the spread crack, gulping it down with lewd swallows. He licked down toward the hole and cleaned up every gob of cum he found. Then he settled on the pouting slot, all sticky with pale nut-cream. While Roberto's hole spasmed and dribbled, Tony licked it sparkling clean.

I had never seen anything so hot. Even though I had just shot my load, I was seized with a mad desire to lick that trembling little hole for myself. "I gotta have that ass," I groaned, my hand still on my cock.

"Go for it, but let's get him on his back." Tony grinned enthusiastically.

Roberto was cooperative, rolling over and pulling up his own legs toward his chest. Tony laughed as he bent the young Italian jock farther over until he was practically standing on his head. His ass was up in the air, spread wide. His hole was gaping open, still quivering with little eager spasms.

"First taste this," Tony smirked as he bent over Roberto's up-ended body and clamped his mouth over mine. The tongue that had just been swiping out Roberto's hot asshole was now swabbing my tonsils. The tongue that had just lapped up my own cum, was now buried in my own mouth. He tasted like ass and cum. It was awesome.

"Now eat that ass," Tony said as his soft eyes bored into mine.

I bent to the task with relish. Roberto's butt looked great up in the air. The two big cheeks were tensed and hard. The soft auburn hair that coated the cheeks disappeared toward the pale crack. The puckered asshole gaped open in the centre, wet and glistening. It trembled in anticipation and I smiled as I first teased it with a light stroke. The tip of my tongue tickled the swollen rim and I almost laughed as I heard Roberto curse with a mix of frustration and excitement below me. His muffled voice was strained as I began to stroke the quivering rim lightly. The responsive flesh gaped apart and then clamped shut alternately with Roberto's excitement. It drooled Tony's spit as it eagerly worked itself into a frenzy. The slot was going wild by the time I clamped my mouth over it and began to suck it inside out. The taste of ass was intoxicating and the smell of Roberto's butt and hole were rank in my nostrils. As I sucked powerfully, I swabbed the pouting flesh of Roberto's hole with my fat tongue.

He was going nuts. He was bucking beneath me and shoving up into my mouth. His own cock was untouched, and I knew all it would take would be a stroke or two and he would blow his own load. But that was not the point, not yet at least. One of the things I love about eating ass is the undeniable frustration of the recipient. Roberto wanted it, he loved it. But he was not going to get off from just a tongue up his ass. It could go on virtually forever, and he would be in an agony of sexual tension the entire time.

I rubbed my face all over his smooth crack as I continued to suck his hole inside out. The slippery flesh trembled violently as I finally began to dig into the steamy orifice with my tongue. I buried the fat thing deep. I explored the yielding inner fuck-tunnel with delight as Roberto grunted and moaned beneath me.

"He loves it, man!" Tony said. "This hot jock loves a tongue up his hungry ass."

My cock had never flagged. It was as stiff as ever. I was as excited as ever. But there was one thing I loved above all else. I wanted Roberto to sit on my face. I wanted his hard cheeks surrounding my own cheeks. I wanted him squatting over me and giving up his hot anus to my tongue.

Tony knew me well. "You want him to sit on your face?"

I rose from my feast with a slurping smack and grinned at my Italian buddy. His eyes sparkled. Without a word, we lifted Roberto up between us as if he was a toy. His hard body was limp in our arms as he moaned out his lust incoherently. He was putty in our hands.

I rested my back on the couch. Tony placed Roberto's butt over my face. The big ass came down from above, spread wide, the hungry hole gaping open. When the hefty cheeks settled over my face, I snorted with satisfaction. Roberto squirmed around, his wet hole searching out my mouth and tongue, eager for more action. He writhed over my face and moaned out loud when I clamped my mouth over his asshole and began to suck and tongue-fuck.

I felt Tony straddling my thighs. I knew he was embracing Roberto, and through the hot cheeks of Roberto's ass, I heard their muffled moans. They were kissing, their tongues duelling, their lush lips mashed together. I increased the tempo of my butt munching. Roberto responded, writhing over my face, his hole gaping wide open, welcoming my tongue eagerly. His asshole had become an open pit, a steamy cavern in which my entire tongue was buried.

The heat of those big ass-cheeks smothering me, and the wet, sloppy asshole my mouth and tongue explored together were the epitome of butt-eating for me. I was in my own personal paradise.

I felt Roberto's asshole suddenly go into spasms. I knew he was cumming. His body humped my face as he shot jizz all over my thighs. More sticky cum splattered my body as Tony also erupted.

I came for the second time as the warm goo ran down my legs and stomach. The wildly spasming asshole over my mouth was the trigger that did me in. It was like a living thing, crying out with its long-awaited and long-denied satisfaction. I jabbed deep up into the dark cavern and held my tongue there as we spilled our mutual loads.

That was by far the best butt-feast I had ever enjoyed. Tony and I are still on the lookout for more hot tongue-anal action though. Who knows what we'll find.

The Crack of Don

ERIC KARNOWSKI

He's lying next to me, sleeping soundly in the morning light, and it's no wonder. We played hard last night, and he came twice: first while I blew him and then with his cock up my ass. Don's an exclusive top when it comes to ass play. He says he wants to take my cock though; he wants to experience it to understand why I love it so much. He actually tried once.

Since he'd never had a dick in his hole, I figured he should sit on me. That way, he could control how quickly and how deep my cock went inside him. He straddled me, his hairy chest heaving as he leaned forward and rubbed my pecs with his hands. I closed my eyes as he kissed me but kept his face in my mind—vibrant green eyes, head shaved bald but his lower face covered by a chestnut beard and sideburns that stopped about even with the middle of his ears. My hard dick pointed straight to the ceiling. When the hairy flesh of his legs and ass brushed the head, it made me shiver.

I waited to let him pick his own moment to start. I've never been a patient person, but I think I did well that night. When he finally moved to stretch his hole with my lubed cock, I smiled and said, "Yeah, baby, that's it, nice and slow." I half-opened my eyes to watch him slide my fat rod inside.

His face was red and his eyes were scrunched closed as tight as I'd ever seen. His muscles were so strained, I thought he was going to explode—and not in a good way.

"Whoa, cowboy," I said. I held his hips and pushed him up, ending the cock-to-hole contact that was barely there anyway. "If you don't relax, you're gonna rupture something."

He collapsed beside me and buried his face in my chest. "I'm sorry, I tried. I'm sorry."

"Shh, sexy," I said. "It's okay. I remember what it was like myself—that first time. Some guys need relaxing, too."

It took me a half-hour of stories—some of mine, some I'd heard, and some over-the-top silly songs I made up on the spot—to calm him down. When he wants to try again, I told him, all he has to do is let me know. No pressure.

Now, this morning, he's lying on his stomach, muscled arms under his pillow, biceps bulging. I could lick his muscles for hours starting with his arms, then down to the small of his back where a light patch of silky hair grows, and continuing butt-ward. During the night, Don had kicked the sheets to the foot of the bed. The hairy mounds now beckon like a muscular street whore. Wanna party?

He has the most beautiful ass. I move carefully, positioning myself over his thighs so I can get a better look. His right leg is bent so the right cheek sits a little higher than the left. An idea forms and I grab what I need. Being careful not to disturb him, I return to my position over his legs. I touch his butt lightly. He doesn't move. I lay my palms firmly against the cheeks, and he sleepily straightens his bent leg to press more completely against the mattress. I slowly push to either side, spreading the deep crack to expose the pink hole, ringed in dark fur. When I put my nose into his crack and breathe his funky sweat, my tongue erupts from my mouth like a hard cock poking through a fly. I make contact with his hole, moisten it, and he begins to stir.

"Reggie?" He speaks softly, groggily.

"Shhh, honey," I whisper. "You relax. Let me take care of you."

"Wha'y'doin'?" he asks sleepily.

"Making you feel good, sailor. Trust me?"

"Mmm. Love you."

I kiss the insides of his ass, the walls of the magnificent chasm. "Love you, too, hot stuff. Relax."

"M'kay."

The muscle ring twitches slightly as I moisten it with my tongue. I lap at his hole, which glistens with my spit when I move back to admire it. But I pause only for a moment. I want to get him ready. I press harder with my tongue, teasing the muscle open. Don moans at the sensation, and I gently knead his cheeks with my fingers.

With condom and lube in hand, I'm ready to go, but I take another moment to play with his hole. I press a lubed finger against it, pushing gently but firmly inside. Another moan escapes from Don, and I pull out. In go two fingers, massaging his muscle to open him up. So far so good.

I move forward, pull my fingers out and spread his cheeks again. I kiss his back and gently move his flesh in circles, each cheek in a direction opposite the other, which pulls at his asshole and massages it further. I take aim with my cock and press against his hole. He begins to tense up and turns his head.

"Reg . . ." he starts, but I shush him and kiss his cheek.

"Relax, babe. It's okay. Not gonna hurt you. Just going to make you feel good."

He relaxes a little, and I press in.

"Hurts," Don says, and I pull back a moment, still making circles with his ass.

Laying my weight on his back, I keep my stubbly cheek against his soft beard as I sing to him quietly, making up words and tune as I go.

"Love my man, all I can, love him much, love to touch . . . ."
Just being silly. He smiles and moans again. "Relax and let me in," I
sing as I sit up to press my hard cock against his waiting hole again.
He responds, and the warmth of his body slowly swallows my cock,
the tight muscle squeezing like a bear hug that would envelop my
soul.

My hips touch him, and I lie forward, letting him hold my
entire weight. The full lengths of our bodies rub together, flesh to
flesh, as I finally fuck him, slowly and tenderly. As our sweaty bodies
heat each other, we both know: we are loved.

2 + 1

M. CHRISTIAN

Okay, it's a bit freaky. I admit it. Some people do whips and chains, put needles through their dicks, or clamp clothespins on their nipples or dress in mommy's old dresses. But me—I get hard from dish soap.

Not just hard, mind you, but rock and steel hard. Same for seeing a roll of paper towels or a pair of rubber gloves. Not latex—that would be obviously kinky. But rather just a pair of yellow scrubbing gloves. Walking through the cleaning supplies aisle at the Piggly-Wiggly can get real interesting, especially while having to hide a throbbing dick from the bag boy.

You see, those guys with pins through their tits and welts on their asses have their dungeons and playrooms. Dan and I, we've got the kitchen. Mostly the kitchen sink.

Can't really say how it happened, not really. I mean, I know the first time was—what?—six months or so ago. There I was, playing wife and doing the dishes, when Dan decided that the view of me bent over the sink, ass out in a pair of old gym shorts, was just too much to bear. It was good. It was damned good. Dan's always been a really great fuck, but that day he was possessed or something. A fuck like you'd find in a porno flick—though I doubt Jeff Stryker would have done someone with their face buried in the sink, breathing lemon-scented liquid that "softens your hands while you do the dishes."

I don't know what was into Dan that day—not that I'm complaining—but I know what kept me bent, open, smiling and happy: Oshi.

Oshi wasn't involved the first time Dan grabbed my shorts, jerked them down, and gave my asshole a good, wet kiss. He wasn't there when one of his fingers, then two, then three, then four went deep in me, feeling where his dick wanted to go, loosening my tight muscles. No Oshi when Dan's dick finally did find my mark, pushing steadily, strongly till his pubic hairs tickled my ass crack and his balls gently tapped against my cheeks.

In fact, no Oshi that first time at all. But the next time—ah, that was different. Great different. Fantastic different. Tremendous different. It must have been about a week later, and I was being the Ms. again. There's something kind of sensual about doing the dishes: water splashing on the china, droplets shimmering on the cutlery, soap making everything slippery. I guess Dan agreed with me, because, sure enough, right when I was between soaping and rinsing, I felt him walk into the room.

Dan. What can I say about Dan? I love him. No duh, right? I mean, not only is he fucking me, but I'm doing his dishes—and I'm not into that "slave, do the damned dishes" thing either. We're lucky, I guess, not that we found each other, but that our domesticity hasn't gotten ugly yet. After five years I guess that's quite an accomplishment. We fuck in the living room. We fuck in the den. We fuck on the front lawn (okay, it was 3 a.m., but still we did it). We fuck with me on top, with Dan on top, and with both of us lying side by side. And, yeah, we've even done it a couple of times in the bedroom. We can sit and giggle at *Sex in the City* and fuck like we're trying out for an Olympic event. We've got it, whatever the hell *it* is, and I'm damned glad. Damned glad that almost every Saturday afternoon, while I'm doing the lunch dishes, we fuck in the kitchen—and I love it. I love it when Dan pulls my pants down, lubes me up—another great use of dish soap—and sticks his very handsome, very big cock up my ass. But it's even better with Oshi there.

Oshi lives next door. He moved in about six months ago. Nice guy. Smiles a lot, you know? I'd hadn't been with many Japanese guys, but there was something about him. Sexy. Very, very sexy. Big, but not like he graduated from the Muscle Academy. Just the right amount of nice muscle in all the right places. Bald, too. Smooth round head, polished like the marble bust of a samurai. The way he moves—it's like he's on well-oiled bearings. Smooth. Watching him walk out to get the Sunday morning paper, wearing a simple kimono-like robe, you can tell that he fucks like an artist: steady, inspired strokes. And his mouth! Plush lips, strong jaw. Just the right amount of suck, a perfect degree of tongue, maybe even a hint of teeth. The blow-job of an artist.

The first time with Oshi was damned good: my hands slippery and warm, face flushed from the hot steam, Dan's hands suddenly on my ass. My shorts around my ankles, Dan's cock pressing against my pucker. Dan's cock pushing inside me. Good, damned good. Then Oshi joined us. Damn. Two was good, but three was incredible.

Maybe they don't believe in curtains in Japan. Maybe he just couldn't find the right chintz for his bedroom. Whatever. There was just bare glass between our kitchen window and his bedroom—the bedroom where he slept and worked out in the buff. When I saw him all stretched out on his futon, defined and strong, I was in lust. Dizzying, distracting, heart (and dick) thumping lust. Okay, the fact that Dan's cock was sliding in and out of my tight little asshole might have had something to do with it. But I don't think it was the only thing: two good, three better. Looking at Oshi sprawled out on his bed, body so well-defined, helmet of a half-hard cock peering slyly out of a dense tangle of scratchy hairs, I was lost. I saw Oshi get up from his bed and smile wryly. The expression on his face transmitting an obvious, "you think that's good, you just wait." He walks towards me, his muscles doing their wonderful dance, his semi-hard cock swaying back and forth, with each back and each forth getting harder and harder until, when he finally walks up to me, he's gloriously and spectacularly hard. He stands in front of me. He's still bobbing, but only because Dan's dick sliding in and out of me is messing with my line of vision. My breath comes in harsh rasps. I break out in chills—a wash of goose bumps, almost like a kind of fear of how good this all is.

I want to grab my dick, I need to grab my dick, but I don't. If I touch it, I'll cum, shotgun-blast hard, and that'll be it. My asshole will seize, my legs will go, and the stars will come out behind my eyes. So I don't. I hang on, trying not to pay attention to the throbbing, pulse-pounding demands of my cock. I focus on the three of us: Dan's big cock in my ass and Oshi's handsome member bobbing right in front of my eyes. Two good, three religious. One cock inside me and one lingering hauntingly, teasingly in front of my face. Cocks are so damned pretty. Just look at one: pale pink shaft, tickling hairs where it connects to its owner, soft yet hard bulb at the tip, that little vertical slit where the good stuff comes out. Nice, damned nice to look at.

Even better to be fucked by one. Filling then emptying, filling then emptying, filling then emptying. From feeling that you might have a whole damned fist in you to really needing to take a shit. In and out. One of the best damned things ever—and Dan was really, really good at it. But better is to have one sliding in and out of your ass while another one bobs in front of your face, lingering, teasing.

At the tip, a pale drop of salty cum, the shaft starting to get that "really, really hard" shine to it. I was in the best of places, between a cock and a hard place. Then it got better, if that was possible. Oshi took a single, small step forward and his cock, that wonderful hard cock, touched my lips. If cocks look great, they taste even better, and Oshi's was just right: skin, sweat, salt, cum, funk, and a bit of soap. I've never been one to do anything halfway. A kiss would just not do, so I licked him—watching his cock lift then drop when my tongue left his head—then wrapped my lips around the head and rolled all of my mouth around and around him. Oshi didn't make a sound, but his eyes—what I could see of them looking down at me from on-high—glazed over and I knew that I'd gotten to him. So I sucked, as I was fucked, and, Lord, it was good. Time vanished. I was just a tube for cocks. Just a mouth and an asshole for these two lovely, hard men. Three is a magic number. Finally, the pressure built too high and I had to, just had to. Tie my hands down and I would have given anyone anything to get them free: my ATM code? Yours! My credit cards? Take them! Everything I own? Cart it off!

But I wasn't tied, so my hand clamped down on my cock. I was shocked by how hard it was, how hot I was. It felt like someone else's cock, a fourth person in our group of three—and the thought of that, yet another person, is what pushed me right over the side. Heaven, bliss, damned hot—that and more. Sex is supposed to be good, right? Well, this wasn't that—it was great.

Or at least it was in my mind. All I have to do is close my eyes and Oshi's right there with us, adding his dick to our fun. I've thought about talking to Dan about having Oshi over some night to see if he'd be game to join us. You can't tell me that Dan hasn't thought about it: he has eyes as well as a cock, after all. But I think I know why neither one of us has brought it up. In our minds, as Dan fucks me and I get fucked and Oshi relaxes on his futon across the way, it's all perfect. No hurt feelings or drama. In our minds, it's always wonderful, never disappointing. Maybe we'll have Oshi over—someday—or maybe we never will. But in the meantime I get off getting fucked while I suck our Japanese neighbor off: the three of us in cock, mouth and asshole ecstasy, with me bent over the kitchen sink with lemon-scented soap tingling my nose.

Evan's Slut

K. TERREGA

It's Evan's ass, of course, that I adore.

The first time he let me close—close enough to see, close enough to smell—I came just from rubbing myself on the sheets. He laughed at me, but when he turned I could see that my excitement had triggered his own. His cock was purple and swollen with desire. He fucked me harder that night than ever before, biting my neck and crying out as he drove himself deep into me.

Now he calls me his little ass-slut, and I can't deny it.

I can't deny that the sight of his naked butt, firm and darkly hairy, makes my cock stand instantly at attention. I can't deny that the scent of his musky bung-hole makes the sweat break out on my body. And I can't deny that the taste of his dark canal practically makes me swoon.

Of course, Evan knows what the sight of his bum does to me and he loves the power it gives him. He knows that I'll do anything for a taste of his crack and he likes to tease me with the sight of his naked ass, dripping water as he emerges, steamy and hot from the shower.

He'll reach for my cock, which is always hard at the sight of his tight butt, and squeeze me through my jeans, smiling lewdly when my swollen dick gives me away. If I'm lucky—and Evan doesn't like for me to get lucky too often—he'll move toward me. He'll squeeze harder on my rod as his smiling mouth touches mine and he'll stroke me while his wet tongue traces its way around my parched lips.

It's then that his naked body presses hard against mine, dampening my clothes as he thrusts his tongue down my throat, and the feel of his nipples through my shirt sends goose bumps across my already flushed skin. Expertly he unzips my pants and grabs hold of me, breaking our kiss to lead me to the bed by my straining knob.

Even then, though, he never gives me what I want right away. Instead he undresses me as I stand helpless at the foot of the bed. He likes to touch me with his rough, calloused hands and run his palms over my unresisting flesh before bending to take a nipple into his mouth. His love-bites are painful as he nips and sucks his way lower—and painfully arousing, which he discovers soon enough when his lips reach the distended knob of my erection.

His mouth, always so warm and wet, closes around the sensitive skin at the tip and I can't help but groan as he laps at the thin, stretched membrane. His hands are on my ass now, pulling me close, spreading my cheeks roughly, even as his tongue gently caresses my knob.

Until, of course, he shoves his head down hard on my cock and his mouth envelopes my thick shaft with its slick depths. He likes to suck me hard and use his groping hands to shove my rod into his slurping mouth as he pulls almost painfully at my sensitive erection.

His fingers begin to probe, and as his mouth tugs at my stiff cock, I feel a thick finger begin to stroke my anus. Instinctively I clench as first one, then another finger thrusts its way up my tight hole. Evan likes this part, too, opening me up, knowing how the

initial tightening of my asshole will eventually turn to gaping ac-
quiescence. He fucks me with his fingers, in perfect rhythm with the
pulsing of my cock, until he knows that I'm close, knows that I'm
weak-kneed with desire.

Then he stops and withdraws both his fingers and his mouth.
Nibbling his way up my belly to my lips, he kisses me deeply.

"Tell me what you want," he says, and I can smell his cock-
scented breath as he bites at the corners of my lips.

"I want to lick your ass, Evan," I say, my voice husky with longing but weak, too, from the need I feel for him. "Please," I whisper as
he presses up against me, his rock-hard cock warm against my belly.
I can hear the strain in my voice as I plead with him, but I don't care
because now his rough hands are on my ass again and he is licking
my ear. He bites the lobe and I squeal.

"Please let me, Evan," I whimper as his teeth and lips continue
their assault. I can feel his own intensity increasing and I continue
in a rush. "It'll feel good, I swear, Evan . . . I'll make it good, I swear .
. . oh, god . . ." I groan, as he forces his tongue deep into my ear. And
then he pushes me away, smirking at my neediness, but he bends at
the waist, his hands braced on the bed, his ass open and inviting.

Gratefully, I drop to my knees behind him and spread his
cheeks wide, the way he likes it. Greedy with desire, I stick my nose
deep in his crack and inhale his musky essence before using the tip
of my tongue to caress the brown puckered folds. My fingers reach
for his swollen ball-sac as my tongue laps at the sensitive puckers of
his anus. I hear his quick intake of breath as I gently manipulate his
swollen balls.

I move lower to suckle on the thin skin of his sac before gently
caressing the hard ridge leading up to his asshole. I feel his muscles
tighten as I work my way slowly upward toward my ultimate goal.
My tongue begins to probe more deeply now and I hear a slight
moan as the tip finally penetrates Evan's tight little hole. The scent

of his arousal as my tongue begins to insinuate itself into his bung-hole is almost more than I can bear. I feel my cock twitch as I feast on Evan's treasure.

My fingers move from his balls to his straining cock. Wrapping my hand around him tightly—the way he likes it—I begin to move more quickly, and soon I am stroking on his smooth shaft as my tongue plunges deep into his tight hole. Evan's breath is ragged and I struggle for breath myself as I fuck him with my probing tongue, trying to burrow even more deeply into his shit-hole. His cock begins to swell alarmingly in my hand as he bucks against me and I can tell by the feel of his quivering balls that his time is near.

That's when he rips away from my probing tongue and shoves me down roughly, not to the bed but to the cool, wooden floor. I'm on my hands and knees now, the way Evan likes me, especially after I've suckled at his asshole. I know I'm about to get it hard and fierce. His hand twisted into my hair, he pulls my head back and without preamble shoves his way deep into my ass with one long, painful thrust.

His other hand reaches for my swollen shaft as he begins to ram himself deeply into my rectum, until my sphincter opens up and welcomes him. My butt-muscles tug at his pistoning cock as he slams my willing hole. He strokes my throbbing dick rough and hard as he pounds his way deep into my hole and he bites at my exposed neck until I cry out from wanting more. And he gives me more, his cock splitting me open as his fingers bring me close to the edge.

When he squirts his load deep into my fuck-hole, my balls swell and I feel my own jizz begin its tortuous journey up my cock. An agonizing second later, I gratefully explode into Evan's hand as his cock-cream continues to fill my shitter. His spewing cock pounds at my butt, lubing my canal with his juice until it dribbles out of my ass the way my own cum is slipping and dripping through his fingers. With a final thrust, he pins me to the floor, his hand still tight on my limp and satisfied cock as his own spent member twitches in my hole.

And then Evan kisses me, his mouth tasting faintly of my cock, my own mouth tasting strongly of the depths of his asshole. As Evan strokes my hair and lightly kisses my neck, sending shivers up and down my spine, he whispers that I'm nothing but a slut, *his* slut.

His words are tender, almost mocking. But when his cock, nestled deep in my quivering hole, begins to swell again—giving me perhaps another chance to lick the sweet sweat from his ass—I feel my own cock twitch in delight, and am almost obscenely grateful at the thought of being Evan's slut once again.

Barry's Berry

MAX SOUTHERN

Barry was standing in the steam room, his body dripping with perspiration. A blast of hot steam had just been unleashed and he had stepped to the corner to cool off. He undraped his towel from his waist and ran it through his hair, offering up a clear view of that ass of his, truly an ass of stunning proportions. To the casual observer, removing his towel might have seemed like an innocent moment. Yet I knew his pointing his globes in my direction wasn't unintentional. It was an ass I had craved for too long.

Barry was short and cuddly and extremely cute. He was in his early 30s and had a farm-boy face, a slightly hairy chest, and a charming disposition. It was his mouth-watering rear that got me going, though. His was *almost* a bubble butt but a beautiful ass just the same—rounded and perky and laced with hair. Not a Bigfoot bum, just a meaty and virile one. In my fantasies, Barry also had a tight hole made for joyrides. Many a night I had jacked my meat thinking of his posterior crammed into my face, or having him bounce up and down on my dick. He was mild-mannered, proper, and seemingly shy, but I secretly hoped that he was one of those guys who gives off an air of decency when his clothes are on, but turns into a sex swine when the lights are out.

For years Barry and I had made goo-goo eyes at one another at
the gym but had never acted on our mutual attraction until Barry
had spotted an online ad of mine (an old one, to boot). He had
promptly emailed me, but our timing didn't work out. I had been
dating someone by then, and later, when I had been single, he was
attached. Now, two years later, it was clear that the heat between us
was still there, but I was happily attached (again) and didn't want to
risk it all for a one sizzling piece of tail. Or did I?

On this particular evening, Barry had come to the gym late,
apparently having missed his usual lunchtime swim. I had discovered him walking toward the pool in his little green trunks just as I
was finishing a turn on the treadmill. I cooled down, showered and
took a place in the warm confines of the hot tub. After I had soaked,
I showered again and headed for the steam room, which was empty
except for a couple of older gay guys who sat for hours checking out
the scenery.

I was dating someone, but like most gay men, I was no angel. I
had fooled around in steam rooms before—in fact, my cherry had
been busted in one by a hung, pseudo-straight frat boy—but I was
in my 30s now and felt too old and responsible for that kind of
behavior. Then again, my boyfriend was away on business (and not
due back for another week) and I hadn't had sex since he had left.
Plus, it was damn near impossible to think angelic thoughts with
Barry's fine ass staring at me through the foggy haze of steam.

I was about to pass out from the combination of the extreme
heat and the sight before me when he draped the towel around his
waist and headed off for a shower. A few minutes later, I went out
for a drink of water and to check the time. An announcement over
the PA informed us that the gym was closing in 10 minutes. The
other men started packing their gym bags and heading out. I, however, went back for more steam. As I pulled the steam room door
open, Barry stepped out of the shower, packing a semi-erection. He

eyed me innocently; I was dying to know what was on his mind. Would he have the nerve? Just as importantly, would I?

I entered the steam room and sat. A skinny, gray-haired man was inside but left quickly enough. Soon after, Barry came in, his eyes immediately finding me. I knew this would be my only opportunity to take advantage of my obsession over him and his ass. I hesitated, then walked toward the animal I'd lusted after for years. Nothing was said for awhile as we surmised the safety of the situation. Then I lost all inhibition, grabbed his shoulder blade and planted a deep kiss on his lips. Our tongues darted in and out of each other's mouths as we explored our passion for the first time. Barry's skin was sweet but manly and I felt his boner rise up against his towel. In another instant he was completely naked, his cock dripping pre-cum. Normally, I would have dropped to my knees and slurped on it for half an hour. Yet it was Barry's cheeks that had inspired me and I wasn't able to waste any more time.

I moved behind him and grabbed hold of his ass. Then I made a single, slow move to his hole, licking it like I would some exotic, never-before-tasted treat. Barry moaned and immediately hunched over as my tongue slid toward his rectum. I dove into his backside, part of me wanting to take my time and luxuriate over it, part of me wanting to wolf it down whole. As my tongue slipped deeper into his nether regions, I pushed farther and farther. His was a salty, sweaty taste and it was evident that Barry hadn't received a good rim job in awhile. We were like wild beasts caught up in the frenzy. It would have taken a SWAT team to dislodge us.

"Fuck me," he suddenly ordered me. "Ram my ass."

It wasn't a polite request. As I had expected and hoped, Barry was no Clark Kent while in the throes of lust. And as juicy as his butt tasted, I knew a good fucking would be even more satisfying. We moved to the corner and I poked a finger up his chute. Our bodies were so moist with sweat, we didn't need lube. With one shove, I lodged my dick up his butt. An audible gasp flew from his mouth. I grabbed his cheeks and paced myself, going in and out with precision, picking up the pace. His hands were on the wall, his backside quaking. God, it was like an oven inside him.

I leaned forward to kiss him and before long we were ready to burst. Barry was first. "Goddamn," he yelled, as his body convulsed and his cock sprayed cum all over the steam room wall, my pole still worming inside him the whole time. Seconds later, I shot a load up his beautiful furry butt, shaking as I unleashed my jism. Then we both nearly collapsed in ecstasy as I continued to hold onto him.

A few moments passed and he tried to drape the towel around him. But I was having none of that. I tasted his ass again, licking my juice out of his pucker and planting sloppy kisses all over his backside. Afterwards, we both sat down, composing ourselves, embarrassed and guilty. A few moments later, a gym attendant poked his head inside and reiterated that the gym was closing. We had gotten away with it. Barry left in a hurry, but outside, as we climbed into our cars, he smiled across the empty parking lot and waved goodbye.

That one steam room tryst would have to forever suffice. A few months later, Barry decided to change gyms, opting for one closer to his house. Once in a blue moon, we see each other out and about, and share a secret grin over our little escapade. Barry even sent me a surprise e-mail not long afterwards. It was an ass shot. Nothing else about the owner was visible in the photograph. Yet, I knew that ass; there was no mistaking it. And I would always remember the taste of Barry's berry.

Smackdown:
Stone Cold Steve Austin's Ass 2

PETER MORSHEAD

I hurried through the empty arena parking lot, heart pounding from the adrenaline pumping through my veins. My dick was dripping pre-cum again. I still hadn't gotten off yet, but who cares? I sure as hell didn't. I had just had the most amazing experience of my life. I planted my ass in the driver's seat of my truck and locked the door behind me. Was I fucking dreaming? I brought the sweaty wrestling trunks up to my nose, then smeared them all over my face. I took a big honking whiff. This was no dream. I was holding and smelling a pair of Stone Cold Steve Austin's used wrestling trunks, still ripe with a healthy dose of Stone Cold sweat, funk, musk and cum. They were mine now. All mine. I earned 'em. Just ask Stone Cold. On second thought . . . .

I wanted to drive off, but my hands were shaking, my legs wobbly, my stomach full of butterflies from some kind of delayed shock. What if Austin changed his mind about not having me arrested for sneaking into his locker room? What if he had second thoughts about letting me eat his ass and suck his cock, then throwing me his cum-soaked trunks before ordering me to get the hell out of his private domain? What if he wanted to kick *my* ass after I ate *his* ass? What if he wanted to bash my skull in or send some of his bodyguard goons after me to make sure I kept quiet? Forever?

"But I will keep quiet!" I almost shouted aloud to myself, as if talking to the mob or something. I had to get the hell out of there, but not before one last whiff. Maybe it would calm my nerves. I put the trunks over my head and let out a long sigh. Make your escape, I told my crazy, impulsive ass. Then you can shove these trunks up your nose and breathe in his ass, balls and cock every night for the rest of your life.

The thought made me laugh. I removed my new treasure from my face and felt better. That is, until I saw him. Stone Cold. The six-foot-three, 255 pound blond giant with the shiny bald head was standing alone next to the arena in the distance, peering at my car with laser-like precision. Was he angry? I couldn't tell. He sure as hell wasn't smiling. More like scowling. More like: *I'm gonna kick your little pussy-boy ass so you don't go around spreading any rumors about me.*

I started the truck and burned a whole lotta rubber bolting from the scene. Maybe Stone Cold Steven Austin had regrets about letting an obsessed fan worship his gladiator glutes, but I could definitely live with what we did, as long as some WWF thugs didn't hunt me down seeking vengeance, pro-wrestling-style.

For the next few days, I daydreamed a lot and walked around in a daze. I never jerked off with his trunks as planned. Instead I sealed them in a Ziploc bag to preserve the aroma and hid them in the back of my closet. After a few weeks, life returned to normal and I began laugh at my worrying about Stone Cold coming after me. I mean, he didn't even know my name, let alone where I lived. I began to enjoy my nightly JO sessions thinking of my one and only time with my favorite pro wrestler. I even thought about taking the trunks out of the Ziploc to inhale his smell again.

But it was the opening of something else that rocked my world: an envelope that came in the mail without a return address. Inside was a crudely-drawn map to some building on the outskirts of the city. Underneath the drawing was a handwritten note: I AL-WAYS FINISH WHAT I START. BE THERE AT MIDNIGHT ON SATURDAY. ALONE. TELL NO ONE. BOTTOM LINE.

That's the bottom line. Austin's trademark saying. He wanted me. At the X on the paper. For what? To beat the shit out of me, scare me, sit on my face, ram his cock down my throat again, fuck me, get fucked by me, fuck me up, make sure I disappeared—all the above? How did he know my name and where to find me? What did Stone Cold have in store for me? I sat on my bed, reading the note over and over, trembling and getting hard at the same time . . . .

I sped through the dead of night as if my life depended on it. It was already after midnight. I was late, nervous as all hell and partially lost. I flicked on the dome light to glance at the map again. I'd been driving for over an hour. Wherever I was going was remote. I found the turnoff and drove down a narrow road. There were no streetlights and I had to pay close attention to avoid going off into a ditch. Eventually the pavement segued into a dirt road filled with potholes, most of them aiming to destroy the underside of my car. When I was close enough to the last turnoff—according to the map—I killed the engine and decided to walk the rest of the way.

I was engulfed by pitch blackness, the only illumination coming from my tiny emergency flashlight. My heart was pounding; I felt like my chest would explode. My cock had been hard since I first jumped in the truck. I'm sure my underwear was drenched in pre-cum. After what seemed like twenty minutes but was probably only five, I came upon a clearing and an abandoned warehouse. A 4x4 truck was parked in front. I swallowed hard, shining the flash-light through the driver side window. Empty beer cans, a blue gym bag and some CDs littered the passenger seat. A cap hung from the rearview mirror that said: *Hell Yeah*. Hell, yeah, I was in for it. And Big Daddy was waiting to lay some kind of smackdown on his ass-licking fan. Oh, God, please let it be of the sexual variety.

The door on the side of the warehouse was half-torn off its hinges and made a rusty squeak as I moved it aside. The air inside the building was humid, hot and stale. I crept down a dark, narrow hallway, the beam from my flashlight leading the way. My footsteps made a loud echo. I could hear my breathing, too. The hallway opened up to a large room with a lone bare light bulb hanging from the ceiling. And there he was, all the way across the room, standing with a cocky grin on his handsome mug. But he wasn't alone. Holy shit! Standing next to him was Chris Benoit, the five-foot-nine WWF stud who was built like a pit bull and a fullback combined. His head was cocked to one side, his face covered by several days' worth of beard stubble. My jaw hit the floor. Both Austin and Benoit were buck-ass naked except for their wrestling boots. Their bodies were glistening with sweat, each man stroking his own missile-like hard-on.

"You made it here in one piece," said Austin. "Guess ol' Stone Cold knows how to draw up a map."

"Just fine, sir, uh, Steve, uh, Stone Cold." I held my ground at the opposite side of the room. I still couldn't move yet. I still didn't want to reach out and grab anything or move forward lest I wake up and kill myself for this only being a dream. "How did you know how to find me?"

"License plate," Austin said matter-of-factly. "I know you've been craving another taste of Stone Cold's ass. Thought I'd bring along a bud. His wife don't like sucking cock. That's where fans and fuck buddies come in, long as they don't piss us off and do nothing stupid like spreading lies about us. Get my drift, son?"

My legs started giving out on me. "Oh, I'm drifting, sir. I mean,

I'll suck your drift. I mean, I get it. Mum's the word. Forever."

Stone Cold nodded for me to join them. I staggered forward. My eyes went from one to the other, my brain unable to decide who to move toward first. Stone Cold made up my mind for me. When I reached them, he grabbed me by the shoulders and forced me to my knees. Benoit then went behind me, grabbed my sweaty T-shirt and ripped it right off my body, tossing the pieces to the grimy warehouse floor.

"You like eating out a sweaty man's ass, huh, kid?" Chris brought his stubbly face right to my ear. His breath smelled of beer.

"Anything you guys want," I stammered. "I'm your man. Or boy."

Chris stared me dead in the eyes, then he straightened up and cracked a smile.

Both men towered over me on either side. I could feel the heat of their bodies and the musk from their ripe pits and crotches. It was intoxicating. My aching cock became even harder. They circled me like sharks, each man spitting in the palm of his hand and lubing up the throbbing pieces of meat circumnavigating my head. They grunted as they made their way around me, snorts and moans, whiffs and sniffs, "fuck yeahs" and "fucking As."

When they stopped moving, Chris Benoit's nine-inch cut cock bounced inches from my face, curving upward toward my eyebrows. I opened up my mouth and leaned forward, but Benoit turned around, and an even more heavenly sight confronted me: his ass. Momentarily, I studied every curve and contour: the short dark blond hair matted to his cheeks due to a heavy layer of sweat; the beefy but high and tight twin mounds of pale ass underneath. His butt was smaller than Stone Cold's, but still it was a fleshed-out, meaty sculpture of masculine perfection.

"You're gonna work for that blowjob," said Benoit. "Get your fucking mug in my crack and get to work."

I shoved my face into Benoit's hairy, sweaty butt and took a deep whiff of that valley of manliness. He was riper than ripe. My mouth and nose and forehead were quickly soaked with sweat. I licked the salty warmth and grabbed his butt cheeks as my tongue explored blindly.

"Yeah, buddy, that's it. Oh, man, Austin, you're fucking right about him."

"You like eating out Benoit's ass, don't you? You like it as much as Stone Cold's?"

"Sure," I mumbled, lapping at Benoit's furry butt-crack and burrowing towards the hole. Stone Cold stepped beside him and grabbed him by the shoulder. Chris did the same, and the two men bent over, giving me an ample view of their massive muscular asses. I traveled from one set of meaty, sweaty glutes to the other, licking, sniffing, snorting, kissing, sucking. I was lost in Butt City and never wanted to find my way back. The warehouse was filled with the sounds of our uninhibited lust. We moaned. We yelled. We cursed back and forth at each other.

As I feasted, I tried to decide which stud had the muskier ass, the tighter butthole, the loudest reaction to my hard-working tongue. Austin had the funkier crack. I swore he hadn't showered in days. Benoit had the tighter ass. No way could I get a few fingers up there like I did with Austin back in the arena locker room. And they both seemed to be equally vocal, with Stone Cold giving as many "Fuck, yeahs" and "Oh, shits" as Chris Benoit.

After a good forty minutes of nonstop rimming, both men turned to me brandishing their cocks. No instructions were needed. I took a dick in each hand and put Benoit's in my mouth. I massaged his meaty mushroom head with my tongue, then swallowed his shaft while I jerked Stone Cold's prick. They put their arms around each other's torsos and I was able to rub both men's cock heads together. Drops of sweat dripped off their bodies onto my face and shoulders as my tongue slipped and slid from one cock to the other. I was taking Benoit's flesh tube down my throat when Stone Cold moved behind me, pulled me up off the floor and yanked down my jeans. I gasped, causing Benoit's cock to slip out of my mouth and smack against his belly.

"Get the fuck back down on my dick!" Chris grabbed the back of my head, shoved me onto his meat and began assaulting my mouth with hard thrusts. "That's it, fucker. Cocksucker! Fucking whore! You like Benoit's meat, don't you?"

I grunted my appreciation as Stone Cold's big hands spread my butt-cheeks from behind. I was so worked up that my asshole was nice and loose. I wanted Stone Cold up my ass so fucking bad I was shaking. As Benoit continued fucking my mouth, Stone Cold put his cockhead against my hole and pushed in a bit. I gripped Benoit's beefy thighs and my mouth released his cock as I struggled to breath.

"Bitch!" Benoit smacked me across my face, then grabbed my hair and pulled me to his face. "What the fuck? Did I say stop sucking?"

"You wanna snoop around in my dressing room and mess with the Rattlesnake's ass, you'd better be prepared to pay the price," Stone Cold said from behind. "And that's the bottom line. Understand, pussy-boy?"

I didn't dare look at him, but I did squirm enough so that my hole was no longer in line with his cockhead. Benoit still had my hair in his hands. His nostrils flared and a look of pure aggression raged in his eyes. Suddenly I was confused. I wasn't sure if they were playing WWF mind games to turn me on or what. I also wasn't sure if I still wanted to be there. These guys could break every bone in my body and leave me for dead if they wanted to. Was I a damned fool to have come here? A stupid, crazy, horny fool?

Benoit released his hold on me. I pulled up my jeans and

backed away. The two of them laughed, but not the kind of laugh that told me, "Okay, kid, this is all a joke." They closed in on me. Each man took an arm. My body froze. I was helpless. I wondered how many other groupies had been subjected to this kind of treatment.

They hauled me back to the center of the room and blindfolded me with shards of my torn T-shirt. Next, they stripped off my sneakers, jeans and underwear.

"Bend over," Austin commanded me, shoving my back with the bottom of his boot. My mouth collided with Benoit's crotch. He clamped down on my neck and made me engulf his cock. A few seconds later, I felt Stone Cold's thick meat entering my ass without hesitation or gentility—just a little spit, or so I hoped.

They proceeded to plug me from both ends. At first, the pain in my anal ring was unbearable. I wanted to pass out but feared what they might do to me if I failed them. I let my body go, sucking Benoit, not resisting the assault. My ass was on fire, and not in a good way. Then I felt Stone Cold ramming past my sphincter and tickling my prostate. I moaned and startled myself when I discovered that I was thrusting backwards in time with Stone Cold's pounding. The sweat and funk that filled the room invaded my nostrils and I heard myself slurping hungrily on Benoit's curved cock. We were all moaning now. Once again, I was a horn-dog in heat and wanted to howl at the moon. Benoit's massive meat was fucking my face, and spit and drool was running down the sides of my mouth.

"Yeah, buddy, you love Benoit's cock. I can tell," said Austin.

"Yeah, man, fuck his pussy-ass," said Benoit.

Still fucking me from behind, Stone Cold grabbed my cock and began jerking me off. I no longer cared that I was blindfolded. What I needed was to work on Benoit's asshole. I reached around, squeezed those firm mountains of butt flesh and rubbed my finger against his hole. He even shifted his legs a bit to allow a bit better access. I rubbed around his tight puckered hole, smearing his man juice around his ring.

"Go for it, fucker," he said and I slid my index finger all the way up his hairy hole. The sweat made entering very easy and he let out a loud throaty moan, bucking his hips while continuing to fuck my face. I was lost in a maze of sensations: Stone Cold's cock up my ass, his hand jerking my cock, Benoit's cock down my throat, my fingers up Benoit's ass, the grunts from all three of us, the smell of sex and man musk in the air. My body was thrashing and bucking and I was drowning in wave after wave of unbelievable pleasure. I never wanted this adventure in the dark to end.

Stone Cold leaned forward even more, his sweaty pecs thumping against my back. He started yelling and growling and blasted inside my guts. His grip on my dick became painful but I treasured the pain. Then Benoit started cursing at the top of his lungs and shot hot jets of cum all over the insides of my mouth. It was bitter, salty and tangy and I swallowed as best as I could. Some spilled out and ran down my chin. I wanted to dive down and lick it up, but Stone Cold still had my dick in a vise grip. He squeezed tighter. I exploded all over the floor. In the next beat, Benoit slipped his cock out of my mouth and Stone Cold pulled out of my ass. I collapsed on the floor, landing in cum, and passed out from sheer mental exhaustion.

When I woke on the grimy warehouse floor, I was alone. I could feel Stone Cold's cum deep in my ass and the bitter aftertaste of Chris Benoit in my mouth. I stood up, a bit shaky. My shirt lay in shreds beside me, but my jeans and sneakers were still there. I got dressed, picked up my flashlight and made my way out.

Night had turned into dawn. I had no idea what time it was, but it looked like the sun might rise in another hour. Their 4x4 was gone and I wondered if they had encountered any difficulty driving past my truck on such a narrow, treacherous road. Walking back to my truck, I saw a blue gym bag on the roof. I broke out in a big smile and ran the rest of the way to the car. It was the same gym bag that was in Stone Cold's truck. I unzipped it and looked inside. Not only was there another pair of Stone Cold's wrestling trunks similar to the ones I had earned back in the locker room, but a pair of sweaty, used socks as well. There were a pair of wrestling tights in there, too. I took them out, buried my face in the crotch and ass areas and inhaled. *Oh yeah! That's him.* Chris Benoit always wore tights when he wrestled.

Before heading home, I knew I'd have to stop by the grocery store. Time to get a few more Ziploc bags.

About the Buttmen

JONATHAN ASCHE ("From Behind") has been writing about the pleasures of the male ass (as well as other body parts) for nearly a decade. His short stories have appeared in *Torso, Playguy, Men, In Touch for Men, Mandate* and *Inches*, as well as the anthologies *Friction 3* and *Buttmen 2*. He lives in Atlanta with his husband (and favorite butt).

ALAN BELL (editor) took his first editing credit on his junior high school newspaper. Since then, he has edited *Gaysweek,* New York's first lesbian and gay weekly newspaper; *Kujisource,* a black AIDS newsletter; and several magazines for the black lesbian and gay community, most notably *BLK* and *Blackfire.* For six years, he was film critic for the *Los Angeles Sentinel,* a mainstream black weekly. His film criticism has also appeared in the *Los Angeles Times.* He is a graduate of UCLA, the University of the State of New York and is ABD in sociology at New York University. Bell, who likes to almost cover his own butt with boxer shorts and baggy jeans, edited the first and second *Buttmen* anthologies.

M. CHRISTIAN's ("2 + 1") work has appeared in *Best American Erotica, Best Gay Erotica, Best Lesbian Erotica, Best Fetish Erotica,*

Best Transgendered Erotica, Friction and over 150 other books, magazines, and websites. He is the editor of over 12 anthologies, including *Best S/M Erotica, The Burning Pen, Guilty Pleasures* and many others. Christian is the author of the Lambda-nominated collection, *Dirty Words* (gay erotica), *Speaking Parts* (lesbian erotica), and *The Bachelor Machine* (science fiction erotica). His website is www.mchristian.com.

MARTIN COX's ("How I Became a Butt Boy") lifelong quest is to find the perfect male butt, a quest that he describes as "most enjoyable." His work has appeared in *Men, Black Inches* and *First Hand* as well as on the web as a video reviewer for ManNet.com, Rad Video and DVD Empire.

JAY O. DICKINGSON ("In Blackhaven Forest") describes himself as "a dreamer, a lover, a teller of tales." He sees himself as a "dream spinner" who can "be anything I want and anything you want me to be." Dickingson lives in a little house on the prairie in southeastern Alberta, Canada, dreaming of knights and squires and days of old. "In Blackhaven Forest" is a glance at a larger epic-in-progress—in search of a publisher—about a gay band of adventurers and butt lovers out to save the world. He also appeared in the original *Buttmen*.

JOHN DOUGLAS ("James, Dean") is an Australian artist and author. He is working hard encouraging rimming as the means to International Conflict Resolution. The John Douglas website is at geocities.com/JohnDouglas_Art

JXW1952 ("Enter the Fist") didn't come to terms with his homosexuality until age 35. But he came with a vengeance. He considers himself a connoisseur of men's butts. He has been partnered for 13 years and has spent the last 11 of those in Florida. His sexual appetite has become more intense and downright kinky over time. After fighting his inhibitions for some time, he has finally opened the door to his true sexual identity and to experiencing it all.

MARC JAMES ("Posterior Power") can't go for more than a few minutes without some butt-related thought entering his head. He claims to have X-ray vision because he is able to determine the kind of butt a man has right through jeans, boxers and sometimes even a robe. He is far more curious to view a man's ass than see his cock. James is a top man turned on mostly by younger guys but who can still appreciate an older guy blessed with nice glutes. When not obsessing about butts his interests run to computer hardware, web design and photography. This is his first published story.

ERIC KARNOWSKI ("The Crack of Don") grew up in a small town in Tennessee and currently lives in Boston with his partner of ten years. His work has appeared in *Harrington Gay Men's Fiction Quarterly* and in the anthology *Bearotica*. He appreciates the finer points of the male anatomy—especially when they're hairy.

JERRY METKO ("The Storm") is a Midwest writer whose topics range from erotica to suspense and science fiction. He is currently working on a novel dealing with gay themes and the supernatural. This is his first published work.

PETER MORSHEAD ("Smackdown: Stone Cold Steve Austin's Ass 2") resides in his native Halifax, Nova Scotia, and has been an avid fan of the male butt most of his adult life. He thinks some of the greatest butts of all time belong to male athletes and his personal favorites are the butts of runners, cyclists, gymnasts, body builders and wrestlers. The first installment of his Stone Cold adventure appears in *Buttmen 2*.

J. SCOTT NEWMAN ("The Groom's Virgin Ass") spends his days as a middle school teacher while his nights and weekends are filled with gay charity work, movies and time with friends. This is the 33-year-old Burlington County, New Jersey resident's first published work.

P.P. REID ("Boys and Pigs") is a 38-year-old single white male who loves to see the bulge of a round cheek in tight jeans or the curve of the small of a man's back as it swells to a hard mound. The muscles of the back of some workin' man swingin' a hammer, shirtless in the sun, make his mouth dry and his heart beat faster. Reid generally takes the top role, but has occasionally bottomed for "special men in my life." He is a skilled computer hardware technician, has a sense of humor and passionate about politics, philosophy and love. This is his first published work.

JAY STARRE ("Spring Break Buttfest," "A Good Spanking," "Razored Rear," "Hungry Bum," "Chow Down: Confessions of an Ass Muncher") resides in Vancouver, British Columbia, and loves ass, any way he can get it. He loves exercise, sports, writing and butt. His work has appeared in *Torso, Honcho, American Bear, Men, Indulge, Mandate, International Leatherman, Bear* and others. He has also written for nearly a dozen anthologies, including *Friction 4* and *Buttmen* and *Buttmen 2*. Starre greatly appreciates the male butt in all its forms.

D'JAHMA SENTWALI ("Jailhouse Rock(hard)") is an African American who began his writing career as a poet and performance artist. His works have been featured in *America's Greatest Poets, Aphrodisiac, Clique* and in a yet-to-be-published Other Countries anthology. Sentwali has been a feature in such venues as Forward & Out, New York Innovators, Brother's Night Out, Music & Rhythm,

Opening Night, WLIB and NYU Radio. He is the former co-host of H.E.A.L. Brooklyn and the present host of Words & Music.

SIMON SHEPPARD ("Lucky Night") is the author of *Kinkorama: Travels Through Queer Desire, Hotter Than Hell and Other Stories* and the co-editor, with M. Christian, of *Rough Stuff* and its sequel, *Roughed Up: More Tales of Gay Men, Sex, and Power*. His next short story collection, *In Deep*, will be published by Alyson Books. Besides the first two *Buttmen* volumes, the work of this San Francisco resident has appeared in over 80 other anthologies, including the *Best American Erotica, Best Gay Erotica,* and *Friction* series. His website is www.simonsheppard.com.

MEL SMITH's ("Baby") stories have appeared in magazines, online and in numerous anthologies. She is not a gay man and in general considers herself a cocklover first and foremost, but she cannot deny the allure of a particularly fine male ass. She has one very special one in mind right now.

MAX SOUTHERN ("Barry's Berry") is an Atlanta-based freelance writer whose work has appeared in publications throughout the country, as well as on ManNet.com. Most notably, he has served as a judge for the GayVN adult video industry awards for the last three years. Max credits his partner Craig, whose butt cheeks have sang to him many a time, as an inspiration.

MATTHEW STEWARD ("Heaven in a Jockstrap") has written online porn reviews and appeared in *Buttmen 2*. He is a college instructor living in New York City.

TROY STORM ("Buddy's Fine Behind") has had over two hundred erotic stories published in gay, bi and straight publications, including *Buttmen 2. Gym Shorts*, his collection of short stories concerning West Hollywood gym jocks, has been published by Companion Press. Troy feels he appreciates every aspect of a well-built male, but he admits the sight of a solidly-constructed butt and the treasure that lies therein makes him really sit up and grab his thesaurus.

K. TERREGA ("Evan's Slut") is the author of over 300 published stories, articles, essays and letters that have appeared in *Gallery, Playgirl, Penthouse Variations* and many other print and online magazines. Terrega is also the author of *It's A Dirty Job...Writing Porn for Fun and Profit* and edits a free newsletter for writers of porn and erotica: www.katyterrega.com/newsletter.html.

TOM G. TONGUE ("Neighborly Rim," "Traveling Salesman Rim") is the pseudonym of an Atlanta, Georgia-based writer. Tom and his tongue have been butt lovers since childhood even when they didn't know why they loved a man's posterior so much. Although his work has been seen on the Internet's Nifty Erotic Stories Archive, "Neighborly Rim" and "Traveling Salesman Rim" are his first print published works.

RICHARD TRAYNER ("Licking LeRoy") is a lifelong connoisseur of bubble butts. Since his teens in Colorado in the 60s he has admired, serviced and worshiped the sacred mounds of flesh most men take for granted. Covered in coarse growth, dusted with blond fine hairs or shaved bare, he loves 'em all and does his best to show his appreciation with his tongue and lips. Now in his 50s, Trayner still finds delight in exploring hot young ass, and he offers to train any aspiring buttmen.

DUANE WILLIAMS ("The Sea in His Ass") lives in Hamilton, Canada. His short fiction has appeared in literary anthologies across

North America, including *Queeries, Quickies, Queer View Mirror I & II, Blithe House, Contra/Diction, Velvet Mafia, Suspect Thoughts, Buttmen 2, Harrington Gay Men's Literary Quarterly,* the *Church-Wellesley Review, Full Body Contact, Frictions 6* and *Boyfriend From Hell.* He can be contacted at duanewilliams@cogeco.ca

THOM WOLF ("Collaboration"), the author of *Words Made Flesh,* lives in the United Kingdom. His work has appeared in *In Touch, Indulge, Inches, Men, Freshmen* and the anthologies *Friction 3, 5, 6, Twink* and *Bearotica.* He likes yoga, music, vodka and sex and is a rabid Kylie Minogue fan. His second novel *The Chain* is published late 2003.

west beach books • more about buttmen 3 •
up next • contact the editor • the booty board •
submission info • contact the editor • contact west
• behind the book • other west beach books •
booty prizes • coming up next • the booty board
• submission info • contact west beach books
the book • other west beach books • more about
• contact the editor • coming up next • the booty
buy • submission info • contact west beach books
the book • other west beach books • more about
board • booty prizes • coming up next • write
• where to buy • submission info • contact west
celebrity butt **surf's up** challenge •
behind the book **surf's up** • more about
buttmen 3 • buttmenfunzone.com • other west
booty board • write your own review • reviews
beach books • ebook info • celebrity butt challenge
more about buttmen 3 • buttmenfunzone.com •
write your own review • reviews • where to buy •
info • celebrity butt challenge • behind the book •
• buttmenfunzone.com • the booty board • booty
reviews • where to buy • submission info • contact
• other west beach books • more about buttmen 3
• booty prizes • coming up next • the booty board
• submission info • contact west beach books
the book • other west beach books • more about

buttmenfunzone.com • booty prizes • coming
write your own review • reviews • where to buy •
beach books • ebook info • celebrity butt challenge
more about buttmen 3 • buttmenfunzone.com •
• write your own review • reviews • where to buy
• ebook info • celebrity butt challenge • behind
buttmen 3 • buttmenfunzone.com • booty prizes
board • write your own review • reviews • where to
• ebook info • celebrity butt challenge • behind
buttmen 3 • buttmenfunzone.com • the booty
your own review • reviews • contact the editor
beach books • ebook info • contact the editor • the

www.westbeachbooks.com

beach books • booty prizes • coming up next • the
• where to buy • submission info • contact west
• behind the book • other west beach books •
booty prizes • coming up next • the booty board •
submission info • contact west beach books • ebook
other west beach books • more about buttmen 3
prizes • coming up next • write your own review •
west beach books • ebook info • behind the book
• buttmenfunzone.com • celebrity butt challenge
• write your own review • reviews • where to buy
• ebook info • celebrity butt challenge • behind
buttmen 3 • buttmenfunzone.com • booty prizes

ALSO FROM WEST BEACH BOOKS
The Novels of Randy Boyd

"Not politically correct."
—*IN Los Angeles Magazine*

UPRISING
The Suspense Thriller

Nominated for two Lambda Literary Awards, including Best Men's Mystery

"A writer to reckon with."
—*Lambda Book Report*

BRIDGE ACROSS THE OCEAN
A Lambda Literary Award finalist for Best Small Press Title

"Boyd has a knack for the controversial."
—*Between the Lines*

THE DEVIL INSIDE
A Lambda Literary Award finalist for Best Science Fiction/ Fantasy Title

Available at bookstores and on the net in traditional print and eBook formats

www.westbeachbooks.com

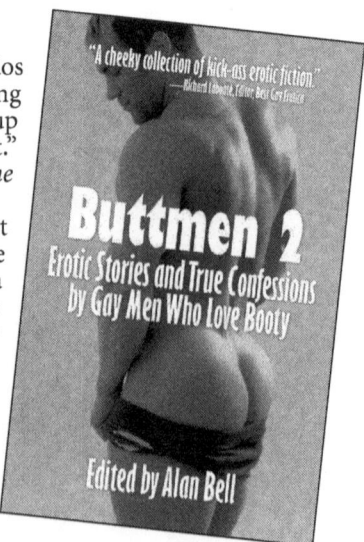

www.ingramcontent.com/pod-product-compliance
Lightning Source LLC
Chambersburg PA
CBHW032037240626
47154CB00003B/950